EDEN'S WAKE

LYNN STEIGLEDER

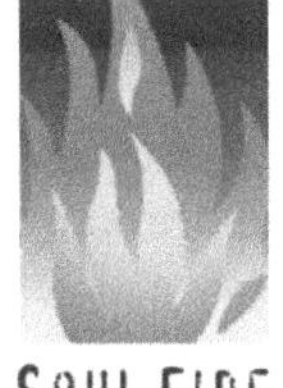

SOUL FIRE
PRESS

an imprint of
Christopher Matthews Publishing

Boston, Massachusetts

Eden's Wake

Editor: Elise Pehrson, Jeremy Soldevilla
Cover design: Neil Noah

ISBN 978-1938985-73-7
ebook ISBN 978-1-938985-74-4

Published by
Soul Fire Press
an imprint of
CHRISTOPHER MATTHEWS PUBLISHING
http://christopher matthewspub.com
Boston

Printed in the United States of America

Rising Tide

**(First book in the *Rising Tide* series and
predecessor to *Eden's Wake)***

The story thus far...

S ET ADRIFT IN AN ENDLESS SEA, Ben Adams can see no escape from his prison. A powerful hurricane has destroyed his habitat, killed his best friend, Pete, and left him alone, floating in a cramped decompression chamber.

Due to unseen forces, Ben is compelled to search for an unknown signal he comes to realize as "C-7." This realization comes in the form of a series of pulses on his otherwise unresponsive communication system. Before time runs out, he manages to contact a passing ship, the Morning Star, and is rescued. However, his eleventh hour saviors turn out to be less than honorable. The ship's crew are modern day pirates led by the corrupt and murderous Captain Evans.

Despite their initial distrust, Stewart, Vinny, and Skull befriend Ben, taking him into their confidence. Ben learns that the ship has been under the control of an unseen force that guides the vessel. Ben also discovers the Captain's ward; a beautiful young woman named Eve and quickly falls in love with her.

While Evans is consumed by an evil metamorphosis, Stewart, Vinny, and Skull, along with Ben and Eve, form an alliance against the Captain. They attempt to uncover the strange events occurring on board the ship.

The ship reaches it next destination: An island that appears on no charts and is populated by a primitive, yet advanced, civilization.

Jhorr, their leader, embraces the Morning Star's crew and confines Evans until his transformation reaches its necessary stage of completion. It is here that Ben learns the object of his obsession; 'C-7' is a ship's transport container.

The crew, along with the newly-transformed Evans (now called Eleazor), once again boards the Morning Star, headed toward their final destination.

Upon reaching the container, the doors open, revealing a vast seascape; a new world totally covered by water.

As Ben, Eve, and Eleazor cross the threshold, water begins pouring from the new world, filling the old.

Acknowlegements

Without these friends this book would have been impossibly possible and maybe even for better or for worse. (Just like to keep all my bases covered).

Suzie Martin: Her laugh, singing when she comes through the door, her crisis we prayed for together, her reading out loud and her occasionally using her fingers to type (when not griping about my keyboard).

Carol Neilan: My personal assistant, my typist extraordinaire, my muse, my editorial partner, my nemesis and friend, plus the only person I know who can survive solely off of peanut butter and jelly sandwiches.

To my wife Donna: For believing in me, putting up with me, her encouragement and helping a computer illiterate husband through the times that would have been resolved using colorful language.

And to my sister Terri Cox and my mother Evelyn Holladay: Without their encouragement and masterful typing skills I can't say where this book would be today.

Table of Contents

Chapter One

EN TURNED TO SEE the container doors close and fade into the surrounding sky, his last link to the only world he had ever known. As the water continued its hasty retreat from the present into the former, the rock ledge took on its true shape as a plateau.

On its face, a staircase curved its way to the valley floor below, no doubt tracing a line that ancient footsteps had coursed for countless generations.

Ben and Eve stood on the top step, as a terrified Eleazor backed away from the edge.

A slight tremor caused her to stumble forward.

Ben reached out, grabbed Eve by the shirttail and pulled her back. "Going somewhere?"

Eve wrapped her arms around him. "Not now."

The water level was falling so rapidly it was as if this world had been flushed. Eddies and whirlpools formed, swirled and then disappeared as they drained into the unseen.

The ground underfoot groaned and swelled. A second later the plateau disappeared in an explosive gusher of mud, stones and tangled roots.

The blast knocked Eleazor backward onto solid ground, covering him in a thick coat of gray slime. As he tried to lift himself under the weight of the mud, another weight (not in the conventional sense, but a dark intelligence) pressed him back to the ground.

Eleazor continued to struggle against the force that held him fast, panic growing in his simple mind until the calming influence of familiarity took over. It assured Eleazor that he was not alone and that he would come to know and embrace what he now feared.

Ben and Eve found themselves intertwined within the full force of the collapse and the ensuing push of debris. They rode one of the flat stone stair treads like a body board along the leading edge of the earthen slide.

Halfway down the slope the avalanche collapsed in on itself. It covered the pair in a layer of sticky mud and coarse sand with the absorbent properties of pumice. Stones that separated from larger boulders during the initial blast pelted the pair as they traveled downward.

No longer able to hold onto their granite body board, their mud-coated fingers unusable, Ben and Eve found themselves pulled into the full fury of the landslide.

As they tumbled through the mass of earth and debris, the couple found they were not being shredded alive.

The porous sand absorbed the moisture from the mud that coated their bodies, turning the material into a lightweight concrete. What would have become a custom made tomb, saved them from the deluge as they slid down the collapsing incline.

The rock cocoon skidded to a stop. It resembled two distorted statues entangled in a comical embrace of finality. Stress fractures had developed where the hardened chrysalis sustained damage during its trip down the hillside.

Several places bulged where the cracks intersected. With a loud 'pop' a section of material fell away, exposing a human knee and partial thigh. A solitary pale hand maneuvered a path from inside the claustrophobic statue, making its way through the only available opening. Oxygen-starved fingers enlarged the hole.

A fist crashed through the top exposing Ben from the neck up. He gasped for air to free his body of trapped carbon dioxide and shook his head as best he could in the confined area to remove small particles from his face. With one massive push, he removed the entire chest section and freed himself.

Eve pushed several holes in her concrete clothing, and with Ben's help, she was soon free.

As Eve's breathing returned to normal, the couple had a chance to survey the path they had just covered.

"Now there's something you don't see every day," Ben said.

Eve looked at him awaiting an answer.

Ben recognized the silent question as his cue to respond. "I'm certain that the saturated soil is what caused the hundred yards of hillside to break free." Ben pondered the entire scenario running it over and over again in his head.

Eve shook her head. "Really?" she said sarcastically.

"Yeah," Ben said, engrossed in his explanation.

He rested his forearm on her shoulder. "One trip down the mountain is enough for me." Ben said.

"I'm trying my best not to make light of your explanation," Eve said, "but enough already." She smiled and allowed her shoulder to droop, causing Ben's arm to slip off, and him to lose his balance.

Eve walked a short distance back up the slope, knelt and rubbed her fingers across the solidified ground.

Ben joined her.

"I guess you're right. The entire avalanche *has* turned to stone," Eve said.

Ben knelt beside her. "Good thing too."

"How so?" Eve asked.

"We'd still be sliding." Ben stood and helped Eve to her feet.

A disparaged wail permeated the heavy air from above. A small orange head could be seen where Ben and Eve had begun their slide.

Ben noticed for the first time that his labored breathing had not subsided even after breaking out of the statue.

"What's up with short stuff?" Ben huffed.

"Looks like our ward is scared again."

Eleazor sat at the top of the landslide's origin with a hand on either side of his head, covering his ears. He rocked back and forth, exuding a shrill cry that echoed off the surrounding rock formations.

"Eleazor!" She screamed. No response. Eve looked around, located a stone, and reached down. She tossed the object up several times, allowing it to fall back into her hand, and then smiled at Ben. The stone flew true and landed beside the wailing gargoyle.

Eleazor paused in mid-scream and glared in her direction.

Eve glared back with her arms extended from her sides, palms up. "Well," she said, placing her hands on her hips, "are you coming or are you going to sit there and whine?"

"You leave me all alone," he squawked, shaking his fists. Eleazor bounced up and down on his rear end. "I'll gets yous mean peoples," he rolled onto his stomach. Cautiously lowering himself, Eleazor began his descent.

Chapter Two

EN TOOK EVE'S HAND and helped her off the end of the hardened landslide. He stood, amazed that the flood had not left a sodden environment devoid of life, but a lush green landscape. Ben could make out birds darting and lighting among the branches.

"Just look at this," Eve said, admiring the rich vegetation that embellished a small clearing forming a canopy over the whole. Walking to a large, red petal flower, she nestled the bud in both hands, pressed her nose close and breathed deeply. "Wonderful." Eve embraced the delicate aroma and then exhaled.

Ben staggered to her side, unable to speak, once again laboring for oxygen.

"You *are* having trouble, aren't you?" Eve placed the palm of her hand on his forehead.

Ben waved her off. "I'll be fine."

He collapsed on the ground beside her until his breathing returned to normal.

Three thuds and a string of curses caused the couple to turn and see Eleazor fall off the end of the landslide. He rolled several feet to an abrupt stop against a small sapling. Ben sensed that the tree was attempting to move from the bulbous creature's touch. If the sapling had not been rooted, he was sure it would have run away.

Eleazor lifted himself up and waddled over to Eve. "You leaves me, you bad girly." He bent down and pounded the ground with his fist. Standing, Eleazor stomped his feet and screwed his face into a wrinkled tantrum. "No leaves me no mo!"

"I see you made it anyway," Eve said. She bent over, bringing herself down to his level. "Keep up, you clumsy little wretch. I won't wait for you again." Eve stood and turned, facing away from the creature. Eve had felt the cold essence of evil as she stared into his lifeless eyes, and knew that, while docile for now, soon confrontation would no longer be an option.

"Okee dokee," Eleazor replied, his demeanor now jovial. "Me be goody good and keepy up."

Eve glanced back and nodded, relieved at his compliance. She thought best not to relinquish even the smallest amount of control as long as it could be maintained.

"Well, if the two of you are done," Ben interrupted, "our first priority should be clean water and food."

"It's either your stomach or the other thing you're always going on about," Eve said. "I'm surprised you're even considering food."

Ben shrugged. "Gotta eat."

AFTER SEVERAL HOURS of near silent hiking, the terrain had changed. Ben, Eve and Eleazor, now found themselves in a shallow slot canyon. The change had been so subtle, that the rising walls and the canyon growing narrower seemed like the natural course for the topography to evolve. Ben, Eve and Eleazor were bound, having traveled a mile or more past, the point of no return.

"We'll need water soon," Ben said. He knelt and scooped up a handful of dirt, scanning two directions. The way they were going and the way they had come. Ben raised his hand and let the dirt trickle out of a slightly opened fist. "Turning back is not an option."

Ben stood. "Guess that means we keep going," he said.

They came to a halt, Ben motioning toward an object protruding from the wall: a twisted tree with oval pods hanging in clusters.

"This is the second tree with fruit I've seen in the last half hour, and this one is low enough to reach." Ben noticed feathered wings rustling in the foliage and bits of fruit falling to the ground.

"The birds seem to like them."

He walked to one of the clusters. "One way to find out . . ." He pulled one of the pods and took a bite.

"No!" Eve exclaimed. "You don't know what it will do to you!"

Ben dug his thumbnail between two molars, dislodging a remaining particle. He purged the chunk with a whoosh of air. "If it's safe to eat, time will be the one to spit that information out."

"Hilarious," Eve said, "We're all gonna die and you're making jokes."

"No one's going to die, sweetheart," he touched the underside of her chin and kissed her. "It'll be all right, you'll see."

"What if it's not?" Eve protested. "What if it kills you?"

"It'll be quicker than starvation." Ben placed both hands on her shoulders. "We have to eat."

Eve slumped. "I just can't imagine going on without you and being left alone with Mr. Personality." Eve glanced over her shoulder. "Make Eleazor eat it. A dose of poison would do him good."

Ben eyed the creature with obvious distaste. "Nah, let him get his own food."

Eleazor perked up sensing himself being brought into the conversation.

Eve shook her head and sighed. "If it kills you, I'll just take a bite myself."

"That's my girl," Ben turned to see Eleazor playing with his toes. "All right, Stumpy, we're hanging tight for a while."

Eleazor looked up. "Me hang, but me no Stumpy." He pointed to himself. "Me Leazy."

"Whatever," Ben replied.

After some time had passed with no ill effects, Ben pulled another pod, took a bite, and this time swallowed.

"Just a little longer, then we'll—" Ben cocked his head, a puzzled look on his face, a low rumble in the distance growing. He turned an ear toward the sound, his expression stoic.

Eve reacted. "What's —"

"Shh!" Ben snapped, holding up his hand. "I thought it was over," he whispered.

"What?" Eve urged. "What is it? What's wrong?"

Ben shook his head. "This world, it's not finished!"

"You're not making any sense. It's not finished what?"

Ben's eyes locked with Eve's. "Draining!"

Chapter Three

T HROUGH A DEEP, SINISTER HAZE, the silhouette of a lone figure faded in and out through the fog. He was communicating with a disembodied presence.

"You realize that we must capture and maintain possession of the artifact at all cost," the entity said, its voice as soothing as a mother comforting her child.

"Yes, Dark One," the figure named Sedah replied.

"Once I have corrupted my host's form," the soothing voice continued, "I will take charge for a short while. You will be my general and number one. Until that time, you will act using all patience and keeping the others within their ranks and undetected by the one called Ben. Do not discount his companion Eve, and the small one who will soon walk with me as one." The presence seemed to close in around the solitary visitor. "And take this to heart; they shall not be harmed until the appointed time."

"It will be as you have commanded," Sedah said. He inhaled deeply to overcome the sudden weight of claustrophobia that threatened to strangle him.

"Let it be so . . ." the voice paused for a moment, its demeanor having changed from placid to one of such evil as to be capable of unspeakable atrocities.

Cracks appeared in the immediate area as shards fell from disintegrating walls of glass. Sedah backed away into the fog as the entity hummed a low haunting tune.

Chapter Four

A WALL OF WATER was now visible at the far end of the canyon, traveling at an incredible rate of speed toward Ben, Eve and Eleazor. Ben turned to glimpse a second wall of water coming from the opposite direction.

That's impossible, he thought, *we just came that way*. Ben seized Eve and pushed her upward.

"Take hold of the tree branch," he yelled over the now thundering sound of the water. Eve complied, and then Ben jumped, grasping the lower branch and pulling himself into the tree beside Eve.

Ben looked down and noticed Eleazor still playing with his toes, oblivious to the events unfolding around him. As Ben and Eve climbed higher in the tree attempting to reach the upper edge of the canyon, the two waves collided on the pair.

Something akin to being squished between two bricks dislodged both Ben and Eve from their treetop perch. The water covered the canyon floor, and Eleazor was nowhere to be found.

Ben and Eve had held fast to each other's hand until a large, fast-moving object missed Eve but kissed the back of her head. The near miss caused the couple to lose their grip and Eve to be sucked under water in the object's wake. Ben dove and freed his wife from the dying turbulence. He grabbed her around the waist and headed upward.

As Ben struggled to reach the life-giving air, he glanced back at the retreating object. Big and orange was the only sight his brain would allow him to process.

Ben burst through the surface of the water, inhaling air between coughs and sputters. Turning his attention to Eve, he found she was groggy and sported a respectable knot on the back of her head. Ben struggled in the torrent of water to keep Eve from slipping away. He had become so turned around he didn't know in which direction he was moving. Was he advancing deeper into the canyon or retreating whence he came?

A large jet of bubbles surrounded them. As they subsided, Eleazor broke the surface and bobbed up and down in the water. "Bennie boys!" he exclaimed. "And Evies, too! Me back! What you two is doin?"

Ben opened his mouth to speak, but a wave stifled his response, prompting a coughing fit.

Eve broke from Ben's grasp. As her head dropped beneath the surface, the cool water partially revived her.

To keep from losing his wife, Ben clutched her floating brunette locks; any remaining grogginess cleared. Eve came to the surface with a shout, her hand searching for purchase. As she found Ben's collar, he pulled her close.

"Good to see you," she sputtered.

Ben smiled. "Why didn't you tell me you couldn't swim?" *If looks could kill,* Ben thought.

"Just trying to back stroke in a shipping lane before I mentioned my lack of prowess in the water." That's when Eve noticed the bouncing orange gargoyle. "I see Li'l Abner is still with us," she said, her voice taking on more than a hint of disgust.

"Hi, Evies!" Eleazor exclaimed. "Me back, too!"

Eve smiled and nodded. Her eyes fixated on Ben, asking, *What now?*

Ben stared back, but before his answer became clear, they began to spin.

"What's happening?" Eve asked.

"We is spinny-spin-spin!" Eleazor replied. "Let's go faster! We need more faster!"

His request did not go unanswered as their speed doubled.

"I'm not sure, Eve," Ben said, ignoring the bobbing orange monstrosity.

Eve held Ben in a death-grip. He watched as Eleazor swam unhindered amidst the churn.

"It's a whirlpool!" Ben exclaimed.

The spinning water increased in speed, until three heads disappeared at the bottom of the vortex.

A SMALL RODENT skittered out of the way as three bodies were spat from the bottom of the whirlpool onto the rock floor below. Eve rolled onto her back, wincing in pain. She expected to see the underside of the swirling whirlpool. What she witnessed defied all logic.

It appeared as if the whirlpool they had just fallen through was actually a self-contained force. Looking up was like staring into the funnel of a dying tornado. She watched the violent mix subside until nothing remained. Eve was able to observe the hole they had fallen through, now bathing the cave in sunlight.

Ben crawled over to Eve. "You okay?" he asked, his breath coming in short gasps.

"'Bout as well as can be, having nearly drowned in what I assume was water," Eve said. She looked at him with concern, "Are you having trouble breathing again?"

He waved her off without speaking a word and coughed several times, clearing phlegm from his throat.

"Giddy up, Bennie, giddy up, Evie!" Eleazor urged. "We go 'splore cavey cave!" As Ben began to survey his surroundings, he noticed shadowy figures darting about, careful not to remain in full view.

Eve sat up, took several deep breaths and arched her shoulders, trying to relieve the spasms wracking her back.

Ben stood and grabbed Eve with both hands, pulling her to her feet. "Well, here we are," he said, "wherever *here* is."

Eve heard unseen scratching in the shadows. "Wherever it is, I think I'd just as soon be somewhere else."

Eleazor had already started his trek through the cave toward a dim light, barely visible in the distance. "Bennie boys, Evie girlys," the mutant insisted, "come quick! Me finds a way out dis cave."

Before Ben could react to the statement, Eve was pulling him toward the exit.

Chapter Five

I TRUST THAT ALL GOES as planned," the disembodied one said, his voice calm.

"It is as you say," Sedah replied.

The response came as an explosion, knocking him backwards.

"Our domain has been invaded by the humans, why?" The disembodied one roared. Sedah's dread grew as the voice paused. "Even as I speak they have entered the very caves we occupy."

The terrified Sedah dropped to his knees. "I did not know!" he stammered, lying prostrate on the ground. "How can this be?"

"That is your responsibility and yours alone to prevent!"

Sedah pulled himself to his knees. "Yes, oh Dark One, I will not fail you again."

"See to it . . ." the disembodied voice trailed off to nothing.

The verbally beaten subordinate, sensing himself alone once again, bade a hasty retreat, fumbling through dense tangles of webs laced with thousands of dangling arachnids.

Chapter Six

ELEAZOR BURST THROUGH the narrow opening in the cave wall and into the sunlight. "Bennie boys, you comie comes and bring Evies."

Eleazor squinted in the bright light as he motioned toward the opening, beckoning Ben and Eve to follow him.

Moments later, Ben and Eve joined their ward standing in a field of grass. The stalks came up to Ben's knees and halfway up Eleazor's torso. As they moved through the foliage, it seemed to bristle and move away from their touch.

Eve detected a thick liquid oozing from the top of each plant. She clawed at several splotches on her forearms. "Whatever this gunk is, it itches like crazy."

The stem ended in a pod resembling wheat, yet twice the size. Anywhere the liquid came in contact with their skin, a red welt formed that would instantly begin to itch.

As Ben, Eve and Eleazor made their way into the endless field, the flora steadily grew taller until it was well above their heads.

"At least this keeps us safe. The pods are too high to touch," Ben said, looking upward, hoping that the pods would not drip the irritating fluid. Ben paused, and pushed the stems over, snapping them at the base, clearing an area for them to rest.

"Let's sit awhile, sweetheart," Ben said. Eve looked at Ben, a puzzled expression on her face.

"What?" Ben asked. "You look like you swallowed a bug or something."

"Nothing," Eve said. "It's just that you haven't called me 'sweetheart' in such a long time. It sounds kinda out of place."

"I know," Ben said. "With everything we've been through I haven't shown you much affection." He smiled and motioned for her to come close.

Oblivious that Ben and Eve were no longer behind him, Eleazor continued to walk through the jungle of grass.

"Aren't you going to stop him?" Eve asked, scratching her left forearm. "He thinks we are still behind him."

"No," Ben replied. "Let the idiot find out for himself."

"I almost feel sorry for the little wretch." Eve said. "Don't you think we're being a tad rough on him? He is just a bumbling little imp who needs our help."

Ben shook his head."Don't let him pull you into that helpless charade. I've got a hunch we'll soon see a 180 out of that precious little imp."

ME GETS AWFUL HUNGRY," Eleazor said, patting his stomach. "Tha sticky stuff at come from tha top o deese weeds was good, but it too tall to reach now. Me look for more yummies." He turned around and stopped dead in his tracks.

"Bennies?" He asked, wringing his hands together. After receiving no answer, he tried again. "Evies? Is yous there?" Still no answer.

"Is you play joke on Leazy? Come out, come out! Leazy get scared." The ground rose under Eleazor. Like a large mole tunneling, the mounding earth moved in a straight line and then circled the terrified little gargoyle.

When it was six feet away, a smooth black snout resembling a moray eel broke through the ground. The creature was black with random orange splatters that ran from the top of its dorsal fin down the length of its body. About twelve feet of the animal protruded from the ground. It swayed back and forth like a snake about to attack its prey.

"Something is wrong," the eel-like creature hissed. "Yes, Laymen knows, very, very wrong" Laymen continued his dance, moving back and forth, trying to decide whether to devour the sniveling blob before it.

A shadow moved in between Eleazor and Laymen. Not a normal shadow, but one that stood upright with no other source than itself.

The dark form was featureless but humanoid in shape. It stood, facing the black and orange creature.

"Very wrong is correct," the shadow boomed. "No harm will come to this one or the two who remain behind."

"For one obviously lacking in strength, your voice exceeds any substance." The snake-like creature wove to and fro, daring the shadow to make the first move.

"Do not trifle with me; lest you experience the wrath of one with little substance. How unfortunate that you should have to face the only one of my kind immune to the cleansing power of the great light in the sky."

With no warning, Laymen lunged for Eleazor. At that moment, the shadow's hand caught Laymen by the throat. As his onyx-black fingers dug into its smooth outer skin, his other fist burst through the animal's head, blasting out a large section of bright pink flesh. The shadow pulled his hand back through the cavity, covered with a clear sticky fluid that dripped from the massive wound.

With a final seize, Laymen dropped to the ground with an enormous thud. An oval shaped hunk of meat hung dripping from the shadow's hand.

"Speak of this to no one," the shadow commanded.

After several moments, Eleazor opened his eyes and uncurled from his version of a fetal position. He surveyed his surroundings, spotting the narrow path he had created after leaving Ben and Eve. Once he saw Laymen's mutilated carcass, Eleazor ambled as fast as his misshapen body would carry him back in the direction he'd come.

Chapter Seven

BEN AWOKE from a deep sleep.

"Bennies, Evies, peas be here!" The gargoyle pleaded.

Eve, too tired to sit up, rubbed her eyes. "He's back," she said, in sing-song fashion.

Within moments, Eleazor burst into the opening, tripped and fell flat on his face.

"Where's the fire, Stumpy?" Ben inquired.

"No fire, silly Bennies," he said.

"Where have you been?" Eve questioned.

"Me looks for yummies is all," Eleazor said, remembering the shadow's final warning.

"Great! Now can we go back to sleep or is there another fascinating tale you wish to regale us with?" Ben asked.

"Sleepy sleep be fine," Eleazor replied.

"Thank you," Ben said.

"Ben," Eve said, first with a hint of surprise and then with total alarm in her voice, "Look at this."

Ben tried to sit up, but only managed to roll onto his side. He looked at Eve, unable to speak. Wherever her body touched the grass, her flesh had become translucent, her muscle tone greatly diminished. Looking down at himself, it was clear the same affliction had befallen him.

Eve touched the affected areas on her legs and then looked at Ben. Her eyes told a story of inevitability.

"We've got to get away from these plants," Ben said. He reached for Eve and the two huddled together. The last vestige of sunlight disappeared and the two melting masses intertwined into a single gelatinous blob.

Eleazor began to cry. "Don't go, Bennie boys and Evie girlys. Peas don't go!"

* * *

AS LIGHT FILTERED between the plant stems wet with the morning dew, a curious globule began to pulsate. As it moved, it grew, and separated into two distinct entities. The entities took on a different form. Four elongated areas extended from each mass, with a fifth stopping well short of the length reached by the first four.

The ends of these appendages developed, two forming human fingers and the two longest of the four, toes. The fifth rounded itself and then elongated. Facial features appeared and then color replaced the translucent hue.

"Bennies, Evies, you is back," Eleazor exclaimed.

"Yeah, but back from what?" Ben said. He sat with his head between his legs waiting for the vertigo to cease.

Eve crawled toward Ben, swaying as she did so.

"What was that?" She asked.

"Not a clue," Ben replied. "But you can bet we won't stay in this place another night." He raised his head and looking around, he finished a thought: At least I hope that only happens after dark.

"Which way?" Eve asked.

"Not the way we came," Ben replied.

Eleazor jumped up and down. "Me knows, me knows," he said. "Bennie boys, follow Leazy. Me show you way." Eleazor took off down the path he had traversed twice the day before, the events of that time firmly locked away in his subconscious.

* * *

AFTER THE TWO and Eleazor had traveled a mile, they came to a small clearing. A clearing not purposefully devised, but one made by violent means. Entering the area, the stench of first death, and then evil, enclosed all present in its claustrophobic grip.

"What happened here?" Ben asked, his breathing becoming more labored.

Eve shook her head at the scene laid out before her.

Eleazor stood dumbfounded, remembering what Laymen had warned him not to repeat.

A huge tube shaped skeleton, half stripped of its black and orange flesh, lay in the middle of the clearing. Other pieces of what Ben assumed were parts of the dead creature lay asunder around the skeleton. Hundreds, if not thousands, of buzzing insects along with small rodent-like carrion feeders continued to remove the flesh from the bones.

"I believe we've seen enough," Ben said. He walked around the creature with Eve and Eleazor following behind, all the while giving the remains a wide berth.

Ben, Eve and Eleazor forged a new path into the dreaded foliage, this time as before with Eleazor in the lead. After several more hours of hiking, the plant life thinned until they were clear of the irritating stalks. The trio found themselves in a field of short grass bordering a forest.

"Looks normal enough," Ben said. "From what I've seen so far, that doesn't seem to mean much."

"Are you feeling all right?" Eve asked.

"Not too bad," Ben replied. "As long as we take it slow."

"Good," she said, rubbing his back. They continued on and came to a small stream.

"Looks like a good place to stop for the night," Ben said.

"As long as we avoid that jelly thing," Eve said. She shuddered, contorting her mouth into an expression of disgust.

Ben looked up into the sky.

"Not to worry. I'm sure we'll have something much more interesting waiting for us." He smiled weakly, "I need to rest." Ben plopped down and hung his head between his knees.

"Are you sure you're okay?" Eve said, kneeling beside him.

"I'm fine," Ben said, placing a hand on her arm. Eleazor waddled up and patted Ben's shoulder.

"Bennie be fine, fine. Bennies need sleepy, sleep."

"You got it, Stumpy," Ben replied.

"Bennie say, Stumpy. It okee dokee long as you member me is Leazy."

"Yeah, yeah," Ben said. "Me member." Ben looked at Eve and lay back. "I'll rest here and then we'll set up camp."

"Sure," Eve said. "You'll feel better after a nap."

Ben didn't hear her reply. He was already snoring.

Chapter Eight

EN OPENED HIS EYES to darkness except for the orange flicker that emanated from behind, spreading in all directions as it danced against the surrounding foliage. Ben rolled over. Eve sat in front of the fire, stirring the glowing embers.

"What's up, hot stuff?" Ben said.

Eve jumped. "You startled me."

Ben propped himself up on one elbow. "You shouldn't have let me sleep so long."

Eve slid beside him. "You needed your rest." Eve brushed his hair back with her fingers and kissed his forehead. "Any better?"

"Much," he replied. Ben looked around and sat upright. "Where's Stumpy and how did you start a fire?"

"Your first question answers your second."

Ben thought a moment and furrowed his eyebrows.

"Okay, I'll bite."

"Not a clue," she began. "I stacked some dry kindling and before I could find anything to produce a spark, Eleazor began to show an interest in the wood I had gathered." Eve struggled with her words. It was as though she didn't actually believe what she was saying and was hesitant for fear of telling a lie. "Evidently, knowing what I was trying to do. Eleazor walked to the pile, breathed on it, and what do you know? Fire."

"Which brings me back to my first question: where is he?"

"After you fell asleep, I gathered wood and some of the fruit. Once Eleazor started the fire, he nosed through the stack of pods. Taking a bite, he spit it out and said he would find more, and I quote yummy, yummies. That's the last I saw of him."

"So now Eleazor's breathing fire." Ben pondered this notion and looked at Eve. "You can bet that will turn around to bite us."

Eve touched Ben's arm. "You and I have been through this before, but couldn't we be a little nicer to him." She stared at Ben trying to determine what he was contemplating. "Who knows," she continued, "maybe if we treat him better now he'll remember it after; you know."

"I realize that he seems to be a helpless little oaf and I admit that I've felt sorry for him, but don't let his placid demeanor fool you. You can bet he'll become every bit as evil as Jhorr warned."

"I guess you're right," Eve replied. "Any idea of when it will happen?"

Ben shook his head."Although I'm guessing that monkey won't climb off our backs for some time." Ben threw his wife an amorous grin. "Which brings me to the most important question?" He grabbed Eve and kissed her.

Something sharp poked his back; Ben whirled to see Eleazor standing behind them.

"Where monkey?" Eleazor asked. "Goody, good, good."

Ben jerked at the voice and looked up into the canopy, expecting legions of simian entrees just clamoring to be eaten.

"Don't sneak up on us like that," Eve chastised.

"Me no sneaky," Eleazor exclaimed. "Me waddles and bring yummies." Eleazor extended his hand. In it lay five tiny legs and three beaks. "Me no like little crunchy thingy parts."

"You ate song birds?" Eve asked, turning her nose up in disgust.

Eleazor smiled, exposing jagged yellow teeth with small tufts of feathers stuck in between.

Eve gagged. She stood, covered her mouth, and walked away.

Ben stared at Eleazor, the bizarre scene causing him to stay his planned assault for the creature's interruption. "Ah, we'll pass on the beaks."

"Okee dokee, Bennie boy's," Eleazor said. "Me go sleepy sleep now."

"Yes," Ben said. "You go sleepy sleep." Ben stood and walked over to Eve, wrapping his arms around her. "Sorry about that."

Eve turned to face him, "I'm not sure how much more of him I can take." Her eyes glistened. Eve shrugged her shoulders and dropped them in resolve. "I guess as much as I have to."

* * *

BEN AND EVE WOKE from a fitful night's sleep. Eve looked around.

"So where is our little bundle of joy this morning?"

Ben yawned. "I guess he's rounding up yummies for breakfast." Ben took a deep breath and sighed "Every instinct inside of me is screaming to make him go away."

Eve nodded, "But what choice do we have?"

"Bennies!" A voice sounded from a distance.

Ben turned to see Eleazor dragging what looked like a deer carcass behind.

"Speak of the devil." Ben shook his head and growled.

"What is it this time?" Eve moaned. The couple stood as the creature approached.

"Bennie boys, Evie girlys," Eleazor announced, "me brings breasbuss." He dropped the carcass beside the fire.

"You brought what?" Eve inquired.

"Breasbuss," Eleazor repeated. "Early time yummies."

"Oh, breakfast," Eve acknowledged.

"Right-o," Eleazor said, "breasbuss."

Ben leaned his head back and waved his hand in front of his nose. "How long has this thing been dead?"

Eleazor looked at Ben. "It runny runs fast. Me catch and take big bitey bite."

"You just killed it?" Eve asked.

"Yep," Eleazor said and nodded. He leaned over and took a huge bite out of the antelope's neck.

Eve shrank back in surprise.

Ben nudged her. "Look," he said, pointing at the place where Eleazor's bite entered the musculature. The area didn't bleed. It turned black and green as the advancing necrotic flesh overtook the exposed muscle.

"It rots where he bites it," Eve whispered.

"Do you remember what Jhorr said?" Ben whispered back.

"Pure evil," Eve said, nodding her head.

"Bennie, Evie, come eat with Leazy," Eleazor pleaded.

"We've already eaten," Ben said, patting his stomach. "Maybe we'll have some for lunch."

"Yes," Eve echoed. "I'm stuffed." Eve puffed out her cheeks to convince him how full she was. "I couldn't eat another bite."

"Okee dokee, me leave some for you." Eleazor took one final bite and waddled off into the forest happily munching away. As soon as he disappeared, Ben turned to Eve.

"We have to keep a closer eye on him."

Eve nodded. "It's hard to think of him the way Jhorr described him."

Ben looked at the ground stroking his chin between his thumb and index finger. "How do you suppose he chased that deer down?"

"I don't think I want to know." Eve wrapped her arms around herself and shuddered.

Ben wrapped his arms around Eve, pulling her close. "I'll move what's left of that deer before it smells up the whole area." As he released his grip and stepped around her, he saw a pile of black dirt where the carcass had been. Ben moved closer and kicked at the pile, causing a small cloud of dust to rise. Ben stared in amazement. "Not only has it decomposed. It's composted."

"At least we know that we don't want to eat anything he brings us," Eve said.

Ben stared at the decayed material on the ground. "No doubt." He turned his attention to a small pile of fruit they had gathered the day before. "Let's start breakfast."

"THAT MAKES FOUR MORE we can eat," Eve said. She dropped an assortment of fruit and a bundle of grass that held the aroma of citrus in front of the shelter.

Ben finished tying two ends of vine together and looked up at her. "What do you mean four more?"

Eve motioned toward her deposit of produce. "I took a bite of each one while you were finishing the shelter, and what do you know . . ." she paused, spreading her arms. "I'm still here."

Ben stood, his anger suppressing the admiration he felt for his wife's selflessness. "What is wrong with you? Don't you understand that any one of these could have killed you?"

Eve placed both hands on her hips. "So you can risk your life but I can't?"

Ben fumbled for words. "Well, yeah, I guess so." Ben pointed an accusing finger in her direction. "That's the way it is, and that's the way it's going to be."

Eve's mouth dropped. "I don't think so! And if you want to keep that finger you'd better get it out of my face." Eve turned and stomped off into the forest.

Ben shook his head. "Women!" Drawing back his foot, he kicked a hole in the wall of the newly constructed shelter. Ben sat down and took several deep breaths to calm himself.

"Bennie boys," came a shrill voice echoing through the clearing. "Looky, looky what me has."

Ben groaned. Just what I need, he thought, a disgruntled wife, and a sawed off freak that wants to be buddies.

Ben rose to his feet as Eleazor lumbered up, carrying a long slender implement.

"Looky, Bennie boys," he said, handing the object to Ben.

Ben's knees buckled, stunned by the piece he held in his hands. He slowly raised his head. "Did you make this?"

"Nopey nope, Bennie boys. Me finds it."

"Where did you find it?"

"In the woods, Bennie boys. It bump into Leazy."

Ben rolled the piece in his hands. "This can't be," he muttered. "It's impossible."

Chapter Nine

E VE TRUDGED through the forest, kicking up dried foliage with each step. She grunted and kicked a large array of leaves into the air. "Men! How can someone I love make me so furious?" Eve continued her spectacle, alternating vocal outbursts with attempts to injure invisible objects. Finishing her tirade, Eve collapsed on the ground.

"Perhaps it is not as you would suppose," a voice said.

Eve jerked to a standing position scanning the immediate area. "Ben?"

"No, dear one, but a friend nonetheless."

Eve turned to see a lone figure standing mere feet away. He stood tall, close to seven feet, dressed in close-cropped fur. A forked beard hung a foot or more below his chin. His right hand held a staff. Eve's first inclination was Jhorr, but she knew that was impossible.

"Who are you?" she questioned, looking for a quick escape route.

"I am called Sedah," he said, laying a fisted arm across his chest and bowing. Sedah raised his head and nodded. "And what may I call you, fair one?"

Eve hesitated and rubbed her palms against her thighs.

Sedah smiled and took a step toward her.

Chapter Ten

EN LOOKED AT THE OBJECT and at Eleazor. He observed a small hole in the gargoyle's chest, which was oozing a thick black fluid. "Bumped into him?" Ben whispered, turning his attention back to the object.

"How does a world covered by water yesterday produce a pristine arrow? This had to have been man made, and even with the deformed end could just as well have been made this morning." Ben rolled the artifact in his hand. He noted how thin the object was and wondered how it would hold up when in flight. He paid close attention to the diminished tip.

"Obsidian," He whispered. Ben glanced once again at Eleazor's wound.

"I agree," Eleazor said.

Ben, shocked at the response, stared at Eleazor. "What did you say?"

"Okee dokee, Bennie boys."

"Yeah, okee dokee." Ben sighed, lowering his head and shaking it as he did so. After several seconds had passed, he once again questioned Eleazor. "Have you seen Eve?"

"Nopey nope." Eleazor looked at Ben. "Me goes back to find more stuffy stuff. If me sees Evie, me let you know."

"You do that," Ben said. Eleazor waddled toward the forest.

"Of course," he said, as he disappeared into the foliage.

"On second thought, I'll find Eve. Better me than our little schizoid."

Chapter Eleven

"E VE," SHE SAID. "My name is Eve."

"Ah," Sedah said. "The name is known among my people."

Eve looked at Sedah puzzled. "How can that be? We just arrived yesterday."

Sedah smiled. "Follow me." He motioned down a narrow path. "It is better I show you."

Eve stared down the path. *What could he show me, but more woods?*

"Sedah, where are you taking me?"

"As I stated, fair one, to my village I wish to introduce you to my people."

"So you do have a village?"

"It is so."

Eve thought for a moment."I don't know," she said. When Sedah didn't press, this piqued her curiosity. "Maybe I will go."

Eve surprised herself at how willing she was to follow this stranger, but she sensed comfort with this man. *It's like being with loved ones again.* She sighed. *But that's a world away.*

Sedah came to a halt, then entered an elevated clearing. Eve came around and stood beside him.

"Observe," he said. "My people." He spread his hand in a circular motion. From their vantage point they were able to see the entire village spread over a vast area.

Eve stared at the settlement with disbelief. A second later she was off her feet tearing through the forest at breakneck speed. She dodged trees so closely, that tufts of hair would become embedded in the bark and then jerked from their moorings in her scalp. Strangely enough, Eve was more concerned with the loss of hair than the beast that bore her.

From her position she saw the creature was a biped, covered in large diamond shaped scales. Each scale was: gray with a blood red edge and down his back a six-inch tall, yellow mane. The mane resembled stiff hair, she assumed it ran the entire length of its body.

Eve, firmly cradled in the beast's front appendages was fascinated by her transport's large yellow eye.

After traveling, what she perceived to be a mile or more, the settlement was still visible.

"We're moving around the village!" she exclaimed.

Eve felt herself being pulled from the creature's arms and placed on the ground. The next thing she noticed was Sedah beating the reptilian kidnapper with his staff. The beast yelped and squealed as the big man struck it, time and time again.

What seemed so unusual to Eve, even more so than the savage beating, were the words coming from Sedah's mouth.

"No more, or you will die before your time, and rest assured, it will be by my hand." With that, Sedah ceased pummeling the creature and stood in defiance as it hobbled away in pain. He turned his attention toward Eve.

"Are you injured in any way, fair one?"

Eve was busy checking herself over."No, everything seems fine." Sedah helped Eve to her feet. "What was that thing?"

Sedah retrieved his staff. "Nothing more than a pet that has yet to learn its proper place."

"A pet," Eve exclaimed, "That *pet* was going to kill me."

"Worry not; there is no danger, merely mischievousness that must be reminded of its place in our society."

"Mischievous," Eve said. "Seems understated, but if you say so."

"Are you all right to travel?" Sedah asked.

Eve nodded. "As far as I can tell."

Sedah smiled. "Then come, fair one; much awaits." They traversed their way down a small incline and into the valley. Eve was able to discern structures through the foliage just ahead.

"How is this possible?" Eve asked, the memory of her last encounter fading.

Sedah stopped and looked at Eve. "What do you mean, fair one?"

"There was not time to construct a complete settlement in the short time since the water receded," she said.

"I do not comprehend," Sedah replied.

Eve saw in his eyes he didn't understand her inquiry, or maybe he excelled at portraying ignorance. She pondered a moment.

"How long have you been here?"

Sedah looked away and squinted. He seemed to mull the question over in his mind. After much consideration, he once again looked in her direction. "Always."

Eve changed her line of questioning. *He doesn't understand what I'm asking*, she thought.

"You could not have always been here, the flood would have killed you and your people."

Sedah once again took a moment to reflect. "What is *'killed,'* fair one?"

Eve was taken aback. "Don't you understand," she said, and then hesitated. "Dead."

Sedah shook his head, acknowledging his failure to identify with her question.

Eve's irritation welled. "Sedah," she stated, as a matter of fact, "you're born, you live and you die."

Sedah expressed recognition. "Yes, born I know, but this *'die'* you speak of, I do not understand."

A notion crept into Eve's consciousness. *Do these people live forever?* She wondered. Unable to accept this concept, a vexed "okay" was all she could muster.

Sedah, satisfied, turned and hurried along the path. A bewildered Eve followed.

SEDAH AND EVE arrived at the settlement to a warm welcome.

"You've been absent quite a while," Eve commented.

Sedah nodded. "Yes, I left at the rising of the first light."

"This morning?"

"If I understand your words, it is as you say, this morning."

Eve stared at Sedah. "I would have thought much longer, considering the greeting you received."

Sedah ignored her comment. The multitude moved in surrounding Eve.

"Dear friends," he said, "please welcome Eve, and treat her as one of your own."

Chapter Twelve

EN TOSSED THE PROJECTILE to the ground. He walked into the forest, searching for any clue that would tell him which direction Eve had gone.

"Nothing," he said. Ben guessed at the path she may have taken and moved in that direction. It seemed as though Eve had disappeared off the face of this Earth.

Unable to locate any trace of her, Ben's heart pounded against his chest as his anxiety level rose. He hastened his pace and called out Eve's name. Several more minutes passed. *Why did I let her go?* He sat down, fighting for air.

Once his breathing eased, he stood, ready to resume his search. Dire thoughts began to race through Ben's head. There's no one here to take her. Where could she be? Then a notion came to him: "Eleazor."

* * *

"ME FINDS MORE stuff for Bennie boys," Eleazor said, "and me will do's it too. Just you watchy watch." He began to forage through the forest floor in earnest.

"Perhaps there is no need to search," a soothing voice said.

"Who there?" Eleazor questioned. He squatted low, turning his head from side to side. "Is that you, Bennie boys?" His voice now reduced to a whisper.

"No, no," the soothing voice replied. "This is not Bennie boys."

"Who you is?" Eleazor asked, pushing himself upright and looking around in terror.

"I am what you are hoping to find."

"You scares Leazy."

"Don't be afraid." There was a slight pause, "I will be your bestest buddy," the soothing voice finished.

"You be Leazy's buddy bud?"

"Oh, yes. Your very, very, best buddy bud."

"You not hurt Leazy none?" Eleazor asked, laying the tip of a clawed finger on his lower lip.

"Not one little bit. We are very best buddies now."

Eleazor furrowed his brow, thought for a moment and came to a questionable conclusion. "How can me looks for you when you is already here talkin to Leazy?"

"There is no need to search for me. I have always been with you; however, you had yet to realize my presence until this moment."

"You be much with Leazy?"

"For some time now."

"For really real?" Eleazor contorted his face into a smile that resembled a grimace.

"Eleazor, you have begun your transition. I am here to help you and help you I will. You must trust me."

"You say Leazy is sansition?"

"Yes, and may I say, you have done a wonderful job."

Eleazor looked pleased with himself, but his expression took on a look of concern.

"Me worries."

"Do not worry, buddy bud, I will teach you everything you need to know."

"Goody good; me likes to be teached. Just watch, me be besty best of all."

"And so you shall," the soothing voice said. "So you shall."

Chapter Thirteen

EN CONTINUED TO SEARCH for another hour, then sat down, gasping for breath. He dropped his head and felt something touch his shoulder. It caused him to whirl around, landing on his knees.

"A little jumpy?" Eve said.

Ben leapt to his feet. He clutched Eve by the arms and held fast. "Where were you? Don't you know I've been going nuts trying to find you!"

"I'm sorry, sweetie, I didn't realize you were looking for me."

Ben eased his grip, his voice a mixture of concern and frustration. "I was afraid something had happened to you."

Eve wiped an errant hair from her face. Remembering the chance encounter, her eyes widened. "Wait until you hear," she said, placing her hands on Ben's cheeks. "There are other people here."

"What? That's impossible."

"No, they're here. I've talked with them and Sedah."

"Sedah?" Ben said.

"Yes. He's their leader."

Ben shook his head and turned away, dismissing the notion. "I guess they've acquired gills," he said. "Or are you forgetting this place being under water a short time ago?"

Eve walked around to face him. "No," she said. "They don't, and why won't you believe me?"

Ben wrinkled his forehead, remembering the artifact Eleazor had given him. "I guess that could explain it."

"Explain what?"

"Our stumpy little buddy found an arrow. It didn't make sense for something that advanced to exist in such a primitive setting." Ben scratched the back of his neck. "I guess that's one more mystery added to the countless others we've yet to figure out."

"I can't do much about that," Eve said, "but I've got something that will interest you." She presented a small bundle.

"What's that?" Ben asked.

"Something we haven't had in quite a while," Eve said. "Meat!"

Ben looked at the bundle and then at Eve. "So you *did* meet someone?"

She smiled and nodded.

* * *

THE LAST RAYS OF SUNLIGHT filtered through the trees as the couple prepared to eat.

Ben smelled the cooked meat. "What did you say this was again?"

"I'm not sure because the names they have for things are different than ours, but I think it's something like, or at least related to, a squirrel."

"How do you know it's safe to eat?"

"What would they have to gain by poisoning us?"

Ben stared, unable to muster a response. Eve took a bite and then urged him to do the same.

Ben sniffed the diminutive leg one more time, shrugged his shoulders and took a small bite. He raised his eyebrows, nodded his approval and ate with increased fervor. Ben cleaned the bone and tossed it to the side, sucking on each finger and removing every vestige of residue. He finished with a large belch.

"Ben," Eve protested, spewing food out of her mouth. "Not while I'm eating."

Ben chuckled. "Sorry, Mrs. Adams. Might I say, your food shower was most appetizing. Please continue."

Eve nodded, extended her index finger with one hand and covered her mouth with the other and swallowed.

"Sedah said a lot of things I didn't understand. It was almost like he didn't grasp what he was saying either."

"I don't follow you," Ben said.

"I questioned him about the flood and how they had survived," Eve began. "Sedah answered by saying that his people had always been there. He didn't acknowledge that there had been a flood. As I was about to leave, he handed me a bundle of meat. It was then he contradicted himself. Sedah said that since the great water had withdrawn, they could eat every fruit or vegetable and even pre-selected animals to slaughter for meat."

"Wonder what water has to do with that?" said Ben.

"I don't know, but it gets even stranger."

"I've got nothing but time," Ben mused. He stretched out on his back, propping himself up on his elbows.

Eve looked at her surroundings. "Ain't that the truth." She paused and stared thoughtfully at Ben.

"You're not out of the woods yet," he warned. "You don't know these people, and there's no telling what could have happened to you wandering around by yourself."

Eve frowned. "If they wanted to hurt me, don't you think they would have done so instead of letting me go?"

"Regardless, you'd best not be so trusting. Doesn't it make you wonder why he lied about the flood?"

Eve nodded. "Sedah and his people, they just seemed so genuine." She waited for a rebuttal, but none came.

Ben, preoccupied, stared into the darkness.

"Ben?" she asked. "What are you doing, other than not paying attention?"

He glared at Eve. "Just keep talking. We may have a visitor."

"Where?" Eve asked, turning her head side to side.

"Stop," Ben said. "Act as though nothing is unusual."

"Nothing *is* unusual," Eve protested, "other than your recently acquired paranoia."

"Maybe so," Ben said, reaching out and touching her nose, "or perhaps one of your new friends is paying us a visit."

She swatted his hand away. "Keep your delusions to yourself and let me finish my story." Eve settled back into her tale, the interruption forgotten.

"Sedah alluded to the fact they never die. Imagine that? They're born, but never die."

Ben looked at her, covering his curiosity with exaggerated disinterest. "Are you done?"

"What? Have you heard anything I've said?" Eve protested.

Ben moved from a reclined position to his knees, keeping a wary eye for any movement in the forest. "Yes, you're all I've heard."

Eve did her best to ignore Ben's comment. "Well, doesn't any of this seem unusual to you?"

Ben shook his head and smiled. "A little over twenty-four hours ago," Ben said, "I was standing on the edge of two worlds inundated with water. I stepped across a threshold into a ship's transport container. The water that filled the container's domain began to pour into the only world I had ever known. The container doors slammed shut. Once the water from the world we entered had receded, there were birds, animals and trees. Now you're telling me there's a complete race of people oblivious to the fact that a flood even took place. I think I've moved way beyond being surprised at anything that goes on here."

Eve opened her mouth to speak. Before she summoned a word, Ben grabbed a stick from the fire and made a mad dash for the woods. The figure he followed was bipedal and a little over six feet tall from what he could tell by the dim light cast from his makeshift torch.

The chase didn't last long as the humanoid stopped and turned to face Ben. He had long, matted, gray hair and his stained, tattered clothes appeared as though they were once light-colored linen. His beard bore hairless scars etched deep into his pale, leathery skin. A large crooked nose dominated his features. His face was expressionless, save for his eyes which told a story of curiosity, confusion, and fear.

"What do you want and why were you spying on us?" Ben demanded.

The man creature tilted his head side to side and uttered a guttural, "No."

"Well," Ben said, "I need answers, and there are two ways I can get what I want; you give 'em or I take 'em." He paused, allowing this to sink in, wondering if this man-creature before him understood. After several moments of silence, Ben spoke, "I had hoped we'd avoid this, but I guess not."

Ben took a step forward, then a blinding flash of light followed by another stopped him in his tracks. The man vanished. The last thing Ben saw were two gray-colored paws and a long tail making a hasty retreat.

BEN WALKED BACK INTO CAMP, still reeling from his experience. Eve ran up to him. "What happened?" she said.

"I'm not so sure." Ben relayed the story of the chase and confrontation with the strange creature to Eve. The conversation moved to other subjects and before they knew it, the sky was beginning to grow lighter.

"It's nearly dawn," Ben said.

"A little past our bed time, don't you think?"

Ben's demeanor softened. He pulled her close and kissed her.

Eve smiled and returned the gesture. "I can see you're ready as usual."

Ben picked her up. Walking into the shelter, he laid her down on a mattress he had woven from tree boughs.

"Nice," she said.

Ben lay down beside her. "You inspire me to do my best work."

Eve rolled toward him. "I bet."

Eve closed her eyes and moved to kiss him. Ben sensed her advance and prepared his lips to touch hers. Both sighed in anticipation.

"Bennie boys," a voice screeched into the shelter. The squat creature waddled through the door. "Is you sleepy sleep, Bennie boys?"

"It had crossed my mind," Ben moaned, and sat up. "Did you want something?"

Eleazor plopped down on the dirt floor. "Me just wants to tell you somefin." The creature looked at Eve. "Me knows where Evie Eve's is."

Ben rolled his eyes. "And where might that be?"

"Evie Eve's is right aside you, silly Bennie boys."

"Thanks," Ben said, "I hadn't noticed."

Eleazor looked around the room. "Where Leazy sleep?" He asked, with an expectant glance toward the bed.

The question took Ben by surprise. He clambered for a clever answer.

"I thought you would want to find yummies."

"You is so smarty smart. Leazy loves good yummies." He raised himself to his feet and walked to the door. "You have been extremely helpful, Benjamin Adams," Eleazor said, and quietly exited the shelter.

Startled, Eve sat upright. "What was that all about?"

"I'm not sure. He's been doubling up since this morning."

Eve shivered. "Do you suppose he's doing what Jhorr referred to as 'coming into his own?"

"I guess," Ben replied. "Now where were we?" He rolled over and took Eve into his arms.

She pushed him away. "Not now. You have no idea when that thing might come back."

Ben rolled over and sat up on the edge of the mattress. "Great, just great."

She moved over and sat beside him. "I'm sorry, but he gives me the creeps." Eve said.

Ben looked into her eyes and saw genuine fear. Smiling half-heartedly he said. "That's okay. Let's get some sleep."

Chapter Fourteen

E VE WOKE TO AN EMPTY BED. She crawled through the boughs and stepped out of the shelter.

Ben sat beside the fire, his breathing coming in labored gasps.

"Are you okay?" Eve asked.

"Yeah," Ben said, followed by a round of wheeze-filled coughing.

"You sit there and rest, I'll shop this morning."

Ben didn't answer, he just nodded, raised a hand and wiggled his fingers.

EVE RETURNED with an armload of assorted produce. She made quick work peeling and slicing half of the fruit, leaving it raw and laying the rest on a flat stone, covering the fire.

"Won't be long now," Eve said, throwing Ben a wide grin. "You seem to be feeling better."

"Yes, much better."

They began to munch on the raw fruit.

"I'm glad your buddy told you we could eat pretty much anything we want," Ben said.

Eve nodded. "You seem to be a little more willing to accept a stranger's advice, I see."

Ben shook his head. "No just hungry."

"Sedah wanted me to bring you to meet them." Eve said.

"And?"

"Today's as good as any; unless you have other pressing business."

"Maybe we should leave these people alone. Something's wrong," Ben said, "I don't know what it is, but it just doesn't mesh."

"You're going to have to trust at some point and they've already shown their good faith." Eve began removing the cooked fruit from the fire.

"Good faith?" Ben protested. "Are you forgetting your new found friend's deception?"

"I told you, he never tried to hide anything, and he did tell me the truth."

"Eventually, when convenience dictated he do so."

Eve glared at him.

Ben sighed. "All right, I guess it won't hurt to meet them."

Chapter Fifteen

"I THOUGHT YOU SAID this place wasn't far," Ben protested. "We've been hiking for hours." He sat down to rest for a moment. "We've only been walking fifteen minutes." Eve continued on, then realized she was alone. She turned.

Ben sat, struggling for air. Eve ran back to him. "I'm sorry, sweetheart, I didn't know you were having trouble."

Ben tried to speak, but couldn't.

"We'll rest here until you're able to go on." Eve said.

Ben nodded. After several minutes had passed, he said, "Okay, I can go now."

"We'll take it slow," Eve assured him.

The couple made their way down the path Sedah had led Eve on earlier, and soon came to the village clearing. The area was empty.

Eve stood gazing in disbelief. "Where is it?"

"I assume you're talking about the village?" he said.

Eve nodded.

"I guess they pulled out, and from the looks of it, in a hurry."

"How did you reach that conclusion?" Eve asked.

"Their fire pits are still smoldering," Ben replied. He scanned the settlement's footprint. "From the size of this place and you having been here less than twenty-four hours ago, I'd say they left in a hurry."

"Point taken, but why leave?"

"No doubt they'll show up again," Ben said. "Bad pennies always do."

Eve shook her head. "Maybe so, it just makes little sense."

Ben, noticing Eve's disappointment, offered a suggestion. "Hundreds of people, moving an entire village this size, can't be too hard to follow."

The corners of her mouth curled upward into a smile. Ben and Eve circled the area until Ben saw what they'd been looking for. Midway down the east side of the encampment ran a well-trodden path.

"If that ain't it," Ben said, "it doesn't exist."

"You're a genius," Eve said, as she passed Ben and trotted down the roadway exodus.

"BEN," EVE YELLED, "over here!"

He joined her. What he saw caused him to dismiss his shortness of breath.

"What is it?" Eve asked, as the pair moved in closer.

"Can't be," Ben murmured. He began to remove vines and overgrowth from a large, orange colored, cylindrical object.

"It can't be what?"

"This is so much larger than I remember," Ben said, ignoring her comment. He rubbed several layers of dried mud from the side, exposing letters that defined the object's unmistakable identity. Ben stared, dumbfounded.

Eve stood beside him. "Ben, what is it?"

"Do you remember the story I told about the oil rig I worked on?"

Eve nodded. "Yes, the Omega Z, back on our home world."

Ben pointed to the three-letter word in bold type.

"It's the lifeboat," he stammered.

Eve thought a moment and then froze. "The Ark!" she gasped.

"Yes and probably what very nearly took your head off, during the flash flood."

NEITHER BEN NOR EVE noticed the large shadow move overhead and dive toward its prey several hundred yards away.

The winged creature swooped low, severing the stag's head cleanly. It circled around, and landed on the warm, still twitching body and began to feed. Once gorged, the creature walked away, too heavy to fly, leaving the remainder of the already rotting carcass.

Chapter Sixteen

"WHERE EBBY BODY BE DONE and goes to?" Eleazor squawked. He stomped around the camp, through the shelter, and settled by the now extinguished fire. "Me no likes loney lone time."

"You're not alone," said the soothing voice. "I told you I am always here for you."

"You no fun," Eleazor replied. "Me cants bring you yummies or thingies that make you says, 'Oh, Leazy, where you get dis'?"

"I can do much better than that."

"How yous do it?"

"I will never leave you by yourself," the soothing voice said. "Ben and Eve are selfish. They consider themselves and no one else. I sense they do not care for you at all."

Eleazor poked his bottom lip out and cried.

"There, there, now. That is not the proper way to handle things."

"How you spect Leazy is feel?"

"As you have expressed to me, very sad; however, the only way to heal yourself of this worthless emotion is to become angry."

"Angy?" questioned Eleazor.

"Yes," the soothing voice replied, this time in a low, wicked growl. "Now is the time to begin your formal training. The first lesson will be revenge."

Eleazor pondered a moment and contorted his lips into a hidcous grin. "Yesss," he hissed, "I am sure that is exactly what I need."

Chapter Seventeen

BEN CIRCLED *THE ARK*, clearing away debris until he came upon an open doorway. The door itself was missing, having been wrenched from its hinges. It lay in a crumpled heap several yards away.

"I hope we don't run into whatever did that," Eve said.

Ben nodded, trying to imagine what could rip through two inches of high strength steel.

He stepped inside. Eve followed. As his eyes adjusted to the diminished light, he became able to discern objects within.

"This isn't *The Ark* I remember," he said.

"What's the difference?" Eve asked.

"To start with, it's too big. The Omega Z's *Ark* would hold 35 people, max. It had four bathrooms and a community sleeping area with hammocks. Prepackaged rations were the only food source. It was strictly for short-term survival."

They made their way deeper into the interior of the grounded vessel. Ben opened a gate constructed from hollow steel pipe for his wife to walk through.

"This place could hold a great deal more than 35." Eve said.

Ben nodded, stopped and did a 360. "Have you noticed all the animal stalls? It even smells like a stable." Ben's next step landed in a soft pile of black dust.

"Eve." He stirred the powder with his foot. "Look familiar?"

Eve gasped, stopping to cough. "Eleazor dragged that horrid thing into our camp for breakfast." She cleared her throat and coughed one more time. "Every time I think of it, I want to gag."

"Well, it looks like our little one has been dining out," Ben said. "They do grow up so quickly."

"Enough with the jokes," Eve said.

"Sorry, just watch where you step, it looks like there's more spread throughout the ship."

"It's more like a floating barnyard than a ship."

Ben chuckled and walked, leaving Eve to keep an eye peeled on the floor, for unwholesome things to avoid stepping in. They came to a walled-in area. Along with a kitchen and bathroom, there were 12 private rooms. Two furnished with bunks, and each of the remaining 10 empty, save for a large stainless steel hook attached to the ceiling. Ben stared at the stainless projections.

"There was someone living here besides your barnyard friends," Eve said.

"Apparently," Ben agreed, "This way." Several yards from the sleeping quarters, a single door set into a wall bade Ben and Eve to enter. Ben pulled the lever and stepped inside.

"Look at this," Eve said. "Talk about the lap of luxury."

Ben smiled, "I'd say this is it."

She rubbed her hands over the rich leather seats and sat down in the one to the left. She clutched the small "D" shaped steering wheel, and turned to Ben who had taken a seat in the chair to the right. "Where to, Mr. Adams? I'll take you anywhere you want to go if you'll show me how to start this thing."

"My dear," Ben said, "do you realize you're sitting in the cockpit of one of the most elaborate animal carriers ever constructed. What I'm trying to say is, I haven't a clue, and in case you hadn't noticed, we're all out of water." The short respite and brief reason to chuckle could not have come at a better time.

Ben stared at the intricate instrumentation on the dashboard, and then something caught his eye."There it is," Ben pointed to a switch labeled, OZ release. "Press this switch during bad weather and you'd drop from the drilling platform into the sea. You would remain tethered—"

Both Ben and Eve jerked at the "clanking" noise, elsewhere in the ship.

"I think we may have overstayed our welcome," Ben whispered. He slid from his seat onto the floor and inched toward the open door.

Eve's eyes were as big as saucers.

Once Ben reached the door, he scanned the interior of the ship, but saw nothing. He was about to stand when a faint scratching sound caused him to stay put. Ben signaled with his hand for Eve to join him.

"What's out there?" she asked.

"Nothing I can see; but listen, do you hear that?"

Eve was about to shake her head no, when she recognized what sounded like someone rubbing their hands through sand. She looked at Ben. "Yes," she whispered, "I hear it." After looking through the cockpit windshield, it took a while for their eyes to adjust to the dimly lit cargo area.

Ben pointed to a space, 30 feet to the left."I count at least 10 possibly 12," Ben said.

"They're so small," Eve said, "like little naked people. I wonder what they're doing?"

"Mixing water with the black dust and eating it, near as I can tell," Ben said.

"You could have kept that to yourself."

"You asked."

Eve shuddered."What are we going to do?"

"If we stay in here long enough for them to finish eating, we'll starve to death." Ben said.

"You didn't answer my question."

"Yes I did." He took her by the hand. "We're leaving." Ben stood and helped Eve to her feet. They moved toward the exit with their backs sliding along the walls. Once they reached the doorway, Eve stepped out first. In his zeal to leave the fetid depository, Ben's foot caught the raised metal lip. He may as well have exited *The Ark* beating a drum.

Ben picked himself off the ground. Alerting the 12 inside became a moot point.

There were several hundred more gathered on the outside. They were accepting a steady flow of the black dust through a hole in the Ark's hull. Several groups seem to process the compost in large mortars, grinding the contents with roots and leaves, using oversized pestles, while others packaged the material in leaf bundles.

This impressive production came to a halt when Ben made his grand exit.

The small creatures moved toward the couple.

Eve noticed there seemed to be no difference, in gender. They were dirty, two feet tall carrion feeders, with dark beards and bald heads

"Do you think they're friendly?" Eve squeaked.

Ben pulled Eve, step for step, away from the advancing crowd.

"No, I think they see fresh meat," Ben said. "We need to pick up the pace."

"What about your breathing? You'll never be able to keep up."

"When I give the word, you move as fast as your legs will carry you."

Eve opened her mouth to speak.

"Don't worry," Ben said, "I'll be right behind you."

Eve nodded.

Ben increased to a slow jog to test the competition. They easily matched his speed.

"No time like the present . . . *Run!*" Ben pulled hard on Eve's arm to slingshot her ahead. The move had the opposite effect. Eve's momentum took her straight to the ground, while Ben toppled head over heels trying to avoid Eve's prostrate frame. Ben scrambled back to Eve, as the first of the tiny humanoids arrived.

One ventured forward, making constant gurgling noises. He kept his distance at first, then inched his way in close enough to touch Eve's hair and quickly retreated.

"He's testing the waters," Ben said.

Without warning, the little man rushed in, grabbed two handfuls of Eve's hair and pulled her over, smashing her face into the dirt. As he released his grip and turned to run, Ben wrapped one hand around its scrawny neck. He squeezed until the thing went limp. Ben released the swollen neck and gripped the flaccid creature by his lower legs. Eve was sitting up, coughing and snorting, trying to remove the dirt packed into each of her facial orifices.

"Are you okay?" Ben asked.

Eve nodded."Where are you going with that thing," she said, in a nasal voice.

"A little house cleaning."

Ben began a purposeful walk toward the column of little people. One stepped out, by reason of confrontation or curiosity. To Ben, it didn't matter. One swing, two fractured skulls means a weapon for each hand. After several dozen tiny corpses lay scattered, Ben stopped to catch his breath.

"I could do this all day." Ben looked at the bodies and at what seemed to be thousands of tiny heads advancing toward him. "Well, maybe not all day." Ben moved back to where Eve was standing. "We need to move, and now."

The advancing line of little people came to an abrupt halt, paused, then opted for a hasty retreat.

"That's odd," Ben said, "I wonder what made them leave like that." A presence descended, settling over both Ben and Eve. The hair on the back of Ben's neck jumped to attention. As he turned around, Eve was already poking his arm, alerting him to what he already knew.

Ben looked up to locate the eyes of the human forms that stood behind him, 100 or more strong. They dressed in simple cotton clothes, sleeveless shirts and pieces of rope looped through their pants for belts. One stood out from the crowd, in that a cotton and leather band encircled his head and in his hands he held a staff.

"My dear, Eve," Sedah said, "It pleasures me to see you again." He bowed to the young woman and turned to Ben. "I assume this to be the partner you have chosen to join with for life."

"Yes," Eve said. "This is my husband, Ben."

"Good to meet you," Ben said, extending his hand.

"It is good for me, also," Sedah said, staring at Ben's hand, deciding what to do. He decided what seemed right and placed his hand into Ben's. "Your name too is known among my people."

Ben nodded, his curiosity building. He looked at Eve and then to Sedah.

"How do you know my name?"

"Both of your names run deep within the rich history of my people." Sedah smiled, "Please come with me, dear ones. I will show you."

His interest piqued, Ben took Eve's hand and followed.

Sedah led them to a mud and thatched structure. "First, I would ask you to join me in the midday meal."

"We would be delighted," Eve replied.

Ben nodded.

"Please be seated." Sedah motioned toward several woven mats spread out on the floor then left the building. A wooden frame made from bent saplings stretched from floor to ceiling. Framework covered with tufts of thick dried grass was lashed and glued with mud to intermediate wooden hoops used to brace the vertical support. It was an uneven and loosely packed dirt floor, which made sense if the building had been recently erected, Ben thought. The couple seated themselves.

"It's dark in here," Eve whispered.

Ben, looking around, noticed that the only light making its way into the room came through bare spots in the thatching. Thin rays of light shot in all directions crisscrossing each other, illuminating dust specks and giving the interior an unnatural glow.

"I guess this is the best they could do in the short time they've had to erect the village."

Eve rubbed her hands together. "I suppose you're right."

Sedah pushed the animal skin door covering open and stepped into the room. He was carrying a small tray. He set the tray before Ben and Eve and then sat down himself."Please, help yourselves."

Ben looked at the tray. There were several bowls containing chunks of meat in a thick brown liquid. The meat came pierced with wooden skewers. He picked up one of the skewers and looked at Eve. She raised her eyebrows as Ben put the chunk in his mouth. He chewed several times and then his lips spread into a wide grin.

"Delicious," he said, as he reached for another. Eve did the same, and soon, both were devouring the impaled delicacy. After several pieces, Ben set another empty skewer down.

"It's good, but it's so rich I believe that's all I can eat."

Eve took another piece. "Just one more."

Ben filled his cheeks with air and released it. "All yours."

Sedah sat watching the couple eat. When Eve had finished, she leaned backward on her elbows and yawned. Ben sat with his legs crossed in front of him, closing his eyes and nodding off. As he leaned forward, he awoke to keep from tumbling over.

"Perhaps I will leave you to rest," Sedah said. "Afterward, I will show you more of our village."

Eve nodded, and without a word, rolled to her side. Ben joined her, and soon they were both breathing in rhythm. Sedah stepped out of the door.

"Our guests are resting. Please make preparations for their awakening."

Chapter Eighteen

EVE YAWNED and opened her eyes. The room was dark except for fires outside she could see flickering through the grass wall.

"How long was I asleep?" She reached for her head and found her hands bound together. "Ben!" she cried.

A silhouetted figure appeared through the door.

"Please refrain from calling in a loud voice. As we speak, your place is being readied."

"Why am I tied up, and where is my husband?"

"Do not concern yourself with such things. This is part of our most sacred ritual."

"I demand to see Sedah this instant."

"You are not in a position to make demands. Be silent, and Sedah will send for you."

"Untie my hands, you coward, and I'll show you what I'm in a position to do!"

The silhouette had disappeared from the entrance. She slumped and fumed. I*t's a good thing I'm so mad,* she thought, *or else I'd be blubbering like a baby.*

A faint sound caught Eve's attention. Her anger shifted to confusion, melted to fear and ended in dismay. Drums pounding a steady beat could be heard in the distance and growing closer. As the sound increased in volume, she noticed voices. Not the calm, soothing type she so longed for, but a mob, building to a frenzy.

The area around the outside of her prison filled with light until it seemed as though the sun had risen and sat on top of her. Sedah moved the doorway skin and stepped inside. "It is time."

"Sedah," Eve pleaded, "they've tied my hands and held me as a prisoner. Why, and where is Ben?"

"Calm yourself, fair one," Sedah said. "You are the host for a great celebration given in your honor. Please come with me. Your Ben awaits his bride's arrival."

Sedah's explanation did little to quell her fears, but having no recourse, she complied. As Eve appeared from the hut, her hands still bound, a great cheer among those gathered erupted. The light from the torches they carried caused her to squint.

Sedah stepped out behind her. He raised both arms above his head.

A deafening cheer rose from the crowd and turned into a steady mantra. "Eve, Eve, Eve," was the chant, echoed by all in unison. They continued this song at a softer level as Sedah led his captive through the village.

The path they took erupted with individuals that would step aside, allowing them passage. The new participants would pick up the chant, as they fell in behind and followed the procession. After what seemed like hours, they came to the center of the township. The villagers moved in to form a circle around a large cleared area, two hundred feet in diameter.

As they moved into the circle, she noticed Sedah was wearing a long-sleeved, black fur wrap that tapered to a point at knee level both front and back. It fit tightly to his neck and extended upward, ending below his chin. A triangular headdress, made of the same black material, adorned his head. The front lay over his face, trailing down to the center of his chest. There were two slits cut for his eyes and one for his mouth. Two wraps, also of identical material, covered his legs from knee to ankle.

Distracted by the sight of the dark figure, Eve didn't notice increased activity in the interior of the circle until a roar moved through the crowd. She turned her attention toward the commotion. What she saw caused her blood to boil.

Two men carried a ten-foot long pole. Hanging beneath it like so much meat was Ben. His hands and feet bound around the pole allowed his body to dangle, unable to offer any resistance to his captors.

Eve moved to help her husband. "What did you do to him?" she screamed.

Sedah clutched her wrist and nodded.

As she struggled to free herself from his grasp, two men moved in her direction. Each man grabbed one of her arms and escorted her toward center ring. Ben was now hanging by his hands, his feet cut loose, and the pole that bore him propped up on each end by two wooden angular supports.

As Eve neared her husband, a single individual supported one end of the horizontal member while two others removed one of the angled braces. Eve slid onto the pole facing Ben. The brace being replaced now allowed the entire structure to be self-supporting.

Ben and Eve dangled several feet off the ground. Two small diameter logs tall enough to offer support wobbled under their feet. By pulling against the ropes that held their hands, they balanced themselves on the logs in a somewhat more comfortable position.

"You okay?" Ben asked, trying to make his voice heard above the drone of the crowd.

Eve looked around and then back at Ben. She raised her eyebrows as if to say what do you think?

"At least you haven't lost your sense of humor." He took several breaths and coughed.

"Still having trouble breathing?"

"Yeah, it's worse than ever, but I'm sure it won't last much longer."

"Still have your sense of humor."

"Yep, and that's another thing that won't last much longer."

Sedah now stood facing the couple. "Silence. It is time to begin."

"Begin what?" Ben demanded.

"The long-awaited surrender," Sedah replied.

"Would you mind explaining?" Eve said.

"As I have told you, the names of Ben and Eve brought recognition to my associates and have for ages untold."

"This place has been around for two days," Ben said. "What do you mean, 'ages untold?'"

"Your conceptual process is significantly limited," Sedah said. "Your feeble mind cannot grasp the notion of an existence void of time. Since this world's destruction, by the one whose name I cannot mention, we have awaited the Dark One to enter and lead us once again. To assure this final victory, we must present as an offering to the Dark One the two that arrived here to begin this new world."

"And by two, you mean Ben and me?" Eve interrupted.

"Precisely," Sedah said.

"I guess your offering would also translate into sacrifice," Ben said.

"You are more astute than I gave either of you credit for," Sedah said. "It will be a shame to offer ones such as you, but necessary." Sedah motioned, and a small group of men hauled tree boughs, stacking the fuel around and under Ben and Eve.

"Enough," Sedah said. "The time has come for fire to rule." He held the torch high. "May the Dark One reign forever!"

The roar of the crowd shook the ground they stood upon. Eve waited for the noise to subside and took advantage of the lull.

"Sedah, are we not to be confronted by our accuser before we die, or is this Dark One of yours a coward also?"

The assembly became silent.

"Nice," Ben encouraged.

She winked in his direction.

Sedah turned toward Eve. "You will experience his presence, mouthy one. In fact, you may endure more than you care to."

At that moment, Eleazor waddled out of the forest, the throng parting as he approached."Bennie boys, what you is do?"

Ben glanced at Eve and then looked to the bumbling creature. "I sure am glad to see you, Stumpy."

Eleazor moved closer until he could almost touch Ben. "Why you two is a hangin?"

"We're in a pickle, little buddy," Ben said. "Reckon you could help us out?"

"Sure thing, Bennie boys, me helps." He bent over searching for something on the ground. His back bubbled, and the mass of his body increased until he became many times larger. He returned to an upright position so quickly that it startled Ben, causing him to lurch backwards and fall from his perch. Eleazor stood face to face with Ben. He reached his hand down and grabbed Ben's legs pulling him tight.

"*Help us, little buddy,*" Eleazor mocked. "What do you take me for, a fool?" He pushed his face closer until his foul breath burned Ben's nostrils.

Ben was stretched to where his arms and legs would soon dislocate. He tried to protest but could not utter a sound. At that instant, a faint something seeded within Ben's being, waiting its moment in time to germinate.

"Let him go, you orange freak!" Eve screamed.

Eleazor released his grip on Ben and turned toward Eve.

Ben bounced several times and came to rest on the brush now piled high enough to afford a foothold for him to lift up and catch his breath.

"That is the kindest thing you have said since our arrival in this world, dear Eve," Eleazor snarled. "So nice, in fact, you deserve something special from Leazy."

Eve found herself attracted in a dreamy, demented fashion. Eleazor's features, though still vile were much more subtle, calling her to follow. She gazed into his burning eyes, wanting to obey his unspoken invitation.

Prying herself away from his trance, Eve closed her eyes and refocused her thoughts. *If you're there, I'm sure You brought us to this place for some other reason than to die.* She considered her plea then shook her head and sighed. "A little help would be nice," she whispered.

Eleazor moved his face within inches of hers. She felt his breath and turned her face away in disgust. He extended his tongue and licked her cheek. Her face burned.

"No!" she screamed.

Eleazor pulled back and chuckled. "My dear, no doubt you should taste much better when you are done."

"Sedah," Eleazor barked, "I command you to worship me!"

"Yes, Master." Sedah leaned forward to place his torch within the tinder. A projectile came from nowhere striking Sedah in the neck, turning him into a red ball of fire. He rained as black dust upon the ground, extinguishing the end of his torch as it fell. The crowd panicked, as wave after wave of what Ben now knew to be arrows, pummeled the spectators,turning them into the same black dust.

Eleazor looked toward the heavens and howled. Eve shivered at the sound, causing her to fall from her precarious perch. A large pair of wings extended from Eleazor's back, arrows pinging off his body as the appendages began to beat. He lifted off with surprising ease and disappeared into the darkness.

Chapter Nineteen

THE ENTIRE SITE had fallen dark, except for the occasional crimson flare, which moved away from the immediate area. Eve felt herself being lifted. The ropes were severed, and Eve dropped to the ground.

"Ben!" she cried, both hands extended, fumbling in the darkness. Something rough brushed past her fingertips.

"Ben, is that you?" Eve heard a dull thud just to her right. "Ben," she pleaded, "where are you?" Two arms grabbed her from behind. Eve screamed.

"I'm right here," a familiar voice said.

Ben wrapped his arms around Eve and pulled her to the ground. "Shh," he whispered. "I don't know what happened, stay quiet and see how this plays out. It can't be as bad as what we were facing." Ben hesitated, "At least, I hope not."

Eve closed her eyes and buried her head deep into his chest. She could hear his heart pound and his breath coming in shallow gasps. When she dared to open her eyes, she looked toward the sky. Eve perceived a dim yellow glow building over the treetops. "Ben, look,"

He turned to see a host of yellow spheres moving across the sky and settling down around the village center. The orbs pulsated and grew brighter, bathing the entire area with a warm glow that melted any remaining fear from Eve's heart. She took Ben's hand and stood.

A group of seven men approached the couple. The probable leader stepped forward. He was of average height, about six feet and clean-shaven, as were his companions. Eve looked at the burlap fabric from which his clothes were woven. *That must have been what I touched in the darkness,* she thought.

Their shirts were V-neck sleeveless pullovers with no fasteners. Around each man's upper arms, a narrow leather strap was tied with both ends hanging down several inches. Their pants were made from the same fabric, also, with no adornment. They wore soft leather shoes. The most striking features were the polished long bows that all present carried and the woven reed quill loaded with arrows strapped to their back.

"I am Belac," he said. "We come to serve." All seven crossed their chest with their right arm and knelt.

"No," Eve protested. "Please stand. We are indebted to you for saving our lives."

"You are the hope of this world," Belac said, standing upright once again.

"And it is to that end we have prepared," Ben said, "but have been treated like the scourge of this world."

"And for that, I must beg your forgiveness," Belac said. "We could not interfere until the time was right."

"You've been watching us?" Ben questioned.

"This is true," Belac said. "Please," he insisted, "come with me. We will speak of all things after we leave this place."

Most of the orbs formed two parallel lines ten feet apart and moved into the forest. Some of the yellow sentries scoured the outlying areas away from the assembly, searching for any hidden danger.

The path was lit for a distance of several hundred yards. Each orb moved along with the procession so that no one walked in darkness.

Ben and Eve walked behind Belac. Eve turned. She only saw silhouettes in the yellow light, and there seemed to be no end to the line of orbs.

"How many people are with Belac?"

"You read my mind," Ben said. He glanced to the rear and at Eve, "Hundreds." He shook his head. "That can't be right; the line of people seems to have no end." He shrugged. "A thousand or more."

Belac turned and smiled. "Fret not for the number, you are among those who care for you." Belac turned back toward the path saying nothing more for the rest of the journey.

As forest turned to field, a gathering of women met the incoming travelers.

"These will tend to you," Belac said. "In a short while we will assemble and talk of many things." Belac bowed. "It is then I will answer any matters you may have pondered."

"Thank you," Eve said. A young woman wearing a plain knee-length dress woven from the same burlap fabric as the men, beckoned Ben and Eve to follow. She led them to an earthen hut. The door was round and woven from a dense foliage Ben had never seen before. It was about eight feet tall and lightweight; so light, in fact, that it could be rolled to cover the doorway or rolled away to uncover it.

The woman escorted Ben and Eve inside. "All you require is within," she said, and left, rolling the door closed behind her.

"How familiar is this little scenario?" Ben asked, remembering back to the Established Place.

Eve moved close and wrapped her arms around him. "Familiar or not, it sure feels right." A yellow orb, hovering at the roofline, brightened recognizing the young couple.

"You seem to be breathing a little better."

"I hadn't thought about it, but you're right." Ben took a deep breath as if to test for himself and nodded affirmative.

"Let's see what the young lady left for us," Ben said.

Eve released her grip.

The building they occupied was constructed much like the one that imprisoned Eve. A wooden frame with vertical and horizontal members lashed together. This structure, however, was covered with sod. Ben had considered it strange before entering the hut that the outside appeared to be green and vibrant. He now knew that it was, in fact, still growing. "Talk about efficient," he mumbled.

"What did you say?" Eve asked.

"Oh, nothing, just thinking out loud."

The room contained modest furnishings. A bench constructed from shaved tree limbs that would seat two people and a floor mat ten feet square were the lone objects. Two piles of cloth sat neatly folded on the bench, with a pair of shoes atop each pile.

Eve held one of the garments up to her neck and let it unfold, revealing one of the knee-length dresses. This seemed to be the normal dress for the women of the settlement. Ben removed his clothes and pulled the new set of pants up to his waist. *I wonder,* he thought. He released his hold on the waistband, and they fell to the ground. "I guess not."

He scrutinized the pants and saw a drawstring. Ben tightened the cord; he then pulled the shirt over his head and down his torso.

"What's the matter, sweetie?" Eve asked. "Did you have to make the clothes fit yourself this go around?"

"Yeah," he replied, with a hint of disappointment. "I guess they're not as advanced as our last hosts."

Eve gazed at him curiously. "That has nothing to do with it."

"What then?"

Eve took a seat on the bench and motioned for Ben to join her. He sat down beside her.

"What's wrong?" he asked.

"Nothing's wrong, neither you nor I can comprehend the power we encountered at the Established Place, or here." Eve looked around, "Wherever *here* is."

"Well, how about an explanation."

"I can't explain it," she said, looking into his eyes, she took his hands into hers. "Right before Sedah set the fire that would have killed us, I remembered something that Jhorr had spoken of."

"And that was?"

"The One Who Sees all; don't you remember?"

"I remember."

"I asked Him that if He was there, would He help us?"

"And?" Ben inquired.

"That's when the first arrow flew."

Ben stared at her for a moment. "Let me get this straight. You suppose some invisible intelligence, who was a total non-participant, saved us?"

Eve shrugged her shoulders, "I don't know, but it seems strange that help didn't come until after I asked for it."

"Their attack was already planned," Ben protested. "Belac said so himself."

"I know what he said," Eve argued, "but that's not the way it played out."

Ben shook his head and sighed. "Don't attribute our salvation to some fairy tale being. It demeans what Belac and his men did to save us."

"What if I think that it enhances what they did?"

Ben ground his teeth in preparation to blast Eve; a knock at the door redirected his animosity. "What is it?" he growled.

"Please forgive the intrusion," a female voice said. "Belac wishes to enter into session."

Ben glared at Eve, "We'll finish this later."

✳ ✳ ✳

BELAC SAT IN THE OPEN with his eyes closed. The flames from the fire danced off his face causing a pleasantly animated smile. The woman motioned for Ben and Eve to move toward him. Belac opened his eyes. "Welcome. Please be seated."

Ben and Eve sat opposite Belac with the fire between them.

"I trust you are well after your ordeal?"

"Yes, thank you," Eve said.

"Though we have many questions," Ben added.

"Of course," Belac said, "and I will do my best to answer each one."

"Belac," Eve said, "who were those people, and why did they want us dead?"

"Dear Eve," Belac said, "Persons they were not, but demons."

"Demons?" Ben's face twisted into a disgusted look of surprise.

"Where did they come from?" Eve asked. Her hand groped for Ben's; she slid close and held tight.

"You brought them with you," Belac said.

Eve gasped, "How is that possible?"

Enthralled by what he was hearing, Ben sat speechless.

"They manifest the evil that crossed into this world with you," Belac answered. "The multitude that will assist Eleazor in his effort to destroy this world before it can begin."

"I had no idea," Eve said. "How could they have been so convincing?"

"Eleazor used what you held to be dear and safe against you," Belac said.

"Jhorr and the Established Place?" Eve asked. "That's why everything seemed so familiar?"

"Never forget what I am about to tell you," Belac warned. He looked, first at Ben and then Eve. "The creature who accompanied you to this world is the essence of evil. You may see him until his transformation is complete. Once it is finished he will pass from sight into another realm. It is then his power increases and he, along with his seed, will spread throughout this world, enticing the inhabitants to turn from all that is good. He can make the vile and the contemptuous appear inviting and desirable. It is for this reason he is so dangerous, for his only power is one of deception, but what a formidable opponent this power can be."

"Why would they want to harm us?" Eve asked. "Eleazor seemed to need our assistance."

"His need was merely one of convenience," Belac replied. "Eleazor used you for his own means. Even he did not realize the part you would play in the Great One's plan until now."

Ben decided that he had remained silent long enough. "I don't think I understand the part we play in any of this."

"You were told it was your destiny to enter this world," Belac said. "It is my job to help you along your way."

"On our way to what?" Eve asked.

"To be sure that this world has the chance to be all it can be," Belac said.

"Instead of answering questions, you're creating more," Ben said. He stood and paced anxiously.

"Please sit, Ben Adams," Belac said. "This is necessary to bring you in line with the Great One's plan."

Ben threw his hands into the air. "Who is this *Great One* you keep going on about?" he demanded. Eve rose and took Ben's hand.

"Ben," Belac said, "please sit down."

"Ben, please," Eve implored.

He sighed and returned to his seat.

Eve kissed him on the forehead. "Thank you."

Ben grimaced. "For all the good it will do."

"Ben," Belac said, "the Great One I have spoken of, you know as the One Who Sees All."

"Enough," Ben said, glaring at Eve. He whirled to face Belac. "Save your oration for her." He threw his thumb in Eve's direction. "You both seem to suffer from the same delusion."

"I do not understand," Belac said.

"Well, let me try to explain it to you. Eve is under the impression that this *Great One* had something to do with you and your men coming when they did." Ben lowered his head, "I guess she thinks it was the answer to some kind of *last resort* plea," he said raising his head once again.

"As unfortunate as it may be, most appeals for help are made as a last resort," Belac said.

"That, may well be," Ben replied. He leaned toward Belac. "But know this, if I can't see it, it doesn't exist."

"Belief without sight cannot be forced," Belac said. "It must be nurtured to grow." He nodded to Ben and then to Eve.

"Assurance can be yours, but it is your choice. We will speak of this no longer, Ben Adams; however, I will leave this thought with you. The love for your Eve runs deep, yet it cannot be seen. We know that your love exists, for we can readily see its evidence." Belac smiled. "So it is with the Great One."

The comment shook Ben. His animosity melted. "I guess," he relented.

"We will now take nourishment," Belac said.

He raised his hand, and a woman appeared carrying a large tray. The fire, diminished to smoldering ash, allowed the woman to place the food over the pit, turning it into a warming tray. A single yellow orb had taken over the job of illuminating the area. There were various fruits, vegetables and seeds steaming in wooden bowls, and two plates, one containing flatbread and the other dried strips of meat.

Belac bowed his head and then looked up again. "I have expressed gratitude for this intake of sustenance," he said. "Please enjoy."

"THANK YOU for the wonderful meal," Eve said.

"Yes," Ben echoed. "I believe it's the best I've had since we've been here."

"I am sure it is," Belac said. The three looked at each other and smiled. A calming hush ensued.

Eve broke the silence. "Ben began having trouble breathing shortly after we arrived. Now it is much better."

"He is away from the evil which infected his body," Belac said. "An evil which we very nearly destroyed. Had we reached the small one while penetration remained a viable option, it would have been over before it began."

Eve looked puzzled. "You mean he's allergic to demons?"

"In a sense," Belac said.

"Can you be a little clearer?" Ben asked, "I'm grateful that it hasn't infected Eve, but why just me?"

"Certainly," Belac replied, "the ones you encountered have a special purpose in mind. Since the first attempt on your life (of which they had no forewarning and no ability to plan) failed, they are forced to revert to their original initiative."

"Which is?"

Belac cast somber eyes upon Ben. "Until the act takes place, knowing what is yet to happen does not exist."

"Makes sense," Ben said, "at least I think so." He shook his head to clear the cobwebs of Belac's last "riddle me this" statement. "Can you tell us about the metal craft we found? On my world it was a water dependent craft called the Ark. We used it as a rescue vessel; except it was much smaller."

"I can indeed," Belac replied. He moved to a more upright position. "The Ark is precisely as you say, a rescue vessel."

"In what way?" Ben asked.

"You see," Belac began, "it also came with you. It was necessary to bring the items crucial to establish the foundation for this world."

"What items?" Eve asked.

"Flora and fauna," Belac replied. "The essentials needed for survival and peace of mind." Belac moved from his seated position to his knees. His voice increased in volume.

"Had your mission begun in this world with nothing, it would have been too difficult to start over from an absolute genesis."

Ben looked at Eve. They both shrugged.

"You're losing us," Ben said.

Belac sat back down. His demeanor became solemn, his voice soft. "Dear, friends," he said. "Imagine seeing naught but a barren landscape after the water had receded from this Earth. Had it been void of not only creatures but of all things familiar to bring you comfort, would you have had the will to continue?"

Eve thought for a moment. "I guess not," she said. "I couldn't imagine waiting around for trees to grow."

"This is why the Great One made these things available to you," Belac said. "It is for your comfort."

Ben raised his eyebrows. "Why didn't He just create these things again instead of going to all the trouble to move them?"

"Why destroy what is inherently good to create again?" Belac queried.

"Point taken," Ben said.

"We ran into a field of plants," Eve said. "Everywhere the fluid from the top of the plant touched us it was very irritating. Once we walked far enough into the field where the plants were too tall to reach, the irritation stopped. As we rested, a strange phenomenon turned both Ben and me to a jelly-like substance."

Eve paused, remembering the comfort she had experienced. It was as if her body was inside and yet, outside of itself, ultimately producing a liberating freedom. "I can say that my subconscious seemed to overtake my conscious being, and I'm only able to remember scant pieces of the experience," Eve lied, not wanting to relate her true experience, but instead felt it something personal she would keep to herself."If you were to ask me what I remembered, I don't believe I could give you an answer."

Belac smiled, "You, my dear friends, were in a field of Clauciun. The irritating effect is to warn those who enter to turn back, for many dangers lie within its borders. If the traveler does not retreat, the Clauciun changes the structure of the person to an inert jelly-like substance which protects him through the night."

"I had no idea." Eve said

Ben nodded, lost in black thoughts during his experience in the weeds, of a monster within, clawing his way to the surface.

The orb wavered. Eve glanced its way and smiled. "I see you have the Keeper," she said.

"Perhaps one day," Belac said, "but for now, the Companion makes our way brighter outside of our being."

Belac exuded a sense of longing. "We await the coming of the Living One," he said. "When this happens, the Living One will show us the way. He will cease to be and then live again. This is when the Companion will move within our being, and we will call this indwelling the Keeper."

Eve looked puzzled. "What about the yellow orbs?"

"They will remain," Belac said. "The Keeper will light our way from within and without."

"Sounds unnecessarily complicated," Ben said.

Belac looked his way with a sorrowful smile.

"I don't know why, but it's making sense," Eve said.

Ben looked her way, his anger now rekindled and growing.

Eve smiled at her husband and then yawned.

"We should bring this evening to a close," Belac said.

Eve yawned again. "Agreed," and then realized there was something else she needed to know.

"If I may, Belac," she said, looking to Ben for support. "Do you recognize the name Jhorr?"

Belac nodded and smiled a great smile. "I have longed for you to ask this of me. Please wait here. I have something of great interest to show you."

Eve watched Belac disappear into the shadows. "Where do you suppose he's going?" she asked.

"I don't care," he replied, "but I hope he hurries. I want to go to bed." Ben yawned and squirmed, placing his elbow on his leg and resting his chin in the palm of his hand.

Belac returned bringing the item he wished to share along with him. A young boy of eight years accompanied him into the yellow light.

"This is he," Belac announced. "The one you know as Jhorr."

Chapter Twenty

"HAVE PREPARATIONS BEEN MADE?" Eleazor asked.

"Yes, Dark One," Sedah replied.

"Good, we will remain hidden for a short time longer, then all will be ours to plunder." Eleazor looked at Sedah and hissed.

A terrified Sedah withdrew, placing his hands over his face and head. This caused Eleazor to burst into a fit of wheeze-filled laughter.

"Make sure the conscripts remain vigilant," Eleazor said. "The one known as Ben will come soon, and we do not want to miss him."

"How can you be sure this man will be there, Dark One?"

"The seed is taking root," Eleazor replied, raising a finger. "Our new recruits—the humans from the grounded vessel—realize they are expendable, do they not?" He asked, his fiery eyes cutting through Sedah.

Sedah shielded his face, unable to return the gaze and afraid to answer.

"See to it they know their place," Eleazor said, "and never question me again or perhaps I shall make an expendable example of *you.*"

Eleazor pressed Sedah's face into the dirt; a multicolored fluid began to flow from his nostrils. "I brought you back to this realm to serve, and serve only me. Do you understand?"

"Yes," Sedah said his muffled voice barely audible through the soft earth.

Eleazor removed his foot from the back of the demon's head. "Be gone with you!"

Sedah wasted no time obeying his master's order.

Chapter Twenty-one

EN AND EVE STARED at the young man in disbelief. Eve wrestled her concentration away from the boy and looked at Belac. "How?" was the only word she could muster.

"It is not a matter of *how*," Belac said, "he is here."

"But," Eve stammered, "he's so young."

Belac smiled. "We were all young at one time."

"Two days ago he was a lot older than this," Ben added.

"Ah," Belac said, "I understand your quandary. When you moved from your world into this one, you became bound to the parameters of this world." Belac looked at Eve. "That also includes time."

Eve pressed both hands into her hair and wildly mussed it. She threw her head back and shifted her gaze from Ben to Belac."That must mean that this era predates the one we came from," Eve said.

"In a manner of speaking," Belac said.

"This world also dictates each aspect of my people's existence, although years, as you understand them, do not apply to us."

"In what way?" Eve asked.

"Young Jhorr here," Belac said, placing his hand on the boy's shoulder. "I am his grandfather 72 times."

"What!" Ben exclaimed. "You mean to tell me you're 72 generations older?"

Belac nodded.

Ben mulled the math over in his head.

"You don't die, do you?" Eve said. Her face glazed over.

"Yes, dear Eve," Belac said. "We die just as you; however, our years number many more, but on a different timeline."

"That's over 2,000 years!" Ben blurted out.

"2,160," Belac said.

Ben stared at Jhorr. "Does he remember us?"

"He cannot remember what he has yet to do;" Belac said, "though recognition in some form may manifest itself within his subconscious being." He placed a hand on Jhorr's shoulder. "Even this I cannot be certain of."

"Who are these people, Grandfather?" Jhorr asked.

"Our new friends," Belac replied. "This is Eve, and this is Ben." He pointed to each.

Jhorr nodded and bowed low. "May I go now, Grandfather?" he asked, turning to Belac.

"Yes, young one," Belac said. The youth wasted no time speeding off into the darkness.

"Now," Belac said, "if there are no other questions . . . "

"No questions!" Ben exclaimed. "How can there *not* be questions?"

Eve touched her husband. "Calm down," she urged. "There'll be time to ask."

"There is much to discuss other than my grandson," Belac said. "However, if there are any pressing issues you feel a need to resolve, please convey."

"When we met Jhorr for the first time he spoke broken English," Eve said. "If he came at a period in time after you, then why do you speak our language so much better?"

"I surmised that you would query this very thing," Belac said. "My explanation may confuse further, but it is the only truthful one I can offer. It is accurate that in time I am Jhorr's predecessor; however, in the sequence in which each circumstance occurred, Jhorr preceded me. It was through this that he assimilated your customs, mannerisms and language to my people."

Ben and Eve tried to wrap their understanding around this concept but could not.

"Please," Belac said, "do not dwell on these things I have spoken to you. They are as they are, and to settle on them will cloud the mind. There are more pressing matters that require our attention."

Ben and Eve both looked at Belac.

"As I have told you," Belac continued, "it is but a matter of time before Eleazor and his followers come into their own."

"I thought you killed the demons at the gathering." Eve said.

"What we did tonight was temporary," Belac confessed. "These factions I cannot destroy; however, followers such as you have also enlisted."

"You mean mortals?" Ben inquired.

"Yes," Belac said.

"How did they get here?" Eve asked.

"Working as tenders of the goods on the Ark," Belac said.

"Well, then, wouldn't they be on our side?" Eve questioned.

"They were," Belac said. He then sighed. "Sadly the Dark One reached them first, and they are now far from our influence."

"What can we do?" Eve asked.

"I will need your help," Belac said, "if both are willing."

"We'll do whatever we can." Eve said. She grabbed Ben's hand. He reluctantly took it.

Belac looked warily at Ben. "We can deal with them," he said, "but we must strike soon, and strike we will on the next rising of the great light."

'WHAT DO YOU MEAN you don't understand?" Eve said. "It's why we were sent here."

"Well, maybe I don't agree with that either" Ben said. He rolled out of the pine bough bed and stood, his back to Eve. The yellow glow in the room increased in brightness.

"What is wrong with you?" Eve demanded. "You've been acting strange all night."

Ben whirled around. "You've been sucking up to Belac and the rest of these fruitcakes around here, and for what?" Ben walked in a straight line and then retraced his steps at the foot of the bed. He stopped abruptly.

"I'll tell you for what," he said, pointing an accusing finger at Eve.

"For some make-believe higher power that everyone around here seems to think has control over their lives."

Ben resumed his trek along the imaginary line. "Do you expect me to swallow that an eight-year-old kid is the same old man we supposedly met a few days ago?"

"*Supposedly* met? Don't tell me Jhorr wasn't real?"

"What difference does it make to you?"

"It makes every difference."

Ben laughed and then bent over until the fit had subsided. He looked at Eve in amazement.

"2,000 years-old?" Ben walked around the bed, sat down and kissed Eve on the cheek. "No one controls me," he said, pointing to his own chest.

"You'd do well to remember that."

Ben stood and dressed.

"Where are you going?"

"For a walk."

"No, Ben," she pleaded. "Please, don't leave."

"You know, I may have made a mistake when I asked you to marry me." Ben pushed his head through the opening in his shirt and paused; savoring the anguish he had created.

"We're just too different."

Tears pooled in Eve's eyes.

Before he left the hut he turned to Eve. "Why don't you go play with your new friends while I'm gone?" A twisted grin crossed his face. "They're more your kind."

A KNOCK AT THE DOOR roused Eve from a fitful sleep. She felt for Ben and then sat upright when she couldn't touch him.

"Come in," she squawked, uneasily.

A woman entered, placed a tray on the ground and left without saying a word. Eve scrambled out of bed, quickly dressed and ran out the door in search of Belac, leaving the tray still steaming on the ground. Within minutes of her exit from the hut, she spotted him.

"Belac!"

Chapter Twenty-two

"HOW COULD SHE let herself be taken in?" Ben argued with himself. "Any logical person knows better than that."

The sun was beginning its morning ascent. He kicked at the loose gravel path and slipped, falling flat on his back. A flood of curses poured from his mouth. Ben picked himself up and began dusting off.

"Hello, friend," said a cheerful voice.

Ben, startled, stumbled and turned a full circle looking in all directions. "I'm not your friend."

"Really," the voice said. "From what I heard a moment ago, it sounds like we have much in common."

Ben's heightened sense of awareness screamed danger. He crouched in anticipation. "If you're so bent on friendship, then show yourself," he demanded.

"Of course," the voice said. "We mean you no harm." Three men dressed in 21st century roughneck garb stepped out from the dense foliage beside the path.

Ben stood upright; his mouth dropped open.

"Better close that mouth, little man, before you trip over it," one of the strangers said.

"I don't believe it," Ben replied. He shook his head. "How?"

"It's not that big a deal," a fourth man said, entering the path from behind the previous three.

Ben smiled and moved toward the foursome.

Chapter Twenty-three

"I HAVE NOT SEEN HIM," Belac said. "Is there something wrong?"

"We had a fight last night," Eve said. "Ben left and I haven't seen him since."

"This is not good. There are things now roaming these wilds that would do him harm."

"What can we do?"

"We leave soon to battle the Dark One's subordinates. We will search for your Ben along the way."

"Thank you," Eve said, sighing with relief.

"For now return to your shelter and take nourishment. You will need sustenance for the journey."

"I don't think I could eat anything."

"Our journey requires that you do so."

Eve nodded. "I'll try."

She left Belac and returned to her hut. Setting the now cold tray on her lap, Eve managed to eat a little. A woman knocked on the door.

"Come in."

The woman pushed her head inside. "It is time. Belac awaits, please follow me."

* * *

"PETE! MARTY!" Ben exclaimed. "I can't believe you are here!" Ben hugged each man. But how?"

"Calm down," Pete said, patting Ben's arm. "Let's get out of here, and we'll explain everything."

"Okay, I guess," Ben said. He was unsure of leaving with his reanimated friends, but he didn't like the four-to-one odds if they failed to accept his refusal. "But if I'm gone too long, I'm afraid I'll be missed."

"Oh, yeah?" Marty questioned.

Ben nodded. "What I meant to say was I don't want to be gone til dark. I'm new to this area, you know, still trying to get my bearings."

Pete put his hand on Ben's back. "Don't worry, old buddy. Would I steer you wrong?"

Pete's voice bore an unusually menacing tone, at least uncharacteristic to the Pete that Ben remembered. The two strangers moved closer, one to Ben's left and one to his right.

Ben eyed all three warily. "Yeah, sure. I guess I'm up for a hike."

"All right," Marty said. "Fall in."

Ben tracked behind Marty through dense underbrush. He noticed his labored breathing returning but attributed it to the excitement of being reunited (and his willful abduction) by ones he had assumed were lost. Pete and the other two followed.

"Here we are," Marty announced.

"Where is *here*?" Ben asked.

Pete stepped up, pushed both hands in between two leaf-laden saplings and spread them apart exposing a narrow cave entrance.

"Here," Pete said, "home sweet home." He threw his head sideways toward the entrance and ducked as he entered the cave.

Ben glanced into the darkness, looked back at Marty, shrugged and then followed.

The five men traversed a stone corridor that broke into an open area about 90 feet in diameter. A fire lit the interior. Ben looked up. The ceiling vaulted 100 feet or more above them. Smoke from the fire filtered into ceiling crevasses, making its way to the outside.

"How about a drink to celebrate our reunion?" Marty asked.

"Sure," Ben agreed and then paused, "what do you have?"

"Have a seat." Marty pointed to three folding fabric chairs.

Ben sat down on one of them. The cave boasted few comforts, three chairs and three sleeping bags. Ben wondered why there were three amenities for four people. A stash of wooden crates, each quite a bit larger than a footlocker, drew his attention. Ben stared at the enclosures pondering their contents.

An enticing aroma once again distracted Ben's attention away from the unexplained crates. He looked toward the fire and noticed something he hadn't seen before. A large piece of meat, pierced through with a wooden skewer, sat between two forked sticks pressed into the ground forming a crude spit over the top of the fire.

Marty noticed Ben's gaze, "Getting hungry?"

"You bet," Ben said, salivating at the mention of food. "I haven't eaten since last night."

"It'll come soon enough," Pete said, handing Ben a metal cup. "Let's talk first."

Ben took the cup, looked at Pete, and then sipped. His eyes widened. "Where did you get bourbon? I haven't had this in years." Ben willingly took another drink, finishing the contents. *Doesn't quite taste the same as I remember,* he thought, *but it'll do.*

"Would you like another?" Pete asked.

"Sure," Ben said, wiping his mouth with his sleeve. The drink warmed Ben inside. Pete refilled the cup and then sat down beside his friend. Marty did likewise with his own cup and sat on the other side.

"So," Pete began. "What have you been up to since you left the habitat?"

Ben almost spit out the liquid he had just taken in. "I should ask you the same thing," he said, wiping his face once again to remove the errant trails of liquor streaming down his chin.

"Please," Pete said, "you first."

Ben hesitated, choosing his words very carefully. "Well, I got married."

"Married?" Pete said. "Tell me about it." His face lit up into that big lug smile that Ben remembered so distinctly.

He wasn't comfortable enough to share all with these men, but he was feeling more at ease. He wove a carefully edited tale. Ben recounted the events after the decompression chamber had surfaced. His rendezvous with *The Morning Star*, his chance encounter with Eve, and the indigenous people that helped them when, according to Ben, *The Morning Star* ran aground. He left out a few details including the Captain's demise, Vinny and Skull's emergence and Jhorr. Other than that, he had mostly come clean.

"Anymore and I'd say that story would be just this side of remarkable" Pete said. He had been leaning forward listening to Ben. He now sat back in his chair, nodding as if agreeing with Ben's story.

"Okay, fellas," Ben said, "your turn."

Pete looked at Marty. Marty nodded. "After our last communication," Marty said, "the entire crew onboard *The OZ* moved into *The Ark*. The storm became so severe, we had to cut loose and float to keep from destroying our vessel."

"I know," Ben said, "I remember seeing it." *Uh, oh, shouldn't have said that.*

"How could you have seen it?" Marty asked. "You were miles away and in 40 foot seas. It would have been impossible to see much of anything."

"I didn't mean I had seen *The Ark*," Ben lied. "I meant to say I could imagine you having to disconnect due to the violent nature of the storm."

"Oh," Marty said, apparently having bought Ben's story. "We floated for two days," he continued. "It took that long for the seas to level out." Marty took a sip of his drink and dumped the rest out. "Once we had winched back in and docked with *The Oz*, I assessed the damage. There wasn't as much as I originally supposed, but it was still bad. The strangest thing I found was that the platform's decompression chamber had been activated. On closer examination, I found it occupied." Marty threw his head sideways toward Pete. "I'll let him take it from here."

Pete nodded then took a deep breath, letting it ease slowly from his lips. He turned to Ben and smiled. "I hated to see you leave, knowing I'd be alone in the habitat for another week." Pete ran his hand through his hair and leaned forward, laying his forearms on his knees.

This is more like the Pete I know, Ben thought.

Through a thin smile, Pete continued. "Day five is when it got bad. I could hear the umbilical lines slamming against the sides of the habitat and could even feel the entire structure move sporadically. I felt it best to don a diving suit just in case." Pete shifted anxiously in his seat.

"The biggest problem I faced was that there would be no time to decompress and get to the surface if the habitat were damaged. Putting on the suit merely bought a few extra hours, and I knew that once the air ran out, it would be a very unpleasant death. When the first umbilical broke loose I grabbed an air bag, stepped into the air lock and cycled the exterior door. Once on the outside, I got as far from the habitat as possible. It blew shortly thereafter."

Pete paused pondering the events in his head and then resumed his story. "I made my way to the surface using the lifting cable that was tethered to what remained of the habitat. When I was down to 10 minutes of air left in my tanks, I inflated the air bag and rode it topside." Pete took several labored breaths as he relived his experience through his own words.

"As I broke through the surface I could see *The Ark* a couple hundred yards away. There was no time to signal. I made my way up the ladder and into *Oz*. Stripping my gear off, I ran to the infirmary and into the decompression chamber with no time to spare. I waited there until *The Ark* returned. I was starving and dehydrated, but in good shape, considering."

"Wow," Ben said. He looked at Pete, the initial mistrust of his old friend now fading. "I don't know how you did it, but it sure is good to see you."

Pete smiled. "It's good to see you, too."

Ben turned to Marty. "I know you hated to leave me down there and I'm glad you made it, but how did both of you get here?"

"It's not an interesting story," Marty said.

Ben smiled. "Try me."

"It turns out that *The Oz* was trashed," Pete explained. "A transport made it to our location two weeks later. After reaching the mainland, Marty and I were cooling down in a bar when a stranger approached us. He offered Marty and me a position manning a livestock barge. Since we were both out of work, we accepted his offer."

"Who was he?" Ben inquired.

"I had never seen him before," Marty said, taking the lead. "We met him the next day at the dock, and I must say, I've never seen an animal transport that was this elaborate. It was called of all things *The Ark*."

"You say you'd never seen him before?" Ben questioned.

"Nope, never," Marty said, "but he was a strange character, all right."

"How so?"

"You're not gonna believe this," Marty said, "but he had one yellow eye and one green eye." Marty looked away for a moment. "I can't be certain but by my recollection he said his name was Sarith."

Ben froze.

"What's wrong?" Pete asked.

"Oh, nothing," Ben said, coming back to his senses. "I thought you said something else."

Pete looked at Marty and smirked. "Tell us about this wife of yours."

Ben struggled to regain his composure. "There's not a lot to tell. We met on the ship, and the captain married us," he fibbed, "and that's about it."

"Where is she now?" Marty asked.

"We argued," Ben confessed, "and I left."

"That's not a good sign for newlyweds," Pete said. "What were you arguing about?"

"Ah, she's got a crazy notion about this all-powerful being that looks over us and controls everything." Ben shook his head, his voice rising in volume. "And it drives me crazy."

"Did you set her straight?" Pete asked.

"You bet I did," Ben said. He could feel his anger elevating.

"Sounds like you did the right thing," Marty said.

"Me, too," Pete chimed. "You've gotta nip those things before they get started."

"I tried to tell her, but she wouldn't listen."

"I know what you mean," Marty said, "I don't want anyone preaching to me."

"So," Pete said, "are you going to answer Marty's question?"

"She's with Belac; and for all I care she can stay there."

"So you've met other people since you arrived?" Pete asked, guardedly.

Ben looked at Pete and then Marty, his anger subsiding and turning to concern for his wife. "Well, yeah," he said, not sure if he should have mentioned his 11th hour saviors.

"Maybe you could take us to these new friends of yours," Marty suggested.

Ben stalled, cautiously considering his answer. "I'm so turned around I wouldn't have a clue how to get back."

"A trained Navy man like yourself?" Marty mused. "I find that hard to swallow."

Ben shrugged his shoulders.

"Sorry, I guess my skills have diminished." He produced a nervous laugh. "You know what they say about getting older."

"No, Ben," Pete said, "why don't you tell me what they say about getting older?"

Marty nodded toward the other two nameless companions, and they came forward standing behind Ben.

Sensing the intrusion, Ben stood and whirled around, readying himself for a confrontation. He coughed sporadically at first, then uncontrollably. His face dropped at the sight of a large winged figure silhouetted by the fire's glow moving toward him from the back of the cave.

Chapter Twenty-four

"THERE'S NO SIGN of him anywhere," Eve said.

"Fear not, dear Eve," Belac replied. "The Great One will look out for your Ben."

"I wish I had your resolve," Eve said.

"As I have spoken, assurance comes to us in times of uncertainty and is imparted to our being as we ford the river of distress." Belac smiled at her, placing his hand on her shoulder. "This is such a time. You would do well to allow your conviction sanctuary."

"Thank you," Eve said, attempting a smile. "I will try."

They continued their trek in quiet.

"Do you think five men are enough?" Eve queried, breaking the silence.

"There are a total of seven," Belac said. "I believe that number to be complete and sufficient for our purpose."

Belac stopped suddenly. He placed his index finger over his lips and motioned for his men to join him. He flanked two to the right and two to the left, concealing both in the undergrowth beside the road. The fifth man took a position beside Belac while Eve stood just to the right and behind them.

Within seconds, a group of men appeared in the distance. Eve counted five. Belac looked at his associate and muttered something inaudible. Both men took their bows and loaded them with an arrow from their respective quills. They stood in the middle of the path waiting patiently for the visitors to come closer.

Chapter Twenty-five

"**W**ELL, NOW, Bennie boys," Eleazor said, "I see we have the pleasure of another meeting."

"*Pleasure*," Ben said. "Is that what this is? And you can stop the 'Bennie boys,' my name is Ben."

"But, my dear Ben, how could you think otherwise?"

Ben crossed his arms and stood defiantly. "If I remember, the last time we met, you tried to turn me into an Adam's roast."

The creature tilted his head back and laughed. "A slight misunderstanding, you can see that, can't you?"

Ben couldn't help but be fascinated by this being, and in a perverted way, attracted to him. He sensed the inner seedling take root, entwining his will in its twisted parasitic squeeze.

Ben looked away, afraid he would be overcome by Eleazor's charisma. "So what do you want from me?" Ben demanded. He labored for a breath and then brought his hand to his mouth and coughed several times, his face still aimed at the ground.

"It is not what *I* want," Eleazor said, laying his hands flat against his own chest. "It is what *you* want. Or rather, what I can do for you." He brought his palms together and cocked his head sideways in a caring posture.

Ben looked into the flaming eyes of evil. The consummating vine flowered in an array of recognition. Ben felt that Eleazor's compassion was genuine.

"Tell me what is bothering you, Ben," Eleazor said, smiling. "I can help you if you allow me to do so."

Yes, Ben thought, *I can trust you*. "It's my wife," he began. "Things were fine at first, but she's become this pious fanatic. Eve won't listen to reason, and there's no getting through to her."

"Tsk, tsk, tsk. Is that not always the way? And what is love, but a silly emotion that causes more pain than it does good?" Eleazor laid a single clawed finger on Ben's shoulder. "Please go on, dear Ben, I wish to hear it all."

"There's not much more to tell. We argued, and I left." Ben looked into the demon's burning eyes. "Am I wrong? Should I go back to her?"

"Oh no," the creature exclaimed, "And have her flaunt these ridiculous ideas over your head! I think not. You should stay here with the ones who care for you."

Ben rubbed his chin, pondering such a move.

"Ben, time is short. Your Eve and her new friends would destroy me and all I have tried to do."

"What?" Ben exclaimed.

"Yes," Eleazor said. "It is sad but true. They do not understand me the way you do."

"Belac," Ben snarled. "If it wasn't for him, none of this would have happened."

"Yes," Eleazor hissed with pleasure. "Whatever can we do about him?"

"I'll take care of that nuisance," Ben said. "Consider him out of the way."

"Ben," Eleazor said hypnotically, "you must understand that I do this, not for myself, but for the oppressed, the misunderstood and the demoralized; just as you were before I rescued you from that woman who would use you as a footstool."

"Yes," Ben said. "It's becoming clear." He felt his chest compress and his breathing become more labored.

"You know that she will try to stop you."

"Let her try." Ben coughed several times and drew another labored breath.

Eleazor's lips curled into something that could only be described as a grin of the damned. "I will take my leave now." Eleazor paused, allowing his comments to sink deep. "Your friends will see to any needs you may have."

"Thank you," Ben said, "not only for your hospitality, but for showing me a different way to look at this."

"No, Ben. You have helped further my cause more than you will ever know." The creature made a hasty exit through the rear of the cave.

Ben watched him leave. The influence which had consumed him partially subsided now that Eleazor was no longer present.

"HERE YA GO," Pete said, handing Ben a cupful of whiskey, "bottoms up!"

Ben nodded and took a drink.

Pete refilled his own cup.

"You're not drinking, Marty," Ben said.

"No taste for it," Marty replied.

"So," Ben said, "tell me more of Eleazor."

"You mean the orange dude?" Pete answered.

Marty cringed.

Pete grabbed his cup and sipped.

Ben nodded.

Pete raised one eyebrow.

"He seems to be a stand-up guy. He's taken good care of me and Marty."

"What do you mean?" Ben asked.

"Well, he hooked us up with a place to stay and decent food to eat."

"On top of that," Marty interrupted, "the Dark One has shown us the way."

"What way is that?" Ben asked.

Marty smiled at Ben and wrapped an arm around his shoulder. Ben shuddered at the coldness of his touch. "It's like this, Ben, old buddy. Eleazor (and he likes to be called the Dark One) is just misunderstood. You've got to admit that you felt a kinship with him as you two talked."

"Well, yeah," Ben agreed. He experienced a deep confusion he could not explain; only that it had a tight grip on his inner being and was beginning to grow.

"Come now," Marty said, "you almost thought of him as a friend."

"Yeah," Ben admitted, "he brought me gifts of a sort when we first arrived here."

"See there," Marty said. "The Dark One wants to be liked, just as we all do."

Ben eyed Marty cautiously. "Pete doesn't seem to be as gung-ho about the whole deal as you are."

Marty smiled. "He's coming around as you will. It takes time."

"Eleazor tried to kill me," Ben challenged.

"Another misunderstanding, as the Dark One has stated. He was merely protecting himself." Marty released his hold on Ben and turned to face him. "The Dark One's real gripe is with that wife of yours."

"Eve?" Ben asked.

"Yes," Marty said, "Eve."

"Why? What has she done?"

"It's not what she's done. It's what she's done to you."

Ben looked puzzled.

"Think about it," Marty said. "What do us guys want outta life but a place to lay our head, a stiff drink, a good meal and a woman now and then? On the other hand, what does Eve want outta life, and by life, I mean your life?"

Ben opened his mouth to speak.

"I'll tell you what she wants," Marty continued. "Eve wants to keep you under her thumb."

Ben nodded his head.

"Oh sure, she's a woman, but they're a dime a dozen. A man wants a woman when he wants a woman and not underfoot telling him what to do."

Ben nodded more vigorously and began mouthing the word, "yes."

"And what has she done?" Marty said. "She's hooked up with another man, this Belac you spoke of."

Ben burned with anger, the fire that only revenge could extinguish.

Marty filled another cup with bourbon and handed it to Ben. "Here, drink this."

Ben emptied the cup. The contents fed the fire that burned inside, but there it was again, something different. It was the same as last time but now it was stronger. Ben decided he liked it and handed the cup back to Marty.

"Getting hungry?" Marty asked.

Ben nodded.

"Afterwards I'll show you where these people live."

"I think this meat is ready," Marty said. He pulled off a piece and chewed. "Yep, it's perfect." A trickle of blood ran out of the corner of his mouth.

* * *

"DID YOU SUPPLY the drink to that imbecile Marty?" Eleazor asked.

"Yes, Dark One," Sedah replied. "He gives it to the others to ready their minds for your control, but why is it not necessary that he take the Kumult blend also?"

"The two have strong minds, especially the one called Ben. He required additional persuasion, which I instilled at our last meeting. The other, Marty, is a weak-minded fool. A mealworm's feeble brain would require more time to direct than that buffoon's. Evil becomes him. I tell him what to do, and he does it."

Sedah looked at Eleazor and smiled.

"Very good," Eleazor said, "smile. When I look upon him, it is as if I am seeing you."

Sedah's grin immediately left his mouth.

Eleazor moved his face to within inches of Sedah's, "and just as expendable."

Chapter Twenty-six

"BELAC!" Eve screamed. "It's Ben!" She moved in his direction. Belac grabbed her wrist, pulling her back. "No. We wait."

"But, it's Ben," she said.

"We wait," Belac insisted.

The five men arrived with Ben in the lead.

"Well, Belac," Ben scowled, "are you about done with my wife?"

Eve inhaled in shock. "Ben, what are you saying?"

Ben glared at her. "I wasn't talking to you."

Eve took a step backward keeping a wary eye on her husband as she did.

"The Dark One pulls you close and considers Ben Adams as his own," Belac said.

"No," Ben countered. "Eleazor has opened my eyes and speaks the truth."

"Deception has taken you, Ben Adams, and know that I will do all in my power to stop you."

"Give it your best shot, but my friends may have something to say about that."

Pete and Marty both unveiled .45 automatic side arms.

A smug grin crossed Ben's face.

"So, these small implements are weapons?" Belac said.

Pete aimed his pistol at the man standing beside Belac and pulled the trigger. The bullet grazed his arm causing him to drop his bow.

"You decide," Ben said. "Just know the next shot won't be as friendly."

At that instant, an arrow cut through the air, piercing Pete's hand and knocking the pistol to the ground. Another from the opposite side connected with Marty's wrist. It penetrated, shattering bone. Marty fell to the ground, dropped the handgun and clutched his wrist.

Ben lurched for the pistol. One of the nameless men that had appeared with Pete and Marty beat him to it. He extended his arm to fire. An arrow entered his torso, causing a brilliant flash of red light, and an ensuing dust cloud.

Marty grabbed the gun with his left hand. No sooner did he feel the cold steel breach his fingers, than an arrow closed his eyes for the last time.

Ben moved to help Pete. Belac sent one final arrow, dispatching the last man standing in a flash of light. Four of Belac's men entered the path from the underbrush. Each man poised to fire. Belac's bow hung in its usual resting place around his shoulder as he approached Ben.

"I hope I did not disappoint in response to your challenge," Belac said, nodding toward Ben.

"What challenge?" Ben sneered.

"My best shot," Belac said.

"No, not at all," Ben replied.

"Good," Belac said. "For my shot, as you call it, can be much more effective than what you have witnessed."

Ben ignored the comment.

"Please go with these men," Belac said. "As much as I regret what must be done, you will be detained as an enemy."

Ben remained silent.

Eve approached him, tears streaming down her face. "What have you done?" she said, confronting him.

Ben snubbed the question; side-stepped around her and left with his jailors.

Two of Belac's men attended to Pete. One restrained him, while the other pushed the arrow the rest of the way through his hand, snapped off the tip, and removed the shaft. He dressed the wound with a spongy substance, wrapped it with a clean cloth and sent him along with Ben.

"It is done for now," Belac said.

"What about Ben?" Eve pleaded.

"I cannot say, for I know not." He placed a knuckle on Eve's cheek wiping away a tear. "Nothing is outside of the power of the Great One," Belac said. He looked toward the sky, "however; it is time to leave this place."

"HOW'S THE HAND?" Ben asked.

Pete extended his arm, wiggled his fingers and curled the digits into a fist."Not too bad. They put some kind of herb on it, and it feels a little too good, considering."

"Good, you must be at your best when we get outta here."

"Get outta here? We're surrounded by guards!"

"You're forgetting about our ace in the hole."

"And what might that be?" Pete asked, the cynicism evident in his response.

"Eleazor wouldn't leave us here."

Pete looked at his hand. "I don't know, Ben. He sent us out alone to face these guys, and I didn't see him coming to help." Pete dropped his head and brought it to rest in the palm of his hand. "And now Marty's gone."

"Yeah, I almost forgot about him." Ben sat down beside Pete. "You two seemed closer than what I remembered."

"We were. It started when we left *The Oz* and worked together instead of him being the boss." Pete looked at Ben. "We had grown pretty tight, kinda like you and I used to be."

Ben smiled, remembering earlier days. "Was the animal transport the only job you two worked together?"

"Yep, for three years that was it."

"Three years," Ben said in disbelief. "From the time I left you in the habitat until now, three years have passed in your when?"

"Yeah, in two more months it'll be four, if that's what you mean by *my when*. Either way, time flies whether you're having fun or not."

Pete noticed Ben's puzzlement. "I gather that four years doesn't work for you."

"Neither does three."

"What does?" Pete asked, not sure if he wanted to know the answer.

"How about a week and a half?"

"A week and a half?" Pete repeated, his voice rising in volume.

Ben nodded. "Tell me what happened after you and Marty took the job on the animal transport."

"It was like Marty said; the transport was the fanciest vessel I'd ever seen used in moving livestock. We met Sarith that first day. The transport was loaded." Pete hesitated and then continued. "Sheep," he said with a puzzled expression. "What used to be normal food stock, cows and pigs were scarce. We hauled animals that were just beginning the domestication process, like mountain goats, deer and antelope. But our first load was full of sheep. I'm not sure who was buying all the lamb, but you can bet they were spending a fortune for it. Sarith gave us the manifest, and that began our new career as aquatic beast technicians." Pete chuckled. "That's what they called us. We preferred *damp ranchers.*"

"Do you remember where you delivered the sheep?"

"It's kinda strange you would ask that because we made so many deliveries over the years you would think they would all run together, but this one sticks out."

"In what way?" Ben's curiosity grew in light of Pete's confusion.

"We delivered to this place more than once. It was an island in the middle of nowhere." Pete moved his thumb and index finger up and down his cheeks and then looked at Ben.

"This place never appeared on any of our charts until we were to make a delivery."

"You made more than one transfer there?"

"Yeah," Pete's same puzzled look returned. "Most likely a half dozen, and each time we made a drop we were prohibited from landing on the island. We would anchor a hundred yards off the beach and flat-bottomed wooden barges and dugout canoes would meet us to unload. Unless the shipment we carried was huge, there would be two men from the island to do the actual off-loading."

This piqued Ben's interest even further. "Can you describe the men?"

"I'd like to tell you they looked like any normal guy, but unless normal is burlap clothes and full-length beards I can't say that."

Emotions he thought had been suppressed began to well up. "The Established Place," Ben whispered.

"What did you say?" Pete asked.

"Nothing important, or maybe *everything*. "Did they say anything?"

"No, not a word; they wouldn't even acknowledge we were there." Pete looked at the floor. "There was one name I caught, purely by accident, as the men were leaving. They didn't know I was within earshot or they wouldn't have said anything."

Ben stood and leaned over. He grabbed Pete by his shoulders."What was it?" he demanded.

"Jhorr," Pete blurted, surprised at Ben's reaction. "I think it was Jhorr."

* * *

EVE SAT, her eyes swollen, unable to comprehend the events that had transpired earlier that day. She rolled to her side on the pine bough bed.

"How?" she moaned. "How could things have gone so wrong?"

"The freedom to rule one's self," came the reply.

Eve jerked and looked toward the response.

Belac's head was visible through the doorway.

"I am sorry if I troubled you. I sensed you were in pain, and I wanted to be of assistance."

"Please come in." She sat up and wiped her eyes.

Belac entered the room and stood at the foot of the bed.

"Please," Eve said, motioning toward the bed. "Please sit down."

Belac smiled, "It would not be proper. I will stand."

"I didn't mean to imply anything improper," she said, shrinking back, feeling guilty.

"Worry not, dear Eve," he said, shaking his head. "There is no need for concern."

Eve sighed. "You said something before you came in."

"Yes, it was in answer to your question."

"Please continue."

Belac cleared his throat. "A wonderful endowment has been bestowed upon us. The gift of choosing to do all we will. The Great One has done this so we would come to know Him. This decision would bring great sadness, for many would choose not to recognize His sovereignty. Many would move far from Him, but a decision He must make, lest our devotion be not freely given."

Eve looked in Belac's direction. "So, you're saying Ben chose this, that's why it happened?"

"Yes, though not to say that enticement was not involved." He took a deep breath and released it slowly. "However, it is as you have said, he chose his own direction."

Eve sat up on her knees; tears welled in her eyes once again. "Well, that's fine, but what about me?" She pointed to herself, her voice cracking as she tried to speak. "I didn't ask for this, so why am I hurting?" She leaned forward, staring intently at Belac. "Tell me, Belac, why?" she cried and collapsed on the bed as convulsive sobs racked her body.

Belac placed a hand on her head. A tear formed in his eye. It traversed his cheek, dropping to the ground, a solemn reminder that consequence afflicts not merely the guilty but the innocent as well.

* * *

"WHAT IS IT?" Pete said, answering the knock at the door.

A young boy entered the room. "I suspected there was a need," the boy said.

"Jhorr," Ben said. "Is that you?"

"Yes," the youth answered. "It is I."

"Are you . . . " Ben asked, sheepishly.

"Yes," Jhorr said. "I am the answer for which you have asked." He walked over and faced Ben. Laying a hand on each side of Ben's head, he spoke, "You have forgotten, Ben Adams, now you will remember."

Ben was back in the habitat having dinner with Pete. The affection that he felt for his friend warmed him. Then to the Orion, *how would he ever get out of this alive*? Ben recalled his first encounter with Eve, Jhorr and the Established Place. The death of Stewart, an enemy turned friend, his marriage to the love of his life, and finally, Sarith telling him above all else to love. He relived it all in a split second. Then it came to an end as quickly as it had begun.

Ben opened his eyes. Jhorr was smiling. Ben's head was still in Jhorr's hands. He nodded, "I understand now, I was never alone."

Jhorr's smile widened. "Indeed you do understand." He lowered his hands, "I must go to Belac. I will return soon."

"PLEASE, YOUNG ONE, enter," Belac said.

Jhorr walked into the room.

Belac was standing over a now subdued Eve. He looked at Jhorr, beckoning a response with his eyes.

"I have been with the one called Ben," Jhorr said.

"Did you show him?"

"Yes," Jhorr answered, "it is time."

"Then he knows?"

"Yes, he knows."

"Further time is required to entirely remove the Dark One's influence. They must be watched intently until this is so."

Jhorr nodded and left.

Eve sat up. "You're talking about Ben, aren't you?"

"Dear Eve," Belac said, "I must leave for a time; however, I will return soon."

Eve grabbed his hand. "Please Belac, tell me, I must understand."

Belac smiled, taking Eve's hand into both of his. "It is for good I go. Know what I have said to be true."

* * *

"WILL YOU TELL ME what happened?" Pete asked.

"I don't think I can," Ben replied. "I don't know myself."

"What do you mean? If you can't, who can?"

Ben thought for a moment. "Pete, do you remember the last time we were together in the habitat?"

"Sure, what of it?"

"We were close back then."

"Yeah," Pete acknowledged.

"That's one place I've been."

Pete smiled, the smile turned to a chuckle, and then laughter. "I'll take 20 credits worth of what you're on." Pete looked around the room and back at Ben. "I could handle a change of scenery."

"No," Ben said, "it's not like that at all."

"Okay, I'll bite." Pete propped his elbow on his knee and planted his chin in the palm of his hand.

"Not only have I been to the habitat, but to the Orion and several other places. There's no time to explain right now, but they all have one common denominator."

"And what was this *common denominator*?" Pete mused then hesitated a moment, "No, don't tell me, it was your guardian angel." Pete bit his lip trying not to laugh again.

Ben smiled. "You are closer than you think."

Pete's grin left his face. "You're serious, aren't you?"

"Yes, In fact, I've never been more serious in my life."

"All right," Pete said, "I'm listening."

"Everything revealed was at a point in my life when the situation was hopeless and I had no recourse or I was surrounded by people that cared about me."

"Okay, but what does that have to do with anything?"

"I can't chalk everything up to coincidence. It was too orchestrated, too scripted to have happened that way." Ben looked at Pete, "I told you about my floating in the Orion?"

Pete nodded.

"What are the odds that a ship would come along and find an object the size of the decompression chamber they weren't looking for. Then, adding to this minor miracle, accomplish this feat in a billion square miles of ocean?"

"It's a long shot, but stranger things have happened."

"Stranger than the ship that located me steering itself to my location despite the efforts of the crew to change course?"

"I'll admit it's getting a little weird, but how do you know that the ship dictated its own course. You weren't there; they hadn't picked you up yet."

"Stewart was the helmsman that day." Ben's expression changed to one of fondness. "We started off as adversaries and ended up as friends."

"So he told you?"

"He did, and showed me much more than that."

A knock at the door interrupted the conversation.

"Yes," Ben said.

Belac entered the room with Jhorr beside him. Ben stood and walked to meet him.

"Greetings, Ben Adams," Belac said. "It is good to see you."

Ben took Belac's hand into both of his. He didn't know how, but he had to apologize.

"It is unnecessary," Belac said, sensing Ben's intentions. "Your eyes speak many words."

Ben smiled and nodded with a hint of embarrassment.

"There is someone here to see you, Ben Adams," Belac said. He stepped to the side making a waving motion with his hand. Eve entered the room, her eyes red, and her hair falling in tangled ringlets around her face.

"Eve," Ben whispered.

She ran to him, threw her arms around him, and cried once again.

Ben pulled her close and resting his chin on her head, matched her tear for tear.

EVE LIFTED HER HEAD. "Where have you been?" She sniffed and shuddered at the same time.

"Away for a short time," Ben replied, "but I'm back now." He wiped her tears with his thumbs.

"I thought I'd lost you."

"Not a chance."

Nestling his hand underneath her chin, he raised her head. "You can't get rid of me that easy."

Eve smiled and kissed him.

Ben pushed her to arms length. "You are looking a tad rough though," he joked.

"Since I can't see myself, I guess that's your problem."

Ben smiled. "It's not such a bad problem."

"Uh hmm," Pete grunted.

Ben looked in his direction. "Sorry, buddy. Sweetheart, I'd like you to meet my reincarnated friend, Pete."

Eve attempted to straighten her hair. "Pleasure to meet you," she said, extending her hand.

Pete took her hand. "You sure know how to pick'em," he said, throwing a wink in Ben's direction.

Eve blushed, and then she too looked at Ben, pointed at Pete and shook her head in disbelief. "This isn't?" she mouthed. "No, it can't be; can it?"

Ben knew what Eve was thinking. "Yes, it can, and it is."

"How?" Eve asked.

Belac interrupted. "Perhaps it would do to discuss these matters after the three have taken nourishment."

Eve glared affectionately at Ben. "Due to a situation beyond my control, eating was not high on the list of activities this week."

"I guess that's my fault," Ben said. He lowered his head, then winced at the pain coursing through his skull.

"Ben?" Eve exclaimed. "What is it? What's wrong?"

Belac nodded at Jhorr and the young one left the shelter.

Ben doubled over and dropped to one knee.

Eve fell to her husband's side. "Belac, please help him!"

Two men entered the shelter behind Jhorr.

Belac placed his hands on Eve's shoulders. "These men will see to the needs of your Ben and the one called Pete. Please calm yourself and I will explain."

Eve stood catatonic, as Ben and Pete were escorted from the dwelling. She turned to Belac, her eye's begging for something, for anything to grasp. Any thread to hold on to that would somehow push away this new cycle of fear, invading her being.

Belac smiled. "Please sit, dear one."

Eve complied. "Why?" she whispered.

"The Dark One has conspired to thwart the chosen ones by any means possible. The struggle your Ben and his companion now face is to rid themselves of Eleazor's methods of coercion."

"Methods of coercion?" Eve questioned. "What do you mean?"

"A mind control substance, known as the Kumult, has been enlisted to turn those who would not otherwise follow onto a malevolent course."

Eve's momentary lull was again turning into full-fledged panic. She rose and faced Belac. "I understand none of this? Is Ben in danger?"

"Dear Eve—"

"Don't, 'dear Eve' me!" She threw her hands up and out to the side in a gesture of futility. "Why aren't you doing something?"

Belac stood and took Eve by both wrists. "Your Ben and the one called Pete are being well cared for."

"You haven't answered my question." She remained firm, glaring at Belac.

Belac nodded. "Indeed I have not." He motioned for Eve to sit.

 She complied.

Belac reseated himself, sighed, and spoke. "I do not believe the Kumult was given in sufficient quantities or for an extended period as to cause any lasting problems. However, the Dark One has placed within your Ben a notion that could well lead to destruction."

Eve lowered her head, cradling it in her hands. "How could this happen? It's not supposed to be like this."

A puzzled look spread across Belac's face. "I do not understand, dear one."

 Eve raised her head.

Belac looked into Eve's eyes. "Please explain."

Eve sniffed several times and then wiped her nose. She stared at Belac. "It shouldn't be like this. Once we married, everything fell to pieces. I'm all for the better or worse stuff, but I can't handle any more *worse*." Eve's eyes became moist again. "You know, white picket fences, the pitter patter of little feet." Again she shuddered as she inhaled. "I think it's time I got some of the *better*." She remained stoic, her gaze fixed upon Belac.

"I understand your remorse, dear one," Belac said, "however you must realize—"

Eve shook her head. "You understand nothing." Her eyes never wavered, ever set upon her guardian.

"What you say is true. I cannot put myself in the place in which you now reside." He paused, returning her cold, hard gaze, with a warm expression of concern. "However, know this. I have experienced the loss of one very dear to me."

Eve softened. "Tell me," she whispered.

Belac lowered his head and then raised it again, a somber expression, embedded much deeper than the facial muscles of a single human could express. "Perhaps another time." He sat, inviting Eve to do the same.

Eve nodded and reseated herself. "I'm sorry."

Belac did his best to form a smile. "If you allow me to do so, I will now tell you of what lies ahead for your Ben."

Eve closed her eyes, nodded, and then sat, waiting for Belac to begin.

Belac took a deep breath, allowing it to escape, as he gathered his thoughts. "Both men have had their bodies invaded by the Kumult. As I stated, this should pass in time with no lasting effects." He paused as this sank its way into her consciousness. He shifted uneasily. "However, your Ben has experienced something more."

"What?" Eve insisted, now becoming more animated.

"A seed of deceit was planted within your Ben; a seed that has taken root and grown."

"You make it sound so final." She slid off her seat and onto her knees in front of Belac. "Please tell me there's something we can do." Her eyes pleaded for help.

Belac took her hands. "There is a chance; however, I will need your assistance."

Eve nodded vigorously.

"We must wait for a time," Belac said, "perhaps my tale of love lost will convince you of my ability to experience your anguish."

"ANIA," Belac bellowed, "Come, look what I found."

The pretty petite brunette ran to her husband's side. "What is it my love?"

"Footprints," Belac said, "and they appear to be from the Liasen." He felt an open palm hard against his back.

"I run to answer your call, and you regale me with children's stories." She wrapped her arms around him and they kissed.

"Children's stories," Belac said. "The Liasen is very real, and a creature I have seen."

Ania pushed away from her husband with an incensed expression. "Why would you utter an untruth to your wife on your honeymoon?"

"Have you ever known your betrothed to speak a lie, even in jest to the one he loves?" Belac said.

Ania's eyes welled, she moved toward Belac. She buried her face into his fur covering pleading for forgiveness between sobs.

"Ania, you mustn't—"

The guttural roar of a beast pulled the newlyweds apart.

"What?" was all she could manage to utter before Belac had her by the arm moving through the dense vegetation.

"Faster, dear one," Belac urged, "For your life, faster."

The thundering footfalls from behind began to subside in intensity. Belac and Ania slowed and then came to a stop.

"I could not . . . have stayed . . . the pace . . . much longer," Ania said, between breaths. Belac bent over with his hands on his knees, not bothering to speak until he had somewhat caught his breath.

"So tell me, husband, was that the infamous Liasen that terrorized my dreams as a child?"

Belac smiled. A large brown form dropped from the sky. A second later, the form rose, attached to a snakelike appendage and disappeared. "I cannot be sure the Liasen I saw as a child—" halfway through Belac's sentence he realized he was speaking to his wife's legs from the knees down still standing.

Chapter Twenty-seven

AN INCOHERENT BEN sat upright and rubbed his head.

"What happened?" His speech was thick and slurred. His head pounded.

What did I do last night? Ben's thoughts shifted to an earlier time. He was 18, in the Navy and suffering from the worst hangover. The image disappeared as soon as it had begun, with a familiar voice.

"Hey, little man," Pete said. "I thought we had lost you."

"We?" Ben said. "Who are we and who are you?"

Pete chuckled. "Here, drink this." He extended a cup containing a light green broth.

Ben wove bleary eyes up to the level of the beaker. "Don't you think I've had enough?"

Pete pushed the cup to Ben's lips. "Drink," he insisted.

Ben eyed the big man offering drink. He glanced at the cup, and once again at the cupbearer. Turning his attention to the pale liquid, he looked, sniffed, and then reluctantly tilted the receptacle and took a sip.

"How's that?" Pete asked.

Ben shrugged his shoulders. "What is it?"

"A compound that will serve to clear your head," a voice said.

Ben turned toward the voice. One of Belac's men stood several feet away. He nodded. "I am called Lyndon."

"When did you come in?" Ben asked.

"He's been here the whole time," Pete said.

"Okay," Ben said, clutching his temples in one hand. "When did I come in?"

"The effect will not be immediate," Lyndon said. "It will require a short—"

Ben waved his free arm. "Enough already, I get it." He kept his hand in place over his eyes and peered through a space between his fingers. "Just keep it down. My head is about to split."

Pete smiled and touched Ben's shoulder. "All right—"

Ben knocked his hand away, crouching down in a defensive position, his finger tips and toes contacting the ground, poised to spring. "Back off!" he growled.

Pete jumped back in surprise. "Ben?" he exclaimed, craning his neck to believe what he was seeing.

"You damned traitor," Ben yelled, with an unnatural resonance that caused Pete to pull back a second time.

Ben swung around, taking a swipe at Pete's head, just missing his intended target.

Pete sensed a hand wrap around his left bicep.

"We will now take our leave," Lyndon said.

Pete turned. Before he could make eye contact, he felt himself pulled through the door of the modest hut. He tried to protest, but the grip around his upper arm remained steadfast.

Once in the night air, Pete pulled away from Lyndon and then turned to face his aggressor. "What are you doing?"

Lyndon raised his hand. Four men appeared, moving promptly through the doorway and into the structure.

"Your friend will be cared for," Lyndon said. "We will now go."

"Go?" Pete replied. "I'm not leaving him alone with those four goons." He turned to re-enter the hut. Lyndon caught him by the arm. Pete whirled around, cocking his arm and throwing his fist as he did so.

Lyndon caught the projectile mere inches from his nose, twisted his hand and in the process took Pete to the ground, landing on one knee. "We will go now," he repeated.

Pete looked down at the ground unsure how he could have gotten so close so suddenly. The one who bought him to this point still held Pete's clenched hand. "Uh-huh."

"I DON'T UNDERSTAND," Pete said. "I wanted to stay with my friend, but your thug here," he cocked his head sideways toward Lyndon, standing motionless, arms crossed, several feet away, "had a different idea."

Eve sat silent beside Pete and across from Belac.

"It is not for you to intervene," Belac said. "You will also have obstacles to overcome."

Pete stood, defiantly. "Then why am I not with Ben?"

Belac made calming motions with his hands. "Again, it is not an assessment you are able to make."

"Okay. That's the second time you've implied that I'm not competent to decide." Pete stepped in front of Belac, arms straight by his side, clenching and unclenching his fists. "I think it's about time you quit talking in circles and start explaining." Pete inched closer to Belac.

Lyndon dropped his arms and moved toward Pete.

Belac waved him off, and the protector backed away, resuming his statuesque facade.

Pete turned his head and glanced at Lyndon."I'm ready for you now, big boy."

"This is unnecessary," Belac said, motioning for Pete to sit. "Please." He waved his hand once again, inviting Pete to take a seat.

Pete hesitated, looked at Lyndon, then at Belac, once again to Lyndon, and sat down. The image of his earlier trip to the ground at the hand of Belac's bodyguard was still vivid in his mind.

"A plague of sorts has infected yourself and the one known as Ben," Belac began.

"Plague?" Pete questioned. "What do you mean *plague*?"

"The Kumult," Belac said.

"Kumult?" Pete wrinkled his forehead. "What is Kumult?"

Belac pursed his lips, a somber expression crossing his face. "A potion given to you by the Dark One. It prepares one for complete mind control."

"I don't understand," Pete said. "If both Ben and I were given this *Kumult*, why am I not in the same shape he is?"

"Regrettably for your Ben," Belac said, "the potion is not the only concern."

Pete once again rose to his feet, glaring at Belac. "Well, what then?"

"Pete," Eve pleaded. "Belac simply means to help." She stood, taking him by the hand. "Please, hear Belac out."

Pete sighed, shook his head, and took a deep breath. "Don't know why I'm doing this." He looked at Belac. "Okay, you've got one minute. Make it good."

Belac nodded, "I suppose that by *one minute* you mean do not tarry. It will take but a short time to explain the position in which we find ourselves."

"You've already wasted ten seconds," Pete said.

"The Dark One supplied you with the Kumult to induce mind control. That, as it now appears, will be of little consequence."

Pete shook his head. "I'm outta here. You haven't told me anything I don't already know." Pete turned to leave.

"You must understand that your Ben faces much more than the Kumult."

Pete slowed, but continued to move.

Belac had now risen to his feet, his voice rising in volume. "Ben will not recover without your assistance."

Pete stopped, turned, and made his way back to Belac. "You've got one more minute. No run around. Give it to me straight."

Belac looked at Pete with an air of surprise. "Once again, the exact meaning of your words escapes me. *Run around—* because of the context you have used, I somewhat comprehend its meaning. I will do my best to impart to you all I know."

"I'm listening," Pete said.

"It would appear that the Kumult will have little if any additional effect on you," Belac said. "I fear, combined with the seed that the Dark One has planted within your Ben, such is not the case."

Pete's expression changed from one of insolence to one of concern. "What *is* the case?" he said.

"The combination of the two have the potential to forever pull your Ben into the realm of darkness," Belac said.

"You mentioned Ben couldn't do it without me," Pete said. "What does that mean?"

"Not just you," Eve said. "It will take us both."

Pete turned to look at Eve, then once again at Belac. "Okay, I'm in."

One of the two men who had earlier escorted Ben and Pete away returned. He nodded at Belac. "It has begun."

BEN MOANED AND OPENED his eyes. He clamped them shut again as he sat upright, cradling his head in both hands until the dizziness subsided. He opened his eyes, squinting as the meager light filtered in. After several minutes, he could discern shapes.

He pulled himself to his knees, pausing as another wave of vertigo coursed through his brain.

Ben stood, placing his hands on his knees for support. In each direction were contrasting shades of blue. As his vision adjusted to the new surroundings, he was able to distinguish that the darker shades resembled trees. These were not the trees that one would ordinarily expect, but distorted abominations. Their broad bases grew tightly together. The wrinkled bark swirled in random patterns, until ending at the first course of limbs, which hung close to the ground. The branches grew in tiers that twisted in a spider web-like fashion toward a darkened azure sky.

Something akin to bats, but larger, darted in and out of the menagerie of limbs. Ben couldn't distinguish details, just the ragged silhouettes as they fluttered by.

He was standing on a path of sorts. From the little he could determine, one way disappeared into darkness; the other led toward a pinhead-sized light.

Ben felt the alluring pull of darkness, beckoning him to follow. It repeated over and over its promise of reward if he would take the first step beginning the journey.

The small point of light also called to him, yet promised nothing, save for help along the way and peace once he reached his destination.

Ben looked into the darkness, hesitated and then took his first step toward the light. One of the flying creatures dipped low, opening a small gash in his forehead.

"So that's how it's gonna be." He swatted at the aberration as it dived a second time, knocking it to the ground. As the creature tried to right itself, Ben brought his foot down hard, twisting until mud oozed up the side of his shoe. The miniature beast shrieked, its shrill cry muffled into a gurgle and ultimately silence as its head sunk beneath the murky goo.

Ben raised his foot, bent over, and reached down. The limp form made a sucking sound as he pulled it from its muddy tomb. He brushed caked-on debris from its body, turning it over several times to examine the lifeless corpse. Its wings hung straight down beside its body, gently wafting each time a light, stagnant breeze pushed its way through.

The creature had a curved beak, similar to an eagle, but with rows of random jagged teeth. The forehead swept back, ending at a dome at the crown of the skull. Black, lifeless eyes grotesquely protruded from either side of its head, just below close-cropped, rounded ears. Its wings were blue, a nearly transparent membrane that stretched between black arm bones. The bottom edge of each wing was so ragged it appeared they were haphazardly torn from tissue paper.

Overlapping, triangular scales covered its chest, and stiff, thick fur its back. Ben noticed a single talon hung from the lower thorax, with no legs to speak of.

That's why they're forever moving. They have no way to perch. He lifted the animal by its wing tips, letting the body dangle. The span was approximately two feet.

Ben loosed his hold, allowing the creature to hang by one wing. He curled his lip in disgust and released his final grip. Before the leathery wing could clear his fingertips, the lifeless head screeched, wrenched upward, clamping its serrated beak onto the soft tissue between Ben's right thumb and index finger.

With the same hand Ben made a fist, squeezing tight around the thing's neck. With his free hand he grabbed its torso, twisted and pulled, removing the head. Black fluid spewed from the body as it writhed on the ground in silent agony.

The beak remained attached to his hand, its eyes wide and still afire with whatever demented life inhabited the disembodied aberration. The fluid leaking from the severed head seemed to crawl around Ben's hand and into the wound, opened by the creature's mouth.

"Ahh!" Ben tried to pry the beak open with no success. His hand seared as though doused with acid. A muffled cackle emanated from the closed mouth. To quell the pain, he grabbed the oozing neck and pulled, removing a sizable portion of his own flesh as he did so.

Ben dropped to his knees. He pulled handfuls of muck from the ground and rubbed it into the burning lesion. Wisps of smoke curled upward as he removed the last of the caustic blood. He bared his teeth, stood and stomped the cackling head deep into the mud.

Ben watched as several bubbles pushed through the mud over the buried head and then stopped. He kicked the decapitated body high in the air and out of sight into the woods on the other side of the path. He stood there, eyes ablaze, staring into a fevered nothing for several minutes until his breathing slowed and his muscles relaxed. Ben took a deep breath, sighed and sat down exhausted.

Chapter Twenty-eight

BEN LAY PEACEFULLY, appearing to be asleep.

Eve stepped through the doorway and smiled. "Poor dear, you're exhausted." She didn't notice the men gathered at the head and foot of the bed. Eve sat down beside her husband and kissed him on the forehead. She pulled back, waiting for a reaction. When he didn't move, she nudged him. "Wake up, sweetheart."

Ben remained still and then jerked, swiping at his forehead. An open wound appeared just above his left eye.

Eve looked on in disbelief, frozen in the moment.

Ben grimaced and jerked a second time, pawing at his thumb. A triangular piece of flesh disappeared from his right hand. It oozed a thick clear liquid as though it was just cauterized. Ben relaxed, seeming to slip deeper into his dark sleep.

Eve shook him violently until Belac stopped her short of pulling Ben to the floor.

"Why won't he wake up?" Eve stretched her arms through Belac's grasp, desperate to return to her husband.

"You cannot arouse him," Belac said. "For now it is out of our control."

* * *

BEN AWOKE from a fitful sleep, sitting on the ground; his head hung low between his legs. He raised his head and took a deep breath.

"Can't stay here all day." He looked at his surroundings, ". . . or night." Ben tugged hard at his shirtsleeve. He managed to rip half of it off to serve as a bandage. After wrapping his hand, he stood and began to move toward the small point of light.

The burning had stopped, but the mud-packed wound between his thumb and forefinger continued to throb. As Ben walked, he noticed that the bat bugs, as he dubbed them, still fluttered around, only now staying out of his reach.

Ben sneered. "You'd *better* not get in my way." He scrutinized one as it flew by. "I'll plant you just like I did your brother." A loud chorus of cackles echoed through the trees as though the creatures were voicing their disdain over Ben's reference to their fallen comrade.

Ben smiled. "Remember that." Another resounding chorus of devilish cackles resonated through the air.

He resumed his trek. The ground was noticeably drier, making his way easier without the mud to course through.

In time, Ben perceived the ambient light slowly growing dimmer. A wave of uncertainty passed over him. He looked toward his supposed final destination. The pinpoint of light had grown to the size of a pencil lead.

Ben groaned. "This is going to take forever." He slumped in resignation as his stomach began to growl. He dropped his head and patted his gut. "Hold on buddy, I don't know if there's anything in this hell-hole that we can eat that won't kill us."

He stared down the path. A brief flicker caught his eye.

Ben froze.

"What?" He closed his eyes, shook his head, opened them and then craned his neck. There it was again. With no hesitation, Ben took off down the path in a jog.

✳ ✳ ✳

"WHAT'S HAPPENING to him?" Eve cried. Belac turned her around and firmly grasped her by the shoulders.

"Your Ben is in the hold of the Dark One. He is trapped in something akin to a dreamscape as real to Ben as you and I are to one another." Belac looked at her with all the earnestness he could muster within his heart. "You must retain your composure if we are to return him to this when."

Eve calmed, momentarily staring into Belac's eyes. "I assume when you say *when*, he is being held captive in another dimension?"

Belac smiled. "Not captive; he is simply there to rid himself of the Dark One's seed, unless the evil within is strong enough to persuade him to do otherwise."

Eve seemed to melt at his words, and yet, displayed a confident resolve. She gathered herself, squared her shoulders and stood tall. "Just tell me what to do."

Belac's smile widened. "Indeed I will." He extended one hand to Eve and one hand to Pete. "Come, let us deliberate."

Chapter Twenty-nine

S BEN NEARED the source of his excitement, he began to discern details. A small fire produced the glimmer that had first caught his attention. Close to the meager blaze sat a solitary figure. The light bathed the form in a warm glow that danced around his bearded face.

The old man sat, stirring the embers as a piece of meat roasted over the fire. Ben's stomach growled at the enticing aroma wafting from the meat.

"Greetings, stranger," the old man said.

Ben nodded, his eyes glazed. He stood, staring at the possibility of dinner, saliva dribbling from the corner of his mouth.

"Please," the old man said, gesturing toward the ground in front of him. "Sit; join with me in the evening meal."

Ben's eyes widened. He smiled and then sat, a small dust cloud rising as he plopped onto the dirt.

The old man took the shaved limb that held the meat and pulled it out of the ground. He twisted one of the forelegs, removing nearly a quarter of the rabbit-sized carcass, and handed it to Ben.

Ben snatched the leg from his hand and greedily devoured the first sustenance he'd eaten in what seemed like weeks. Ben could not recall a time he had ever been this hungry. He felt ashamed and then dismissed the notion to fulfill his insatiable appetite.

The old man removed a hindquarter from the sizzling carcass, extending the entire mass to Ben.

Ben finished sucking the last scraps of meat from the foreleg and dropped the bones on the ground, focusing on the bounty placed before him.

Ben mangled the second course. Once done, he wiped his mouth, looking at the old man. "Sorry," he said, breathing heavily, his face covered in grease. "I couldn't help myself. I had to eat."

The old man smiled. "This I know. It is for that very reason along with ones I will make known to you that I am here."

Ben cocked his head. "Okay, you've got my attention."

"Please," the old man said, "finish your meal. You will require the nourishment."

Ben paused, alternating glances between the old man and the half eaten carcass. He quickly made his decision and began to devour the last of the meat.

* * *

"I'M NOT SURE I understand," Pete said. "From what I can see, Ben is lying down asleep, just as any other night." Pete's voice rose in volume, signaling his growing irritation. "I know this because I saw him, and now you're telling me he's somewhere else. Stop talking in circles and please speak so that I can understand."

Eve extended a hand, laying fingers across Pete's wrist. Pete looked at her.

Eve shook her head and whispered, "Listen."

Pete grimaced and faced Belac. "Okay, I'll shut up." He glanced at Eve and back to Belac.

Belac eyes, acknowledged their compliance. "As I have said, your Ben is in the hold of the Dark One. He has entered into a realm that exists within."

"*Within?*" Eve said. "I don't understand." Her face fell as she slipped into the grasp of desperation.

"The place in which your Ben dwells," Belac said, "is planted entirely in his mind. Even though his physical being remains among us, his true self is in the grasp of the Dark One." Belac paused, gazing sternly at the two gathered before him. "And what I have said is true, death in this realm would be every bit as real as if it had happened here."

"What can we do?" Eve asked.

"I want you to stay close, touching him at all times," Belac said. "This will give your Ben a sense of comfort and a purpose." Belac addressed Pete. "You share a kinship through ingestion of the Kumult. I have great hope that in some way this will work to our advantage. We must watch and wait. For now there is nothing more."

* * *

BEN WIPED HIS MOUTH, took a deep breath and released it, deflating as the air left his body.

The old man chuckled. "Had enough?"

"Yes, and thank you." Ben smiled. "I'm sorry I burst into your camp like a mad man, but I felt that without something to eat I would die . . . " he paused, pondering his last sentence. Ben looked into the nothingness and then at the old man. "I think had I not found you, I may have gone mad with hunger."

The old man continued to smile. He lowered his head and raised it again. "I am called Dalon Com."

Ben opened his mouth and then stopped. A curious look spread across his face. His complexion faded to a washed-out shade of gray. Ben focused on the old man.He opened his mouth a second time, hesitated, and spoke in a shaken whisper. "I don't know who I am."

Dalon Com nodded several times over and smiled grimly, saying nothing.

"How can I not know my own name?"

"That I cannot answer; however, I can tell you this. What you lost must be searched out to reclaim. Toward the light is the correct path and must be traversed in all haste."

"Not that I don't want to finish . . . " Ben paused, "whatever I'm supposed to be doing, but what's the big hurry?"

"The meal you have eaten is the only nourishment I can offer. The completion of your quest depends upon the strength it supplies. Much beyond that time and you will certainly go mad with hunger."

Ben shifted uneasily. "That's a good reason, but why?"

"Even though we dwell within the confines of the Dark One's world, you have a way to escape."

Dalon Com stood. He was much taller than Ben had imagined. His garment was modest, a robe of a pale cotton fabric that flowed to the ground. The only visible flesh was his face and hands.

He produced a blade three feet long, a dull pewter color with a double-sided edge. The hilt extended another foot. On its end, a bright glimmer caught Ben's eye. It wasn't constant; instead, it flickered with its bearer's subtle movements.

Ben kept his gaze on the weapon and extended his hand. The old man placed the sword into his open palm. Ben's fingers closed around the leather windings on the handle. A warm presence engulfed him. He didn't understand it, but somehow sensed it was there to provide comfort.

If only I could remember who I am, he thought. He looked at Dalon Com and at the weapon in his hand.

Ben looked up as he spoke, "I'd like to thank—"

The old man had vanished.

He turned in a complete circle. *Did I imagine it all?* The mangled carcass still glowed by the light of the fire. He raised his hand. The sword remained firmly in his grasp.

Ben remembered Dalon Com's last warning. *"You will certainly go mad with hunger."* Ben knelt and gathered the discarded bones.

* * *

EVE SAT DOWN beside Ben. His face bore the look of obvious distress. She placed her hand on his, and his expression began to ease. Eve jerked her head toward Belac, terrified she had done something wrong.

Belac smiled, giving her a silent nod.

Eve relaxed, smiled and turned her full attention to her husband.

Pete looked at Belac. "What's going on?"

Belac placed a hand on Pete's shoulder. "Nothing more than what is necessary."

* * *

"MAYBE A MILE, maybe ten, there's nothing to reference time, distance or anything else in this place." Ben sighed. "Even the point of light I'm headed towards seems to shrink and then grow again." He chuckled. "Guess I'm not the only one who doesn't know whether he's coming or going."

The calm Ben had experienced when he was with Dalon Com was still with him. Now it took on an air of recognition, something akin to a friendly companion traveling alongside. Ben wracked his brain trying to understand why it was so familiar.

A dark, claustrophobic heaviness seemed to drop from nowhere, covering and weighing him down. He came to an abrupt halt, the calm supplanted with an overwhelming sense of danger.

Before Ben could react, a single tentacle, followed by four more, wrapped him in a constricting embrace and pulled him slowly backwards.

His sword fell from the makeshift holder, which was the drawstring around his waist and hit the ground. Ben watched the weapon grow smaller and disappear from sight as his methodical retreat continued, unabated.

* * *

BEN STIFFENED, his arms pulling tight to his side and straight down his thighs. Eve yelped as his hand jerked from her grasp.

She looked at Belac. He raised a hand in her direction signaling for silence. Belac nodded to one of his four men. The attendant left and returned carrying a cot setting it down next to Ben and then stepped aside.

Belac motioned for Pete to join him beside the cot.

Pete, intrigued with the surrounding events, moved to Belac's side without question.

"Do you know why I have summoned you?" Belac asked.

Pete nodded, his expression, one of willing compliance.

"Belac," Eve pleaded, "you have to tell me what you're doing." Tears welled. "Ben's my husband!"

Belac paused and turned. He looked deep into her eyes and realized the pain that encompassed her. "Of course, my dear Eve; however, you must remember that time is of the essence. Your Ben has reached an impasse. I will now enlist the Krang, an ancient power that has yet to be used in this age. The Kumult has given these two a connection that in all hope will make this possible."

"But—" Eve said.

"I have spoken," Belac interrupted. "We must begin."

Eve sank back and meekly nodded.

Belac instructed Pete to lie on the cot beside Ben. Pete complied.

Belac hovered over Pete, chanting, and waving his arms until a pale yellow light appeared. Pete's eyes rolled back and his hands twitched. The light's energy coursed through his arms and legs until his entire body vibrated, emanating a low-pitched hum. The light continued to intensify until the room glowed.

Eve noticed movement out of the corner of her eye, "Belac!" she gasped.

* * *

THE BACKWARD PROGRESSION slowed and soon came to a halt. Ben jerked several times and then locked into a tight fitting space, like a door closing in a snug fitting jamb.

He could turn his head in either direction well enough to see himself wedged into a cavity in a huge tree trunk.

The bindings that held him were in fact appendages from a complex root system, woven eons before, that now laid entangled deep beneath his feet. Each time Ben struggled, the living roots pulled him tighter into his hollow niche.

He stopped fighting and took deep breaths to calm himself. Every breath brought an increase in pressure the constricting tentacles exuded, like a python squeezing the life from him.

Ben felt multiple taps on his right leg, continuing a steady beat, rising upward as it did so. A steady clicking sound accompanied the ascent. Reaching his thigh, the thumps increased in speed, stopping on his abdomen.

Another round of taps started on his left calf, circling around to his thigh before coming to a halt. Whatever had paused on his abdomen made its way up his chest until coming into view.

Ben grimaced as the three foot long black, scorpion-like creature crawled across his face, onto his shoulder and down his right arm. The creature bore eight legs. Its segmented body tapered into a blunt tail. There was no visible stinger, although Ben sensed an inherent danger, as the arachnid continued its advance. A separate pair of forelegs ended in huge claws, revealing the source of the constant clicking.

The second creature and two others, moved to their respective places, one at his left hand and one at each ankle.

The tentacles and the bugs re-assumed restraining Ben. One claw clamped his ankles and wrists and the other to the coarse bark of the tree. Blood trickled down his arms, as the claws dug into his flesh.

"Ahh!"

The tentacles released, and an ominous shadow moved in his direction. As the silhouetted figure lumbered closer, its features came into view. It was the size of a large dog and virtually identical to the scorpion bugs save for its head and forelegs.

"What are you?" Ben struggled against his bindings, causing the blood flow to increase into multiple rivulets flowing down his arms, gathering on his elbows and drip, forming shallow puddles, onto the ground.

He experienced no pain as he tried to absorb the repulsive entity before him. The body and legs were the same as the things that held his arms and legs. The face, that horrific face, is what caused him to tremble.

An elongated tongue, split three ways, lapped at the puddles of crimson liquid at Ben's feet. It finished its feast and imbibed the clots forming at Ben's elbows.

It wove its head upward, or moreover, fluttered, curling its coarse, black tongue around Ben's forearm, removing the blood trails as it moved.

The head attached to a slender neck several feet long. The neck roped from the body. Its black, sagging skin lightened to a pale blue as it reached the back of the skull. This color covered the entire head.

A pair of wings, similar to that of the bat bugs, protruded from the top of the human-like head, allowing it to hover or dart about in any direction. The face was pale, appearing as a skeleton with a tight latex skin stretched over it. Black eyes set deep into hollow sockets and black lips completed the aberration's ghostly appearance.

In place of claws, there were hands with long slender fingers, colored the same washed-out blue. They appeared soft and supple with dark knuckles and long fingernails. A smaller set of wings allowed each hand the same mobility as the head. The wrists as spindly as its neck, its nails mimicking the same clicking sound as its smaller cousins.

As the entity continued its trek up Ben's forearm, it reached his hand, taking his middle finger in its mouth. There were no teeth that Ben could see. He soon found that teeth weren't necessary. A shiny, guillotine-like projection dropped from its upper jaw, bottomed out and then returned.

Ben's finger dropped into the creature's mouth. It swallowed without chewing and then grinned a devilish grin.

Ben screamed, "No!" He struggled against his bindings, the surreal situation eliminating any pain he may have experienced. The creation's claws tightened, causing a fresh flow of blood to pour from his wrists.

The bat bugs fluttered about, like buzzards awaiting scraps from a carnivorous feeding frenzy. Ben watched in horror as the mouth wrapped around his entire hand.

❋ ❋ ❋

BELAC WHIRLED AROUND, attempting to cover the anger that was evident on his face.

Eve pointed to the far corner in the room. "Eyes," she stammered. "I saw a pair of eyes just floating . . . " Her hand was shaking. "Right over there."

His gaze followed her finger to the origin of her fears. All that remained were the remnants of a pale yellow orb vanishing from sight.

"Belac!" Eve screamed, a second time.

He spun his head in answer to her cry. To their dismay, Ben tensed as his middle finger disappeared.

He jerked again. A red cut appeared, encircling his wrist.

Eve grimaced and wailed, "No!"

❋ ❋ ❋

THE HEAD SHRIEKED and rotated around Ben's wrists, opening a circular wound that dug deeper with each revolution.

Ben fought back the only way he could. Gathering all the saliva in his parched mouth, he sucked on his cheeks until they bled. He took a deep breath and sprayed the aberration with the mixture.

It released its grip on Ben's hand, shaking its head like a dog to shed the spittle, howling as it did so. It moved to within inches of Ben's face, opening its mouth wide and continuously slamming the guillotine up and down.

Ben braced for impact. The mouth was now open wide enough to cover his entire face. He tried to jerk his head from side to side avoiding the jaws, but the winged hands fluttered in, holding his head fast.

The guillotine stopped at its open-most point as the mouth slid into its final position blotting out Ben's vision and filling his nostrils with a nauseating stench.

❋ ❋ ❋

'WHAT DO WE DO?" Eve pleaded.

"Trust in the Great One," Belac quietly replied. "Other than this, there is nothing."

Ben jerked, tossing his head left and then right. His movements came to an abrupt halt, his expression one of desperate finality.

❋ ❋ ❋

EVEN THOUGH BEN could not see, he sensed the swipe of the guillotine. The head pulled back and hovered in front of him for a moment.

"What?" he gasped. *There's nothing in its mouth.*

He saw what he had misinterpreted as the beast's deathblow. The sword, given to him by Dalon Com swung again, severing the fluttering hand and shattering the claw that held Ben's left hand. The same fate befell the quivering hand and claw to his right.

Ben's hands, now free, reached for the trailing neck that hung from the aberration's head, waving erratically and squirting a clear fluid, laced with red and black.

He grabbed the swerving appendage with both hands and swung hard, driving the head into the tree between his legs. The skull cracked and a fist-sized chunk dropped out with more liquid oozing behind it.

The head continued to hover. It rose and turned towards Ben, fluid and brain matter still dribbling down its cheek. A wide grin spread across its face as the fluttering hands moved in and united with its dangling appendage.

Ben felt the bindings holding his feet release as the blade shattered the remaining two bugs.

The disembodied head darted sideways, just avoiding the sword, as it swung, contacting nothing but air.

After several more near misses, the head cackled and sped away with the bat bugs in tow, its song trailing off as it disappeared into the gloom.

The decapitated body rose and wavered unsteadily in front of Ben. The sword came down one final time, impaling the creature and pinning it to the ground.

"Well, hello there, little man," the blade wielder said.

This man was more than familiar to Ben. He sensed he should have recognized him as well as if he were looking in a mirror. *But then who am I, even a mirror can't tell me that.*

"Do I know you?" Ben questioned. "I think I do, but I'm not sure." His eyes pleaded for an answer.

The man put a foot on the grounded beast, removed the sword, and rolled it out of the way. He moved closer to Ben. "It's me, your old buddy Pete."

Ben looked at him and shook his head.

"C'mon you've gotta remember me."

Ben shook his head a second time. "But you know *me*?"

"Of course, we've known each other for years." Pete put a hand on his friend's shoulder. "We've been to the ends of the world and back, literally."

Ben glanced at Pete's hand and stared into his face. "Tell me who I am."

Pete stared back. "You have no idea, do you?"

"No," Ben said, "but you do, don't you?"

"Yeah, but first, how do we get outta here?" Pete asked.

Ben nodded. "Toward the light is as near as I've been able to figure."

"You're one up on me. Lead the way and I'll fill you in."

Chapter Thirty

"WHAT DO YOU SUPPOSE is happening?" Eve asked.

"I believe the two are united," Belac said, "however, time is most urgent."

"Will they be okay?"

"Their chance of success is much greater now that they have come together." Belac paused, taking Eve by the hand. "Even so, danger resides in each step they take."

"Belac, what did you mean when you said success?"

"I hesitate to say, though I recognize that I must." He gathered his thoughts in an attempt to lighten the effect his words would have on Eve. Realizing this would be an impossibility, he continued. "The most excellent outcome would be their return to this realm unscathed." Belac paused once again.

"I must know," Eve said

Belac nodded. "The least desirable result, though acceptable, would be to die in battle against the Dark One rather than succumbing to his influence."

Eve tightened her grip on Belac's hand. "I understand." She was solemn, a tear just beginning its course down her face.

* * *

"I'M MARRIED?" Ben said. "What's she like?"

"Yep," Pete replied. "I just met her, so I can't tell you much more than she's definitely a looker."

Ben smiled, delighted at the notion. They continued their trek toward the light without a word spoken between them.

A half an hour passed before Pete broke the silence. "Are you sure we're heading in the right direction, that point of light isn't getting any closer."

"Give it time."

"*Time*! This is more like one step up and ten steps back."

No sooner had the words left Pete's mouth than the far off glimmer moved close enough to touch. Details were now discernible. It was a portal as near as they could tell. The light swirled like iridescent clouds moving in random patterns. As quickly as it began, it moved away, but this time, not as far.

Pete turned and faced Ben. "So how do we go through, assuming that's what we're supposed to do, if it keeps popping in and out?"

"I'm not sure, but I think we'll know when the time is right." Ben's stomach growled, "I could sure use something to eat."

Pete looked around. "I doubt there's anything here that I want to put in my mouth. Let's keep moving. We'll get something as soon as we get outta here."

Ben nodded. As he walked, he remembered Dalon Com's warning. "You will surely go mad with hunger." He pulled out the bones he had stashed in his pants and began to munch.

* * *

"THINGS DO NOT go well," Eleazor growled. "I must resort to forces from within to achieve my goal." The gargoyle howled, causing Sedah to shrink back. The orange giant slammed his fist down, causing the entire room to shake. "That meddling Belac will pay for his interference; oh yes. He will pay!"

The meeting ended as it usually did with Sedah backing away, leaving Eleazor alone in his tirade.

* * *

I'VE GOT TO HAVE something to eat, Ben thought. He looked at Pete, who walked to the left and just ahead as something more than his long lost friend.

A thought entered Ben's head. Something caused him, against his nature, to consider acting upon this notion.

Ben shook his head to clear the fog that had gathered, but the hunger still remained, gnawing at his soul."Hey, Pete, old buddy," Ben said, "how about you let me hold that sword? It is mine."

Pete stopped and turned to Ben. "Sure, I'm tired of the extra weight anyway."

He removed the weapon from his belt and handed it to Ben. "Sorry I didn't wipe the gunk off after pulling it from . . ." he considered his thoughts, "whatever it was."

Ben took the blade. He leered at Pete. "Thanks." He examined the sword, wide-eyed and smiling as he did so.

Pete tapped him on his arm, breaking his entrancement. "We should keep moving."

"Oh yeah, sure, lead the way." Ben stayed just behind Pete, chewing the last of the bones. He swallowed and stared at the rest of his severed finger. Ben removed the stained bandage and placed the nub in his mouth.

Savoring the taste, he sucked on the appendage until the fluid no longer oozed and the finger throbbed. Ben dropped his hand and grinned, the pain serving only to intensify his hunger.

Ben licked his lips and pulled the sword. Pete turned his head and smiled. Ben brought his head up, in a gesture of camaraderie, and returned the smile. Pete resumed his methodical march as Ben raised the weapon over his head.

* * *

"WE NOW HAVE REACHED the apex of this journey," Belac said. "I am fearful that the evil of the Dark One may have permeated the gathering of the two."

"Is there anything we can do?"

Belac didn't answer, but moved to Pete's side and placed a hand on his forehead.

Ben jumped convulsively.

Eve still clutched his hand in both of hers. She let out a cry as a searing pain coursed into her hands and up her arms. Jerking several times she pulled away and collapsed on the floor.

Eve raised her head. "Belac, he needs help!"

With his back turned, he waved his free hand to silence her. She complied, rising to her husband's side, yet careful not to touch him. Despite Eve's concern she kept her eyes on Belac.

Belac pushed his thoughts into Pete's mind. *Turn, you must turn. Do not delay. You must turn now!*

* * *

PETE DID TURN, and just in time to minimize the damage as he raised his arm, taking the brunt of the attack on his forearm. The blade sliced into the thickest part of the muscle, stopping with a clink, as it dug into bone.

"AHHH!" he screamed.

Ben pulled the sword back, bringing it to rest in both hands just above his head, directing the point of the blade toward Pete. Squatting down, he snarled at his intended meal. "I promise not to devour you all at one time." His mouth twisted into a maniacal grin, "I want to save a bit for later."

Pete clamped his hand over the wound.

"What are you doing? It's me, Ben! It's Pete!"

Ben ignored the plea and lunged a second time. Pete dropped and swept his leg, bringing Ben down. The ground knocked the sword free and before Pete could react, Ben was upright wielding the weapon again.

Too fast, Pete thought. He squared off against his friend, both men circling, in search of an opening.

Ben struck first, cleaving Pete's shoulder and shattering his collarbone. Pete fell to his knees; his head drooped as the loss of blood began to take its toll.

Ben raised the sword over his head to strike the final blow. Pete felt his skin inundated with pin pricks as static electricity coursed through his body. His hair began to rise toward the source.

Light from the portal that had appeared just behind him bathed his adversary in a glow that was, more than anything, a directional beacon.

Ben brought the blade down and at the same time Pete countered.

With his remaining strength he raised both legs upending Ben and tossing him backward into the portal.

Pete managed to climb to his knees and fall in behind his friend.

PETE SAT UP suddenly, gasping for air. He surprised Eve and Belac, causing them to let go of the blood-soaked fabric they were pressing over his wounds. At first the fabric stuck, but then, like a turning page, it peeled off and down to the floor.

Eve scrambled to retrieve the cloth. She stopped before reapplying the makeshift bandage. "Belac, the wounds have healed!"

Belac nodded. "Once he reentered this *when* the injuries from the evil realm were nullified."

A hand touched Pete's shoulder. "Sorry, buddy, I could have killed you."

Eve whirled around. "Ben, you're back!" She jumped to her feet and threw her arms around his neck.

Ben wobbled and almost fell. Eve released her hold on his neck and steadied her husband, helping him back to his bed. He stretched out and placed a hand over his eyes.

Eve noticed that his missing finger had returned. She sat down beside him.

Belac laid Pete down and then stepped back. "Most of all rest is needed. We will gather afterwards."

Chapter Thirty-one

EN OPENED HIS EYES and saw his wife staring back at him. Eve's face was exhausted and worn, dark circles sagging under her eyes. She was smiling, her expression bright, to cover her obvious fatigue. "How long?" Ben asked.

"Almost two days," Eve replied.

Ben yawned and then sat up. "Two days? Have you been up all that time?" he said, through another yawn.

She nodded, wearily.

Ben stood, and taking her by the shoulders, laid her down on the same place he had occupied for so long. Eve didn't protest. She smiled and mouthed, "Good night."

Ben kissed her on the forehead. Hearing a rustling noise, he turned as a tray of food slid into the room and the door rolled back into place.

He glanced at Eve and then moved, seating himself on the floor in front of the tray.

Ravenous, Ben pushed food into his mouth, hardly chewing before he swallowed.

"If I join you, you won't try to eat me, will you?" A voice from behind said.

Startled, Ben whirled around, rising to his feet nearly choking.

Pete patted his back until he could catch a breath. Ben removed his hands from his knees and rose to an upright position. He coughed, cleared his throat, and blew a wad of mucus and food out of his mouth.

Pete chuckled, "Didn't mean to choke you up, little man."

Ben coughed again. "You know that you're not supposed to compromise someone by beating them on the back when they're able to breathe on their own, don't you?"

A wide grin spread across Pete's face. He hit Ben across the back another time. "I think you were way past the point of compromise." Ben lurched forward from the force of Pete's gentle impact.

Ben looked at his friend, his face alive with affection, hesitating and then smiled. "Huh, I wasn't in my right mind—."

"Whoa right there, little man. You'd never hurt your ole buddy, so forget about it."

"Kinda tough to forget about hacking your best friend to bite-sized pieces for lunch."

Pete looked down at the tray of half eaten breakfast. "I always knew not to get between you and your food, but do you think I could have something to eat now?"

Ben rubbed the back of Pete's head, mussing his already frazzled hair. "Sure, have at it. I'm done."

Both men took a seat on the floor; Pete devoured what remained of the meal.

'DON'T YOU THINK you've had enough sleep?"

"What?" Ben mumbled.

"Get up."

Ben blinked several times.

Eve was shaking him. "I said, 'get up'."

Ben rubbed his eyes and sat up. "Didn't we just go through this?"

"Yes, and it's getting to be a habit, and not a good one."

Ben was on the floor in front of the breakfast tray. Pete was snoring a few feet away. He yawned and scratched his head. "Musta fallen asleep again."

Eve knelt down on the floor and wrapped her arms around Ben. "It's so good to have you back."

He pulled her close. "You're not mad at me?" Ben asked.

Eve placed a hand on his cheek. "Why would you think that?"

"You yelled at me for going back to sleep."

Eve slapped his chest. "I didn't yell at you!"

"Well then, what would *you* call it?"

"I've been so worried about you." Eve kissed him on the forehead, "I wanted to spend some time alone with you before—"

A knock on the doorpost interrupted Eve's proposition.

"Belac has requested your attendance. I will return soon to provide an escort."

Eve threw her hand up and dropped her head, shaking it, and sighing.

"That!"

"Could you keep it down?" Pete protested. "How do you expect a man to get any sleep around here?" He placed both hands over his face and groaned.

"Rise and shine," Ben said. "We're being paged."

* * *

"WELCOME, DEAR ONES," Belac said. "It is so good to see you." He sat in front of a newly-kindled fire that was just beginning to blaze. Jhorr stood just behind and to Belac's right. The sun hung low in the sky, signaling darkness within the next two hours.

Belac rose. "There is no need to be seated. We will convene later for the evening meal. I am sure you would like to cleanse yourselves first." He motioned to Jhorr. "He will show you to your respective places."

"A bath," Eve moaned in delight. "Thank you."

"Until this evening," Belac replied.

"Please come with me," Jhorr said.

Ben chuckled.

"What are you laughing at?" Eve asked.

"Jhorr doesn't realize how often he'll be leading us around when we meet again," Ben said. He threw a thoughtful glance in Jhorr's direction, *or maybe he does.*

"Irony at its best," Eve said.

They came to a series of small bathhouses poised at different locations over the top of a slow moving stream. The underground tributary surfaced at the base of a stone projection. It continued for a hundred yards above ground and then dipped beneath the earth, resuming its subterranean route. Wisps of steam rose from the water's surface for its entire length.

"Look at that," Eve said.

"Amazing," Ben muttered, "geo-thermal."

Jhorr led each to a separate bathhouse. "I believe everything you require is within," he said.

The single stream turned into many parallel tributaries about ten feet apart, by carving each one into the soft rock basin. A bathhouse sat over the top of each. This arrangement kept the houses out of a single line, allowing each occupant to bathe simultaneously without the uppermost house contaminating the ones downstream.

Within the thatched covering, an area six feet in diameter and one foot deep in the center of the tributary allowed water to flow in. This would fill the pool, and flow out again.

Ben removed his clothes and slid into the water.

BEN WAS THE LAST to emerge from his bathhouse. Eve, Pete and Jhorr were talking several yards away.

"Jhorr," Ben said, "that was very refreshing, thank you."

Jhorr nodded. "It is time for the evening meal. I will show you."

Jhorr led them to the same clearing that Ben and Eve had shared their first meal with Belac. As before, Belac sat quietly in front of the fire. He opened his eyes as they approached.

"Welcome." He spread his arms and smiled, "Sit, and we will talk before taking nourishment."

They took a seat around the fire, Jhorr to Belac's right, Ben, Eve and Pete.

Belac looked at Ben. "I wish to know of your time in the alternate domain." Belac said, his gaze intensified, "Leave nothing out."

Ben nodded and gave the group a detailed account of the event. Pete chimed in at the appropriate moments, describing his part in the tale and filling in holes that Ben couldn't quite remember.

Belac nodded pondering the name of Dalon Com. *If they only knew.* He turned his full attention to the three. "We have many things to discuss," he said. "The meal will arrive as the fire wanes." Belac looked at all in attendance. "Please begin as you so feel led."

"I'd like to start with Pete," Eve said. "We were talking about him when—" She stopped and pondered Ben's experience, "Before Ben was drawn within."

Belac nodded, "Please proceed."

"I'm trying to understand his reincarnation," Eve said, throwing a cynical glance toward Ben. "You told me he was dead, killed in the habitat accident."

"I can shed some light on that," Pete said, as Ben opened his mouth to speak. Pete looked at Ben, leveling his hand in a quieting motion. Pete recalled the events in the habitat that led to his ending up in the decompression chamber aboard the Ark.

"Did you think I was crazy when I introduced you to Pete?" Ben questioned.

"I didn't know what to think," Eve said. She looked at Pete and then at Ben. "So, how did he get here?"

"Remember the animal transport?" Ben said. "It and your head became rather well acquainted during the flood in the Slot Canyon."

Eve looked at him.

"The big orange vessel we found a few days ago; the Ark in this world?" Ben said.

"That's right," she said, "the floating barnyard."

"That's the one," Ben said.

"Maybe I should take it from here," Pete said.

Ben nodded, "Be my guest."

Pete began the story from where he'd left off. When he relayed his and Marty's orientation to the Ark, Eve interrupted."Sarith," she said, "You've seen Sarith?"

"I've seen him, but that's about as far as it goes." Pete said. "We met a few times after we accepted his employment offer."

"What was he like?" Eve asked.

"A nice guy," Pete said, "all the usual attributes of any normal person; long hair, pale complexion; two eyes—one green, one yellow."

"Please, go on," Eve urged.

Pete continued his story, and once again Eve interrupted when he told of delivering goods to the Established Place.

"I can't answer your questions," Pete said. "I never saw more than a few of them at one time, and they wouldn't make eye contact, much less engage in conversation."

"Did you see Jhorr?" she asked.

Pete shook his head and chuckled. *Eve just doesn't get it*. He got ready to speak when something hit his conscious like a ton of bricks. He looked at Jhorr with a familiarity he did not understand.

"No, I never saw him," Pete said. "At least, I don't think so," he mumbled, *until now*.

Jhorr sat in silence. Pleased at the mention of his name.

The fire reduced to embers, two women brought a large tray laying it across the coals. A single yellow orb glowed assuming the illumination duties.

As the five ate, the conversation continued.

"Pete," Eve said. "You still haven't told us how you arrived in this world." Eve stared at him more intently. "In fact, I know very little about you, other than what Ben's told me." Eve glanced in Ben's direction.

"I don't believe you've told *me* that part of your journey," Ben added.

"First things first," Pete said, looking at Ben, "and you, my friend, will have to wait your turn." Pete thought for several moments.

"I've led an uneventful life, at least what I would consider uneventful. I grew up along the coast in the Blue Ridge Mountains. We were poor like everyone else, not knowing when or if there'd be another meal."

Pete paused, remembering his brother, the story of his death being malnutrition when he was six years old. He thought better of saying anything since the circumstances of his death had been questionable, possibly including cannibalism. Pete pushed these notions to the recesses of his mind and continued his story.

"I got out as soon as I could and joined the Navy. That's where I met Ben." He threw a quick smile in Ben's direction.

"After basic, we went our separate ways. Ben favored action, so he went with the UDT. Me, well, being the smarter of the two—"

"Hold on a minute," Ben protested.

Pete held up a hand. "I'm telling this story, and there will be time for rebuttal when I'm done."

Ben nodded and backed down.

Pete smiled and continued his story. "As I was saying, Ben joined the UDT, and I moved into oceanographic studies. We didn't see each other for several years. He was busy blowing stuff up and learning to weld under water. And I was busy drilling holes in the ocean floor. It wasn't until we both worked on the oil rig, *Oz* that we hooked up again."

"Thanks for sharing," Eve said, "I feel at least I know who you are now." She smiled. "Now you can finish your other story."

Pete furrowed his eyebrows.

"You remember," Eve said, "the epic conclusion of how you arrived in this world."

"Yeah, yeah," Pete said. He grinned and began his second tale. "Our last load was a little odd. Every stall in the transport was full, and this time it wasn't just one species but a different one in each stall."

"What's so different about that?" Ben asked. "I would've thought that a load is a load is a load."

"No," Pete said. "Each type of animal tares out differently. Different prices per pound and prices for each vary depending on the time of year. Another thing that made little sense was the head count. In most cases there were two of each kind or seven pair of the same species. It wasn't an efficient business decision to ship livestock that way." Pete took a bite of bread, swallowed, and resumed his story.

"Once we'd received our manifest, we shipped out. Now, I want you to stay with me on this one," Pete warned, "because this is where things go from strange to bizarre."

"We had twelve crew member cabins on board. Two were Marty's and mine. The other ten were locked and sealed. Our papers gave us strict orders not to open them, and as far as a destination, there was none, per se, just a compass heading."

"Boy, that sounds familiar," Ben said, remembering Evans and *The Morning Star*.

"How so?" Pete asked.

"Later," Ben said. "Finish your story."

Pete nodded. "I set a course using the supplied coordinates. We came no closer than a quarter mile of what you call the *Established Place* even though our instrumentation showed open sea where the island should have been. After traveling some time on a westward course *The Ark's* engines slowed and came to a halt. Try as we might, we couldn't get the vessel to move."

"Did you notice any other anomalies?" Ben asked.

Pete hesitated for a moment. "Yeah," he said, shaking his head in disbelief, "yeah, I did." Pete looked at Ben. "There was a yellow aura engulfing the nose of the ship."

Ben looked at Eve and then at Pete, a curious grin on his face.

"What?" Pete said. "You know something you're not telling."

"All in time," Ben said. "Go on."

"Wait a minute," Pete said. "I think I'm being setup."

"You're not being setup," Ben said, "you're just confirming some of the things I've already seen."

"Okay," Pete said, "but you will have a lot to explain after I finish my story."

"Then finish," Ben insisted.

Pete eyed Ben and continued his tale. "We sat still in the water for a short while and then began to move slowly. After a minute or two, we began to rotate. The rotation became faster, and faster, until we were pinned in our seats. The nose of the ship dipped downward and at that point I would swear somebody pushed the handle and flushed us."

Ben chuckled, "flushed," he murmured.

Pete looked at Ben puzzled, his expression turned somber.

"Belac," he said. "What happened to Marty?"

"Dear, Pete," Belac said, "your Marty was too far removed to return from the hold of the Dark One. He proved this with his actions. Had he continued, he would have become partnered with the earthly incarnation of the Dark One once he entered the spirit realm." Belac's expression turned to one of remorse. "I regret this had to be done. Your friend is now at rest. His interment garnered much dignity."

Pete nodded. "Will you show me some time? I'd like to say goodbye."

"It would pleasure me," Belac said, "but for now we must take nourishment. You will need this sustenance."

Pete hesitated, unsure if he should vocalize what truly preyed on his mind. He fidgeted a moment and then decided. "Belac," he said.

"Yes?"

"Why did you spare me, and not Marty?"

"It was you who spared yourself. Had you shown continued aggression, as did your companion, you would lie beside him now," Belac smiled. "It was that very reason which conveyed your worth of a second chance."

Pete returned the smile, "Thank you."

AFTER THE MEAL, Belac spoke. "Please take up your tale once again, my curiosity grows."

Pete took a drink from his cup, wiped his mouth, and continued. "Where was I?"

"You had just been flushed," Ben said, smiling.

"Right," Pete acknowledged. "We spiraled downward." Pete paused for a moment in deep thought. "I became so disoriented I couldn't say for how long. We stopped abruptly and popped to the surface. Marty and I both figured we were back where we had started, thinking we had been caught in a whirlpool of some kind."

Pete looked at the ground and scratched his cheek. "It was then we noticed that our surroundings were different. There were trees everywhere, and we were floating among them. We didn't stay that way for long. *The Ark* dropped, coming to rest in a mass of soggy undergrowth. Once grounded, we became survivalists on dry land in a new world."

"What about the animals?" Eve asked.

"Well," Pete said, "after our exit from the ship it didn't take long to assess the situation. The water had receded; *The Ark* has to have water to move; so it's let 'em loose or leave 'em there to die."

"Where are they now?" Eve asked.

"Procreating, I guess," Pete said, a wide grin spread across his face.

Eve looked down and blushed.

"Curious story," Ben said. "Who's next?"

"Hmm," Pete grunted, "I'm not done yet, and you won't want to miss the next installment."

"Sorry," Ben said.

"Once the cargo was unloaded, minus three crates, we determined that we had about two weeks of food if we carefully rationed it." Pete shook his head and grimaced, "That ain't what happened."

He sat back and pursed his lips. "Later that same day, we went into the forest to gather firewood. When we returned, someone had gone through our stores and taken everything. Not only that, but the doors on the ten sealed cabins were open. After two days with no food was when big, orange and ugly showed up."

"Eleazor?" Eve asked.

"Yes," Pete said, "and bearing gifts."

"Let me guess," Ben said, "food."

"And drink," Pete said. "He moved a dozen or so deer and antelope into *The Ark* itself." Pete grimaced. "This became his private feeding ground. He gave us what we needed, so we listened to him. Before I knew it, he had us." Pete looked at Ben, his eyes filled with remorse, "Even to the point of killing you, if I had to."

Ben reached out, laying a hand on his friend. "I made it there myself," he reassured.

Belac interrupted. "That is how strong his influence can be." He looked around at each one in attendance. "You have heard enough to ponder. Any more at this time would only serve to overwhelm. However, I must make an additional inquiry before the evening comes to an end." The circle of people quieted and stared at Belac, listening attentively.

"Pete," Belac said, "you spoke of three crates that were part of your cargo."

"Yes," Pete replied. "Eleazor had the crates taken to the cave."

"Do you remember the way to this cave?" Belac asked.

"Of course," Pete said, "but to go there would be a death sentence."

"And not going would be much worse," Belac said. "We will adjourn for the night. I thank each of you for your attendance. Tomorrow will begin your training."

Chapter Thirty-two

JHORR ESCORTED THE THREE back to the previous night's meeting place. The sun was just rising when Belac joined them.

"Pleasant morning," he said.

"Good morning," echoed through the circle.

After breakfast, Belac addressed the group. "Dear ones, as I told you last night, your training will begin today."

"What type of training?" Ben asked.

"First, I will explain your objective," Belac said. "You will seek the Andor."

"The Andor?" Eve said.

"Yes," Belac replied. "The Great One instructed followers to construct a vessel that would hold the declaration which had been given them. The staff of the high cleric would also rest in this vessel." Belac paused and sighed. "These items are of no use to Eleazor; however, they are of great import to those who would ally with him."

"Slow down a minute," Ben said. "Where is this Andor and why do we want it?"

"The Andor holds the edicts that govern all who abide on this earth," Belac said. "It is the foundation for the new world you three will establish."

"Back up a minute there," Pete said. "I didn't sign on to establish anything."

"You were chosen to do this," Belac said, "being spared from the last confrontation for the reason I have described. There is none of what you would call, 'signing on.' It is now your purpose."

Pete scratched his head, "I don't know . . ."

Belac raised a hand to silence him. "Trust in what I say. You would not want it otherwise." Belac's mood took a solemn turn. "You must understand the significance associated with the reclamation of the Andor. It is vital to the ultimate success of your mission."

"Why is it vital?" Ben asked.

"It travels with its people being the manifestation of the Great One." Belac said. "Along with the sacred objects it contains that we must learn and obey, it is a source of great comfort even in battle."

"Battle," Ben said. "What battle?"

"Confrontation is inevitable," Belac said. "I will explain this as the need for the three to know arises and not before."

"Do you know the Andor's location?" Ben asked.

"As far as its whereabouts, it lies within the crates taken from *The Ark*."

✳ ✳ ✳

THE ARROW FLEW, missing its target by three feet.

"Outstanding," Belac said. "It was much closer than your last attempt."

"Thanks, I think." Eve looked at the bow and then at Belac. "Do you have one that's not so hard to pull?" she asked, twanging the bowstring. "I shake so much when I'm holding it back I can't aim at the target."

Belac smiled, "Three long bows are being made; one for each of you. Construction of these weapons will take your strength and body structure into consideration. Until the new bows are complete, the ones you are using will increase your power and make your new armaments more effective."

"I suppose it's my turn," Pete said. He stepped forward, loaded his bow, pulled back, and released. The arrow flew true, landing just inches from the center of the target.

"Excellent," Belac exclaimed. "A near perfect shot."

The target was an elm log, eight inches in diameter and twelve feet long. It stood on end bolstered by stones at the bottom and supported by guy lines at the top. There were five horizontal slashes; six inches apart cut halfway down the log, the center of the target being the middle slash.

"I guess you chose not to be the cowboy when you were a kid," Ben mused.

Pete grinned. He brought the bow to his mouth and blew, clearing the imaginary smoke away, as if it were the muzzle of a revolver.

"I reckon not," he said, with a manufactured Southern drawl.

Ben shook his head.

"Here goes nothing." The arrow grazed the side of the target, skewing to the right and into the ground. Ben dropped his arms and sighed.

"Don't worry, little man," Pete said. "It'll come."

"At least you hit the target," Eve said.

"Barely," Ben replied. He looked at Belac. "What are we going to shoot at?"

"Whatever shoots at you," Belac said. He tried to maintain a stern expression; then his face cracked into smile.

"Oh, I see," Ben said. "Everybody's a comedian."

Smiles turned to laughter.

"It is good to laugh," Belac said. "Even the Great One takes time to do so."

"Seriously," Ben said. "Is it the human aberrations of Eleazor that we'll be fighting?"

"They will be there," Belac said. He looked at Ben. "However, they are not your only adversary."

"Eleazor?" Ben questioned.

"No, not even the Dark One," Belac said. "It is the Tamar."

"And the plot thickens," Pete said.

"Belac," Eve questioned, "who are the Tamar?"

Belac motioned to Jhorr and the boy left. "You recall the ten sealed cabins that Pete spoke of onboard the Ark?" Belac asked.

"Yes," Ben replied.

"We found them opened when our supplies were stolen," Pete added.

"Each cabin held a cocoon of sorts," Belac said. "In each chrysalis was a sentient being. Once their metamorphosis is complete, these creatures will serve as the Dark One's corporal presence on this earth and the Dark One will enter the demon realm to rule. It is then he and his demon seed will attack each of us from within and the Tamar will do his bidding, waging war outside of our bodies. They will be among all those who live on this earth."

"Sorry I asked," Ben said.

Jhorr returned with leaf-wrapped bundles and handed one to each person. "It is time for midday nourishment," Belac said.

BEN SWALLOWED the last bite of his sandwich. "Belac, can you give us any details of our mission?"

"I will tell you of your ultimate goal. You must provide, *as you say*, the details."

Ben opened his mouth to speak.

Belac raised his hand. "Please, allow me to finish."

Ben nodded.

"After the three enter, a detachment comprising myself and six of my finest will secure the Andor after all is done. It is my hope that this will be accomplished before the Tamar emerge, if not—" Belac stopped in mid-sentence.

"What is it, Belac?" Eve asked. "What if we don't get there before the Tamar emerge?"

"It is not for me to say," Belac replied. "However, there is more that you must concern yourselves with. The Tamar also employ ones who will protect their brood. These defenders are known as *the Guardian*."

"The Guardian?" Pete repeated.

"They are masters of concealment," Belac said. "Being made from the minerals as the cave itself, it is possible for these cumbersome beasts to take on any shape they wish."

"So they're made of rock?" Eve asked.

"In a sense," Belac replied. "However the bodies of these protectors are much softer than the stone itself, enabling them to conceal their forms within the cave walls."

"They're invisible?" Ben asked.

"Yes and no," Belac said. "They are crafty, staying hidden until their victims, unaware of their presence, are subdued."

"Explain, *yes and no*," Ben said.

"The Guardian are able to become part of the rock itself that surrounds them," Belac said. "In this way they may achieve invisibility."

Ben nodded slowly, pondering the thought of living rock.

"How can we eliminate them?" Pete asked.

"These cannot be killed," Belac said, "only reduced."

"Then tell us how to reduce them," Ben said.

"As I said," Belac began, "they are soft-bodied creatures, almost as soft as sand, but not quite. Once you are in their grasp, it is nearly impossible to escape on your own; however, they can be reduced to their basic elemental structure by an outside force applied to their body."

"So a punch to the face will take one out?" Pete asked.

"Only the part of their body that absorbs the strike," Belac replied.

"So multiple strikes are needed?" Ben asked.

"Yes," Belac said, "either by fist, as you have mentioned, or by implement. Enough of these and the reduction will be complete and the Guardian rendered harmless."

Ben sat in deep thought, absorbing Belac's last comment.

Belac looked at Eve. "Time is short. We must continue."

EVE RAISED HER BOW. Taking a deep breath, she drew back and sent the projectile on its way. The arrow came to rest, quivering in the log slightly above the target area.

"You are nearly there," Belac said.

"It's better," Eve said. "I almost hit the top slash."

"Good shot, sweetheart," Ben teased. "I'll get behind you when we get to the cave."

"Save it," Eve replied.

"This will conclude your first day of training," Belac said. "Your individual weapons will be ready tomorrow. Then empowerment will enter, replacing fear and indecision."

"When will the training end?" Ben said looking at Eve. "I guess what I'm asking is when do we leave?"

"In two more risings of the great light," Belac said. "There will be one more day of training and the last we'll spend in session planning our strike."

"Strike?" Ben exclaimed. "I thought this was a covert mission, you know sneak in, sneak out."

"I am afraid you cannot avoid confrontation," Belac said. "And while I wish to keep it to a minimum, we must prepare for the worst."

"Understood," Ben said.

"The day has come to an end," Belac said. "Jhorr will take you to bathe. Fresh clothes have been made ready. He will return you to the place of nourishment, where we will gather once again." Belac nodded, "Until then..."

✻ ✻ ✻

"SOMETHING ABOUT THIS is very familiar," Ben said, taking another sip. "That's it, the night before our wedding." Ben looked at Eve and winked.

"I don't know," Eve said. "That drink may be a little too much competition."

"Not a chance. Although I must admit that it is nice having you both around."

Once again, two women brought a tray of food and placed it over the dying coals. As if on cue, the orb glowed brighter.

Belac blessed the food. "Please, eat as you will. The heart of a warrior requires much to fuel such a fire."

Eve noticed Jhorr. "You've said little these past few days," she said, reaching around Ben and rubbing his head.

Jhorr smiled and continued to eat.

"Jhorr gathers information," Belac said. "I believe you refer to it as reconnaissance."

"I don't understand," Ben said. "What need could you have for one so young?"

"He will go ahead," Belac said.

"Ahead of what?" Eve asked.

"We must know what the Dark One, his followers and the Tamar are doing," Belac said. "Jhorr will go ahead of you and report back."

The three stared at each other in disbelief.

"A boy," Pete said. "You expect us to rely on recon from a *boy*?"

"Maturity," Belac countered, "is not always measured in years."

"Belac," Eve said, "you can't put Jhorr in this position; it's too dangerous."

"He has known much in his few years," Belac replied.

"Jhorr's just a boy," Eve said.

Belac stood. "Forgive me if I offend anyone of you, but this must be said. The Great One has chosen each one of us, including Jhorr, to assist the three in establishing a foothold in this world. Along with his work, he also empowers us. So rest assured we have everything we need to accomplish this task."

"I would like to speak," Jhorr interrupted.

"Of course," Belac replied.

"My years are few," he began, "but my awareness spans millennia. I do not understand how I perceive these things; only that I do."

"What things?" Eve inquired.

Jhorr thought for a moment, "I met you a short number of days ago."

"Yes," Eve acknowledged.

"In my consciousness, I realize that I will know you many years from now, even though it was before now."

"That kinda thinking could drive you nuts," Pete remarked.

"I drove way past nuts three days ago," Ben replied.

"It's not the time for jokes," Eve said. "Jhorr, please go on."

"It is the same for the one known as Ben," Jhorr continued. "I am aware of his presence before and after. I even discern things of the one called Pete. Events from the future remain within me even though woven in a tale by the Ben of the past."

Eve squinted her eyes and looked at Ben, "Please disregard my last comment. Was I around when you took your little drive?"

"Jhorr," Ben said, "instead of saying 'Ben,' you addressed me as 'the one known as Ben,' why?"

"It seemed like the correct thing to do," Jhorr replied.

"What does that have to do with anything?" Pete asked.

"That's what he called me the first time we met," Ben said, "I'm speaking of the future Jhorr . . . " Ben hesitated, "the older one that lives in the past." His voice trailed off. He mulled over what he had just said. "Ah," he groaned, "you know what I mean."

"I'm still concerned about his age," Pete said.

"No more than I am," Eve said. "Even though he has proven that he is older than his years, he is still too young to put in harm's way."

"It makes no sense to risk the life of one so young," Ben said, looking at Jhorr with deep admiration. "I believe him to be as mature at this point in his young life as I am now." He stared at the youngster. *If not more so*, he thought.

Jhorr smiled. "Do not let my age concern you. With my size, I can fit through places that no other can. This will allow me to observe our quarry without being detected and report back to you."

"I guess I'm overruled," Pete said. He stared at Jhorr for several moments and winked. "Welcome aboard, short stuff."

Jhorr smiled and politely bowed his head.

"It is pleasing to see all here in agreement," Belac said. He clapped his hands and three women appeared bringing more food and drink.

"Belac," Ben said. "There's something I've been meaning to ask you. Something I've tried to make sense of, but can't."

"It seems to trouble you greatly," Belac said. "Please, ask and I will do my best to answer."

"After I argued with Eve and left," Ben said looking at his wife, "I sensed turmoil inside. It was small at first, but after I met Pete and Marty, it didn't seem so bad. Once I talked with Eleazor it felt right, almost like it belonged." He took Eve's hand. "I despised what I had once loved. How could that happen? How could I turn against the things most precious to me?"

"It happens to the best," Belac said. "When you became angry at your loved one, you gave the Dark One an avenue with which to enter. In his present form, he at some point during his evolution had touched you and planted a seed. Once a hold had been established, it began to grow within. Eleazor's power is limited while still in his physical form, so he turned to the power of the Kumult to strengthen his hold. Once he leaves this realm and enters into his own, he will accomplish this same task from within those he targets."

"What is Kumult?" Ben asked.

"It is an herb that can be brewed to make you more susceptible to suggestion," Belac said. "In this case, the suggestions of the Dark One. He gave it to both Pete and yourself. It was evident upon your return. Its effect is temporary unless administered in excess; however, it allows the Dark One to control what you do. The longer it continues, the harder its power is to break. In your case, it was blending Kumult and the Dark One's seed."

Ben shuddered. "The bourbon," he mumbled and turned to Pete. "That was the strange taste in the whiskey that Marty was feeding us."

Pete's expression darkened. "Belac explained the Kumult to Eve and me when you were out of it. That's why he wasn't drinking," Pete said, slowly shaking his head. "I don't feel so bad about him now. He was trying to bring us down with him."

"Why, Belac?" Ben said. "Why would Marty sell us out and why was the Kumult not needed for him?"

"Forgive me for using your own words," Belac said, "but it was for the same reason you sold your loved one's out."

Ben suffered great shame at Belac's comment.

"As for the Kumult, easily led minds require no outside assistance."

An expression of unpardonable remorse nestled firmly into Ben and Pete's faces.

"It is not to be as this," Belac said. "The Great One will grant you pardon if you ask, but you must now learn to grant the same pardon unto yourselves."

"That's going to be tough," Pete said.

"If not impossible," Ben agreed.

"Nevertheless," Belac said, "it must be done." He stood and bowed to each person. "I must now depart. Enjoy the evening. Tomorrow we will begin the last day of training." Turning to leave, he paused and once again faced the party. "We will begin very early. It would be best not to tarry." Belac smiled. "Once again I bid you a pleasant evening."

Chapter Thirty-three

"WHAT . . .?" Ben said sleepily.

Eve opened her eyes. "Shh, go back to sleep."

A knock on the doorpost came once again. This time Jhorr's head pushed through the door."It is time," he announced.

Ben cracked an eyelid, "Time for what?"

"Training," Jhorr said.

"It's still dark outside," Ben complained.

"It is time," Jhorr repeated, firmly. The young boy withdrew from the hut and retreated in silence.

Eve moaned, "No, it's too early."

Ben sat upright and slapped Eve on the hip. "Rise and shine, sugar. Time to go out and learn how to kill stuff." Ben sighed, plopped back down, and began to snore.

Eve moaned once again, sat up and shook him. "Up already. Belac wants us."

Ben rubbed his eyes, sat up, and looked around. "I learned at an early age that you don't always get what you want," he said. "How come that rule applies to no one except yours truly?"

"Just get up," she said, tugging at his arm.

"Yeah, yeah. I'm up, now what?"

THE MEETING AREA was dark save for a small fire. A packaged breakfast of meat and vegetable sandwiches wrapped in leaves sat warming beside the fire. Jhorr handed a breakfast bundle to each person as they arrived.

"It is good to see you again," Belac said.

"You weren't kidding when you insisted we arrive early," Ben said. He unwrapped the leaves and ate.

Belac smiled, "It is necessary, as you will come to understand."

Ben nodded and then raised his eyebrows. "Wow," he exclaimed, "this is an eye opener."

"There is a long day ahead," Belac said. "The nourishment in what you are eating will supply your needs."

Pete nodded vigorously, as did Eve, acknowledging Ben's delight over the unique flavor and Belac's comment regarding its content as they chewed the pleasing mixture.

Once the morning meal was complete Belac rose to speak."Dear ones, today begins our final day of training. Tomorrow evening we will confront the enemy." Belac motioned to Jhorr. "Your new weapons are complete."

Jhorr appeared from the darkness carrying three long bows, each of a different size. He handed one to Ben, one to Eve and the last to Pete, his being the longest of the three.

Pete ran his hand down the shaft's smooth surface. "Can't wait to try this."

"You will soon," Belac said looking at Ben and Eve. "As will you all. Please come with me."

The three followed Belac through a narrow path guided by a single yellow orb. The trail concluded at a large rock projection.

"It is here that we will begin," Belac said.

Jhorr appeared carrying three woven quivers, each full of arrows. The quivers and their contents were similar, varying slightly in size. He handed one to each of the three, taking care to extend the proper quiver to the one for whom it was made. After completing the distribution, Jhorr moved back several steps.

For the first time Ben noticed that the boy's appearance had changed dramatically. He dressed in a dark colored fur. His face was colored black, only his eyes visible. Ben reckoned his teeth would show if he talked or smiled, but somehow, looking at Jhorr told him that neither of these would happen. A small bow hung around his shoulder, a quiver, with arrows scarcely longer than darts, was slung over his back. A belt laden with pockets and pouches drew his fur covering tight around his waist. His arms and legs, shaded black, gave him the façade of a shadow. Jhorr blended with his surroundings, save for the frontal view of his body basking in the glow of the pulsating orb.

Belac stepped closer to the rock out-crop. He pulled a bush to one side, exposing a split in the rock face. Belac nodded and Jhorr disappeared into the narrow crevasse.

"Jhorr will return soon," Belac announced. "He is seeing the test for the first time and will bring back what he has seen and tell you of all he can retain."

"Test?" Ben said.

"Yes," Belac replied. "A test I have comprised to depict how our enemy would act."

"And after that?" Pete asked.

"You three will enter and do whatever you think necessary," Belac replied.

"That's it," Ben said, a sense of urgency in his voice. "No direction what to do once we get in there?"

"No," Belac replied. "It will be as new to you as it is to Jhorr."

"You're just going to send us in there blind?" Pete questioned.

"As I have said," Belac replied, "this is but a test. It will better equip you when the time comes for it to no longer be a test."

After another ten minutes the bush rustled and Jhorr appeared. He moved to the waiting trio, explaining what he had seen and the various positions.

Belac pulled the bush to the side and motioned for the three to enter. Ben picked up his bow and threw the quiver over his shoulder.

"No," Belac said. "Observe first."

Ben stared at Belac and then dropped his armament. "Okay," Ben said, the skepticism evident in his voice. He glanced at Pete and Eve then disappeared into the cave.

"You heard the man," Pete said, nodding at Eve. She smiled weakly, and the two followed Ben into the darkness.

Ben froze ten feet into the cave. Pete slammed into him and Eve into Pete. "Well," Ben whispered, "aren't we stealthy as the night."

"I can't see my hand in front of my face," Pete said. "How am I going to fight anything?" Just then a slight, yellow flash illuminated the area.

"What was that?" Eve questioned, peering nervously into the darkness.

"If you're talking about that flash," Ben said, "it was so fast I'm not convinced that it actually happened."

"Did you see it or not?" Pete said. "I want to know whether or not I'm having a stroke."

"There it goes again," Eve said. "Where is it coming from?"

Ben turned toward Eve's voice. At that moment the light flashed once again. Eve let out a high-pitched yelp.

"Guess that answers that," Ben said.

"Answers what?" Pete inquired.

"Each of you," Ben said, "give me your hands."

They fumbled around in the dark until they stood in an inward facing circle, holding hands.

"Look toward the center," Ben said, "like you're trying to look into each other's eyes." The flash appeared just long enough for six tiny dots to pierce the darkness.

"I don't believe it," Pete said.

"Move in closer to the center," Ben urged. They stepped in toward each other until their faces were almost touching. This time the flash produced the same six dots and danced off the face of each of the three.

"It's us," Eve exclaimed. "It's coming from our eyes."

Ben turned and moved his head from side to side. As the light emanated from his eyes it pierced the darkness with two slender beams allowing him to illuminate twenty feet or more in front of him. "Let's work our way into the cave and see if we can make sense of Jhorr's recon."

After several minutes, Ben noticed that he could control the light pulses using his eyelids. Whenever he would blink the light would project as soon as his eyes were fully open. He passed this information on to Pete and Eve.

The three quickly became accustomed to the dark interior and the brief periods of illumination. Soon they could identify the cave's topography and straw figures propped against the walls.

After spending thirty minutes in the cave's interior, the three exited the same way they had entered. The sun was beginning to rise. Belac stood as a dark silhouette in the new morning wash of light.

"That was amazing," Ben stammered.

"Tell me of your journey," Belac said, playing the role of teacher.

The three relayed their story from the time they entered the cave until their exit.

"Excellent," Belac said. "I trust you have learned of the special tools the Companion will supply for your undertaking."

"We have," Ben said. "I now know why we started before sunrise."

"Yes," Belac said, "to utilize the darkness, it was necessary to begin so early. The cave you will enter will be totally void of light."

"How do we continue now that the sun has risen?" Eve asked.

"That is next," Belac replied. "Don your weapons and we will begin."

"CLOSE YOUR EYES and imagine the cave," Belac said.

"I'm there," Eve replied, attempting to concentrate.

"Good. Now I want you to observe the pulse of light."

"I can see it, but it's so dim."

Belac touched Eve's arm. Eve opened her eyes, Ben and Pete drew near.

"I am speaking to all when I say this; the light you have seen is your guiding beacon." He shifted his weight and then looked in earnest at the three.

"Each of you have seen the miracle of the Light. I ask that you place all of your trust in the Light, knowing that it will take you full circle to where It desires you to be."

"And where is that?" Ben inquired.

"That is between you and the Living One," Belac said. "Only He knows; but rest assured that the path on which He directs you will be the perfect path." Belac paused, allowing the three to ponder this notion.

"Time is short," he continued, "and there is much to do."

Eve closed her eyes, as did Ben, and Pete.

"Once again," Belac said, "envision the cave. When you are there, invite the Light and allow it to enter your being."

The three slowly nodded.

"Now, as you begin to walk, allow the Light to guide you. Move about freely, not permitting your eyes to open. Only the will of the Living One is of any import."

The three began to move, slowly at first, and then with a deliberate and intricate choreography.

BEN OPENED HIS EYES. Pete and Eve followed as if on cue. They were standing in a sparsely wooded glade.

"Where are we?" Eve asked.

"You have come far," Belac replied.

"How long?" Ben asked.

"It will be dark soon," Belac said.

"We've been wandering around for hours," Pete stammered.

"Not wandering," Belac replied, "but following."

The three nodded, vaguely understanding Belac's explanation, but not wanting to suffer through a long-winded clarification.

"When the great light sets tonight," Belac said, "we will resume your instruction in the cave. Until then, take your weapons and grow to know them as though they were an extension of your body."

"We left them at the cave entrance," Ben said.

Belac shook his head and waved a hand at Jhorr. The young spy brought the longbows forward and handed each one to its proper owner. Each of the three strapped a quiver to their back and cradled their bow in hand.

Belac lined Ben, Eve and Pete side-by-side about three feet apart.

"Load your weapons." The three pulled an arrow from their quiver and pushed the notched end into the string.

"Belac," Ben said, "these arrows are so thin. Will they be effective without breaking?"

"Yes," Belac said. "These projectiles are constructed from a very resilient grass. The small diameter allows for the combatant to carry several hundred in their quill."

Ben nodded, eyeing the arrow with a newfound respect.

"Sense your target," Belac said. "As the Light directs you, release at will."

"What target?" Ben whispered to Eve.

"You tell me," she answered.

"Shh," Pete hissed, "it's right in front of you." The arrow left his bow, stopping seventy yards away in the middle of a quarter size circle, carved into a stump projecting eight inches above the ground. At the sound of Pete's release, Ben and Eve discharged their bows. The arrows contacted one another as their paths crossed, rendering both ineffective.

"Come with me," Belac said. They walked the seventy yards to where Pete's arrow had found its mark. Eve inspected the strike more closely.

"How?" she asked, looking at Belac in amazement.

"The Light," Belac said, "cannot be forced. You must allow it to lead. There are multiple targets set up around the perimeter on which we are now standing. Don your weapons. We will try again."

Once again Pete's arrow flew true. Ben's was closer, and Eve's errant flight was worse than before. More attempts ensued with similar results.

"I will return soon," Belac said.

The sun was setting when he returned and announced. "This will be your final attempt. If you are unsuccessful, then so be it. You will enter the Dark One's lair unprepared."

Eve anxiously rubbed her palms against her thighs. "Where is Jhorr?" she asked. His absence instilled in her an uneasy feeling.

"We will join him later," Belac said. "It is now time to focus." The three loaded their bows and readied themselves to release one final time.

"Close your eyes," Belac said.

"What?" Ben said. "We can't shoot with them open!"

"Close your eyes," Belac insisted.

Pete complied. Ben and Eve did the same.

An expanding dread crept back into Eve. *Jhorr*, she thought, *Jhorr's in trouble*. She brought herself back.

"Focus," she whispered, harshly commanding compliance within. "You have got to focus."

"Aim your weapons according to the Light's direction," Belac said, "then release."

Pete leveled his bow to fly at a low arc above the ground. Ben took aim for a higher arc creating a downward shot. Sensing increased confidence in Ben, Eve relaxed. She realized the tip of her arrow's location melding into a visual entity in her mind's eye.

Eve could see the target, a small dot of light in the distance. She brought the two points into line. Jhorr crept back into her thoughts, and the target began to fade. *No*, she screamed inside. *Concentrate. Let the Light guide*. The dot came back into focus. When she realigned the two points, a loud proclamation reverberated through her head, *"Release,"* It demanded. The soft, almost non-existent sound of three arrows moving toward their intended target engulfed the area in an eerie silence.

"Jhorr," Eve whispered, opening her eyes. She felt more at ease.

Belac motioned for the three to follow as he walked, tracing a path behind the three projectiles.

As they neared the landing area, a scene that could only be described as surreal unfolded. Two logs forming a "T" were lashed together, the form laid flat on the ground. An arrow protruded from the end of what would be the bottom of the vertical portion of the "T" if it were standing upright. Two arrows jutted from the horizontal portion of the "T" about six feet apart.

These pointed straight into the air. In between these three points, a pair of leather shoes, toes pointing upward just above the first arrow. Between the six-foot placement of the two remaining arrows, lay two outstretched arms. Fingers twitched just inches from the arrow shafts on either side and the darkened face of an eight-year-old boy.

"Jhorr!" Eve ran to his side and untied his bonds. "What have you done to him?" she demanded.

Eve finished loosening the ropes around Jhorr's wrists and ankles and helped him to an upright position. He stood and walked to stand beside Belac. Ben and Pete stood motionless, not believing what they were seeing.

"It was necessary," Belac said.

Eve dropped her bow and moved toward Belac. "Necessary?" she screamed. "He's just a boy." She stopped, throwing her arms in the air and brought them to rest on her hips. "Who do you think you are? I can see enlisting adults for your outlandish antics, but to willfully endanger a child!" Eve moved closer with malice in her eyes.

Jhorr stepped in front of Belac. "Cease your advance," he said.

Eve came to an abrupt halt; her malice momentarily turning to surprise, then back again. "So" she chastised Belac, "you're gonna let a child do your fighting?"

"Come no further," Jhorr warned.

Eve melted. "You don't understand," she pleaded, pointing at Belac. "He had no problem with you dying and for what?"

"Eve," Jhorr said, "it is not Belac; it is you that lack understanding."

Eve slumped and began to cry. "You're right. I don't understand any of this."

Ben came to her and then faced Belac. "I think you owe us an explanation."

Belac nodded, "Indeed I do." He stepped forward and spread his arms. "Please, sit, and I will tell you of these things that have distressed you so."

The three, along with Jhorr, sat down on the ground, as did Belac. He folded his arms onto his lap and spoke.

"As you know, our time is all but gone. I had no other choice than to try reaching you using desperate methods."

"How did nearly killing Jhorr reach anything?" Eve challenged.

Ben nodded toward Belac. "I think that question's been answered."

"Did you not feel the spirit of Jhorr calling out to you?" Belac asked.

"Well, yeah," Eve stammered, "but—"

"Did it not lead you to aim true?"

"I guess so, but that—"

"It also led your Ben down the correct path," Belac finished.

Eve glanced at Ben. He nodded.

Eve whirled around to Belac. "What if one of us had hit Jhorr?"

"It would not have mattered," Belac said.

"What!" Eve said, standing in a defensive position. "How can you say that?"

"Please, dear Eve," Belac said, making calming motions with his hands. "Return to your seat."

Eve stood defiantly and then melted as the genuine truth in Belac's gaze pushed her to the ground.

Once she sat, Belac resumed. "If I sent you into the Dark One's lair without the guidance of the Living One, you would not have returned." He glared at all present. "You *cannot* do this alone."

"Do not dismiss my question," Eve argued. "You said that if we had killed Jhorr, it wouldn't have mattered."

Belac shook his head. "No, dear one, it would have been an unbearable consequence, but one I would accept if it brought you into the Light." Belac looked at the three with genuine fatherly concern. "You must understand that without the three all would be lost. Not that the Great One could not wipe out the menace that is even now growing, for He could do so with a mere thought; however, it must be said that the Great One uses such as ourselves to accomplish what He so wills."

"But why?" Ben asked. "Wouldn't it be easier to get rid of Eleazor and his cronies and just let us live our lives in peace?"

"Easier, yes," Belac said, "but it would nullify one of our greatest gifts."

"What gift?" Eve questioned. "I've failed to notice anything but trouble since we've been here."

"The gift to choose for ourselves," Belac said. "We are given the freedom to follow the path He has laid out for us, or not to follow; that alone is our choice."

"That makes no sense at all," Eve said. "I choose what I want to do every day. What has this Great One of yours got to do with the choices I make? Are you going to tell me if I brush my teeth before I go to bed He has something to do with that?"

"Only if you allow him to do so" Belac said, then explained. "The Great One has the desire—"

"I'm just about fed up with, *the Great One this* and *the Great One that*," Eve interrupted. "Do you ever talk about anything else but His majesty? There are real people in real trouble, and all you can talk about is this Great One."

Belac cringed in an attempt to control his rising anger. "The Great One," he repeated, "desires to be involved in every aspect of your daily life."

Eve opened her mouth to speak.

Belac raised his hand, his face displaying a rage under control. "You will be silent until I am through."

Eve pulled back.

Belac drew a deep breath, releasing it slowly. "The Great One does not wish to control mindless beings. He gives each one the gift of choosing his or her individual path. You must be willing to trust even though the trust you place is in the unseen."

"How do we trust what we can't see?" Ben asked. "I have a hard enough time trusting things I can see."

Jhorr stepped forward. "Then how would you explain me? How would you explain any of the many things you have experienced since you have been here or the events that led to you being here?"

"I can't," Ben admitted.

"Your seed of understanding has grown," Belac said. "However, this germination takes time. We must now continue your preparation for the time of confrontation grows near."

Chapter Thirty-four

"THE TAMAR ARE SOON to emerge," Sedah said. "I should think another day at the most."

"Show me," Eleazor ordered.

Sedah nodded, and Eleazor followed him through a maze of subterranean corridors. They passed through the open area containing the wooden crates from *The Ark*, then into another passage way. After several turns and detours, the tunnel narrowed and then broke into a smaller undefined room.

The floor and ceiling were uneven, littered with stalactites, stalagmites and various rock formations to where it was difficult to walk until one reached the upper plateaus. Anyone entering the room from this point would have to climb, traversing the obstacles. The walls were so jagged and broken up they appeared as random hallways ending on top of one another.

Ten leather-like, slime-covered sacs, six feet in diameter hung from the ceiling. They pulsated at regular intervals exuding their own light. Eleazor extended his wings, pushed several times and landed on a protruding ledge beside the pulsating sacs. He stood waiting impatiently for Sedah to traverse the rugged terrain to join him.

Sedah's labored breathing supplied incentive to finish his climb, pulling himself over the edge, collapsing at the feet of Eleazor. A hard kick to the ribs brought him to his feet. Eleazor turned his attention to one of the egg cases. He pulled a single claw through the mucus, looked at it, turning his finger from side to side. Eleazor smiled, placing the finger in his mouth, wrapped his lips around it, and pulled the digit out with a sucking sound.

"Yes," he whispered, "soon." Eleazor turned to Sedah, nodding his head in approval. "Good," he said, laying his hand on Sedah's shoulder. "I just may keep you around a little longer."

Sedah, still breathing heavily and nursing the spot that received the brunt of Eleazor's foot with a sympathetic hand, replied. "Thank you, Master. It is for you I do what I do."

"Hmm, exactly what is it you do?"

"I live to serve you, Dark One."

Eleazor chuckled. "Live is the operative word," he said, looking at Sedah with disdain. "You would do well to remember that."

"Of course, Master," Sedah replied, bowing his head in submission.

Eleazor shivered. "We must raise the temperature in the brood chamber."

"How?" Sedah queried.

Eleazor raised a hand. Bringing it down, he knocked Sedah to the ground. "You fool! Can I not trust you to perform even the simplest of tasks?"

Sedah rolled into a ball to avoid the worst of a barrage of savage kicks that flew his way. "You are indeed fortunate to still draw breath," Eleazor bellowed, with a final jolt to Sedah's lower back.

He bent over, placing his face inches away from the injured servant. "Adjust the course of the hot spring flowing into this chamber." He wrapped a hand around Sedah's neck lifting him to his feet. "Do I need to tell you how to accomplish this?"

Sedah, unable to make a sound clutched the hands that encircled his throat.

"Before you respond, you should know that if the answer is yes, I will warm the Tamar with your blood."

Sedah's eyes widened as he emphatically shook his head.

Eleazor grinned. "I did not think so." He dropped the nearly unconscious creature on the ground at his feet. "Do not try me again, lest my good nature turn sour." Eleazor extended his wings and departed.

Chapter Thirty-five

JHORR ONCE AGAIN slipped through the narrow crack.

"This will be your final test," Belac said. "Once Jhorr returns, he will convey to you the essential information. You will enter; secure the cave and signal for my men to recover the Andor."

"Sounds simple enough," Pete said.

"Simple to voice," Belac replied, "however, difficult to execute."

"Is there something you're not telling us?" Eve asked.

"Yes," Belac said. "I held the information for this very moment. As you are aware, the Tamar are soon to emerge, and we must do all in our power to procure the Andor before this happens."

Ben fumed. "Maybe you should tell us what we don't know."

Belac looked at Ben. "You were not ready to hear what I have to say until now. There were too many encumbrances invading your minds. If the Tamar surface before our goal is accomplished, you must eliminate the brood as they emerge from their cocoons. Once loosed, it is an entirely different story." A grimace rolled across his face. "They are all but impossible to kill once they are free."

"All but impossible?" Ben said.

"Yes," Belac replied.

"So there is a chance?" Eve asked, rubbing her hands together. "I mean if they do emerge?"

"There is a chance," Belac said. "The window is narrow; however, a chance nonetheless."

"What would we have to do?" Pete asked. "In case it's like Eve said."

Ben could see the concern on Belac's face as he mulled over the likelihood of the success of this new development. "We need to know," Ben prompted, "no matter how unlikely it may be."

"Of course," Belac said. "The egg case cannot be penetrated by your weapons. The Tamar have a claw on their left foot. This they will use to slice open the cocoon and free themselves."

"As they emerge from their egg case their bodies are soft and a well-placed arrow will kill them immediately. After they are free and begin to develop, their bodies harden within seconds. This brings about the difficulty in killing them I have been reluctant to share with you."

Pete raised his eyebrows in anticipation.

Belac laid two fingers on the left side of his neck just below his earlobe. "This is the place where you must aim." He touched the tip of his thumb to the tip of his middle finger forming a circle, two inches in diameter. "This is the size of the area you will strike. The Tamar use this orifice to breathe." Belac took a deep breath and sighed. "It is not as hard as the rest of the demon's body; however, it will take two, possibly three strikes, in quick succession to weaken, pierce and ultimately kill the creature."

"Three direct hits into a two-inch diameter target, one after another?" Ben shook his head. "Will we get to practice the shot?"

"It has been arranged," Belac said.

Just then Jhorr emerged from within the cave.

"There's your answer," Ben said. He and Eve joined Pete and began to debrief Jhorr.

Chapter Thirty-six

"WAIT FOR THE LIGHT," Ben said.

"It's here," Pete replied. "I noticed it as soon as we entered the cave."

"It seems to be stronger with you than Eve or myself, I guess that puts you in the lead,"

Ben stepped aside, allowing Pete to pass.

As the three pushed deeper into the cave, both Ben and Eve recognized the light, and Ben once again took the lead.

"Jhorr alluded to a room on the right about ten feet ahead with two targets inside," Ben whispered.

"Affirmative," Pete replied.

Each time Ben blinked, a flash of light illuminated the cave wall. Spotting the opening within arm's reach, he signaled to Pete by whirling a finger in the air and pointing to the far side of the door. Pete nodded and moved around Ben falling into position at the opposite side of the doorjamb. Eve moved in behind Ben. All three loaded their weapons.

As if on cue, Ben and Pete burst into the room firing. The arrows crossed in midair striking their targets.

Eve stood between both men, ready to fire. She relaxed her weapon. "I hope you two don't think you're going to have all the fun."

"There'll be plenty to go around," Ben said. "Let's keep moving."

The three moved through the corridor scoring kills in each of the six rooms they encountered.

They broke into a large open area one hundred feet square then regrouped.

"The crates are to the right about halfway in," Ben said. "There should be four targets posted as guards."

Pete dispatched the first, Ben the second and Eve the third, with Pete reloading and eliminating the fourth.

"Now the Tamar," Ben said.

At the rear of the open area the three gathered around a jagged breach leading to the mock brood chamber.

"There's only room for one of us at a time to go through," Ben said. He looked at Pete. "I'll go first, Pete next, then Eve."

Pete and Eve nodded.

Ben started to go and then stopped. "We must do this quickly. Remember what Belac told us about the Tamar once they've emerged." Ben loaded his bow and disappeared into the abyss.

There were ten hanging bags attached to the ceiling. Seven were unopened while two had splits with straw figures dangling out of each gash. Ben placed a shot into the head of the first figure. He felt air displace as the arrow from Pete's bow whooshed by his head striking the second in the chest.

Both men reloaded as Eve screamed.

"It's out!" Her arrow flew true as it shattered, striking the center of the metal disc positioned in the neck of the supposed free Tamar. Pete fired, nicking the plate, and Ben's missed entirely bouncing off the cave wall.

"Not the outcome we'd hoped for," Ben said. He knelt down and picked up his last shot. He slid the arrow back into his quiver. "Not the outcome we had hoped for at all."

* * *

THE GROUP ONCE AGAIN sat around the fire at the Place of Meeting.

"Let us take nourishment," Belac said. He took a deep breath, sighing as it released. "It grieves me greatly to do what I must do."

"What is it?" Eve questioned. "What's wrong?"

Belac looked at Eve, a grave expression on his face. "After this meal," he said, "I will send you into the Den of Evil."

"You have trained us well," Ben said, "and considering the limited time frame I'd say we're as ready as can be."

Belac looked at Eve and Pete. "How say you?"

"I think I speak for Eve when I say, Ben's assessment is correct."

"Tell me," Belac asked, "how do you know this to be true?"

"We completed your test," Ben said.

"You are sure of this?" Belac inquired.

"Yes. It wasn't a perfect run, but I believe it gave us enough of an idea what to expect so our assault will be effective. You said it was just a test and as near as you could surmise the interior of the cave to be."

"The confidence you have gained is admirable," Belac said, "but armed only with this assurance you will most certainly die."

"What do you mean?" Eve protested. "We passed the test."

"And your triumph led you to become arrogant in your own abilities," Belac said.

Ben stood to face his perceived attacker. "I don't get you," he stammered. "You sent us into a dark cave with archaic weapons. We do what you ask of us, and now you refuse to acknowledge our accomplishments!" He glared at Belac. "What's the matter? Are you jealous?"

Belac looked at the three with great sadness. "You fought straw objects that could not fight back." Belac's voice took on a solemn tone. "The ones you will soon face shall not fall so easily."

Ben stared at Belac, allowing his words to penetrate, deeply into his resolve. The glow of success that once surrounded him had now dulled to the gray sullenness of doubt.

Belac stood and placed a hand on Ben's shoulder. "I do not wish to destroy your confidence, merely redirect it." Belac extended his arm, "Sit."

Ben nodded and returned to his seat.

Just then a tray of food arrived. "You will need the energy that these specially prepared provisions will supply," Belac said. "For now we will consume nourishment."

TELL ME OF YOUR TIME in the cave," Belac said.

Ben finished chewing and then swallowed. "There's not that much to tell."

"I desire to hear all," Belac said, "no matter how small—"

He stopped speaking, a stoic expression on his face. "I sense a new life form, one I have never before encountered. I cannot tell if it is one or many; however this entity has no part with good."

Six men arrived at Belac's behest.

"We must leave this place," Belac said, "no harm must come to the three."

Belac convened a brief meeting with the new arrivals.

"Go with these men," Belac said, "we will reunite soon."

Belac's men herded the three and Jhorr through the dark forest at breakneck speed. Ben could feel the leaves brush against his face and sense the huge trunks anchored to the ground. He imagined the damage they could do to the soft flesh of a human body, running full speed, but was confident that would not happen.

Ben detected a faint yellow glow. Upon reaching the light, he found Belac, sitting, eyes closed, illuminated by a single orb.

"Were you able to get any information?" Ben asked.

"Only that a Pentack has been employed to prevent the three from entering into the cave where the Andor is being held."

"Makes sense," Pete said, "if we never make it into Eleazor's lair, they stop it before it starts."

"I'll deal with that later," Ben said, "right now I want to know everything Belac knows about this Pentack."

"This beast is three-dimensional, yet able to become two-dimensional. It sheds vertical slices of itself that possess a height and a width; however too thin to have a measurable thickness. To look at the Pentack sideways is to view invisibility."

"How dangerous is this thing?" Ben asked.

"When it is whole it can take any shape it chooses. Once it sheds these full size, ultra-thin pieces of itself, it can no longer change its shape. But make no mistake, it can steal your life before you know it is gone. And each slice that separates from its body, is just as dangerous as the host, if not more so."

"How does it kill?" Pete asked.

"The creature appears as any normal humanoid, but with enormous strength. Once it separates, each slice will retain a head, two arms, with working fingers, legs and feet. This single piece as with each of the remaining 49 will be sharper than anything imaginable. The Pentack may lose all or any portion of its whole, and by the same token recall any pieces not destroyed."

"How many pieces can this thing produce at one time?" Ben said.

"Penta, meaning 50 would tell us the number of which we must contend," Belac said.

"Can it be hurt?" Pete asked.

"Yes," Belac said, "a single arrow strike is sufficient, although given time it can regenerate if at least one piece remains undamaged."

"Regenerate?" Ben said, "we can kill 49 of a 50 piece monster and have them all come back (I can only assume at their leisure) and hack us to pieces."

"If it is your desire to allow another to hack you to pieces, then so be it," Belac said. "As for me, my eyes will be closed forever before I allow such a thing to take place."

Ben knelt and placed a hand on Belac's shoulder. "How did you learn so much about this creature in the short time we were apart?"

A wide smile spread across Belac's face

"To put it into terms you yourself would use, I'm privy to inside information."

"The Great One?" Ben said.

Belac turned to Ben and smiled, when a sound like the wobble of a thin piece of metal tossed into the air, severed a large tree directly behind the two men. The object continued its flight clearing Belac's and Ben's head by inches. Both men scrambled to avoid being crushed.

"Everyone," Belac ordered, "on your backs and flat to the ground as possible."

"I hear more slices of the Pentack circling." Ben said.

The orb that had supplied the meager light for Belac grew in brilliance. It left its position and moved erratically through the tree tops, diving toward the ground. Then moving left to right in a pattern that made no sense, all the while falling tree boughs littered the area.

"It's following the piece of Pentack," Pete said.

One of Belac's men took aim and placed an arrow through the left hand corner of the intruder. It ceased all movement and fell to the ground.

The orb hovered over the dead slice of Pentack.

Everyone gathered around.

Ben knelt and touched the surface of the anomaly. "It's hard, no give at all."

"Take all care not to touch the edges," Belac said, "Even the slightest pressure could sever the digit."

The slice of Pentack was shaped as a person with both arms at its side, legs straight and toes pointed.

A barely audible sound, like that of a knife entering its sheath caused all but one of the group to duck. The man who brought the creature down stood erect, a confused expression on his face and a slight gurgling sound emanating from a fine red line encircling his neck. His eyes rolled over white as he wobbled. His head hit the ground first, soon followed by his body.

The sky filled with a dozen or more orbs moving randomly about the sky. They dipped to the ground one minute and out of sight above the treetops the next.

They found that the Pentack pieces were possible to hit. Judicious tracking of the orb tailing the target and the insight to apply the correct amount of lead to the arrow made this possible. The success rate hovered somewhere between sixty and seventy percent.

"How many do you count?" Pete asked.

"Seven, maybe eight," Ben said, "They move like drugged out bats."

"What's the matter, little man, getting to be too much for you?"

Ben's next shot drove another one into the ground. He said nothing but his silence said volumes.

Belac approached Ben scooting along the ground on his elbows, legs bent in frog fashion.

"Come with me," Belac said, "the battle here grows nigh."

Ben followed Belac, moving close to the ground until they were 30 yards from the foray. It was then that Ben knew as the aberration stood he had not been following Belac, but the Pentack instead.

The creature had concealed its missing pieces by pressing itself low to the ground.

"What do you want?" Ben demanded.

"The three must be eliminated at all costs." The creature sounded remarkably like Belac.

"Who sent you?"

"You know him as the evil one."

"Who is the evil one to you?"

"My present benefactor."

Ben made no sudden movements or any movement at all that would cause the Pentack to feel threatened.

"Of what benefit would you realize to murder my wife, friend and me?"

The creature seemed puzzled. "Murder? What is this murder you speak of?"

"It's like the pieces you first sent to eliminate myself and my kind."

"That is of no consequence; the pieces you waylaid for a time will regenerate and then return."

Ben thought deeply for a moment and then smiled. "Do you have a name?"

"If you mean a noun by which others refer to me, then to you I answer yes."

"Would you care to tell me, so I know whom I am addressing?"

"No one has ever requested this information before."

"Perhaps no one has ever cared before."

The creature thought for a long while and then seemed to smile even though no outward change was evident in his appearance. "Chester, my name is Chester."

"Well, Chester, I'm very pleased to meet you." Ben partially extended a hand and quickly drew it back, knowing it would otherwise return as a nub.

Chester appeared to mull over this friendly greeting. "I think," he paused searching for the correct words. "That I maybe also pleased."

"Do you recall the word friend?" Ben asked.

This response required less time.

"Yes," Chester replied, "it suggests a familiarity and a desire to spend time with a selected subject and to have the same sentiment reflected back to you."

"Do you suppose that you and I could become friends?"

"You would desire to facilitate a mutual understanding of goodwill between you and me?"

"Very much so," Ben replied.

"Then, yes," Chester replied. "I have never had a friend. Tell me how and I will learn."

"First would you answer my question?"

"Of what benefit is it to dispose of you and yours?" Chester replied.

Ben didn't expect his new found friend to recall the question so readily. "Yes," Ben said, "that is it exactly."

"Why, the benefit of being useful, what other reason could there possibly be."

"Do you understand that we do not regenerate once we have been attacked? If injured or even killed that remains for eternity. We do not return to ourselves."

"I do not understand," Chester said, "the one I eliminated is no more?"

Ben nodded. "Sadly enough, this is true."

"I am very . . . what the word is I believe it to be sorrowful . . . Yes, I am very sorrowful that I have caused this to another being."

"It's okay. You didn't know that you were harming another." The next question that Ben was about to ask caused more apprehension than when he first found himself face to face with the Pentack. "Does this mean you will no longer cause harm or impede my group?"

"But of course," Chester said, "we are friends, and to that end we cause no harm to one another."

"What about the others traveling with me?"

"The ones who travel with you—"

Ben saw movement behind Chester, a single orb lighting the entire area.

"NO!" Ben screamed. A single piece of Chester separated from the rest and hovered over the decimated sections of his body. The orb hanging over Ben increased its illumination tenfold while another tracked the last piece of Chester into the sky.

Six men stood and made their way toward Ben. What remained of Chester's body, pierced by six arrows fell to the ground.

Belac, Pete, Eve, Jhorr and two of Belac's men joined Ben.

"What are you looking at?" Eve asked.

Ben watched the orb bounce out of sight before he answered. "Either the best friend or an enemy I wouldn't wish on my worst enemy."

"What do you mean?"

"Never mind that now, Belac, where's Belac?"

"Is the Pentack no longer a setback to our cause?"

"Before you attacked I was turning the creature from an enemy to a friend. Now that you have interfered, the Pentack, known as Chester may be a force to be reckoned with."

"So we were unsuccessful in destroying the beast?"

"Yes," Ben said, "One piece still remains."

"It will take some time for regeneration to take place—"

Jhorr interrupted. "The darkness is now complete. We must make all haste; the time to enter the cave has come."

BELAC, JHORR, Ben, Eve and Pete gathered several yards from the cave entrance. Belac hugged each one.

"You will do well," he whispered. Raising his hands over his head and looking upward, he spoke to the Great One on behalf of the three and Jhorr. When he finished, he placed his hand on Jhorr's shoulder and nodded. The youth disappeared into the darkness.

"I will now leave you and join my men," Belac said, in a whisper. "Wait for Jhorr, speak softly, so as not to draw attention, and when you are ready, enter the cave." He placed a hand on Ben. "Lead them well, and may the Light go with you."

Ben smiled and nodded. Before he could utter a word, Belac was gone. Ben looked at Eve and Pete. "Guess it's up to us now."

"And the Light," Eve added.

Chapter Thirty-seven

JHORR CROUCHED until his eyes became used to the darkness. Once they had adjusted, he moved cautiously, staying close to the cave wall. After ten minutes of progressing deeper into the cave, he perceived a dim glow. As he advanced closer he could hear voices. Staying at the edge of the light's reach, he chose a vantage point. This afforded him a view of two figures around a fire allowing him to hear their conversation.

"If you don't like it, Maylan, then don't eat it," the lofty figure said. He was taller than average. His head resembled a frog but with a longer snout. Two fangs protruded downward from his upper jaw and two upward from his lower jaw. The lower tusks spread outward from base to tip. The rest of the mouth was lined with rows of small, jagged, ill-fitting teeth. Long, wrinkled fingers pushed meat into his mouth, expelling pieces of masticated flesh from his lips as he spoke.

The shorter of the two screeched. His body slumped almost to the point of touching the ground. Thick legs supported the rear portion of his torso, while four arms held the front aloft—two placed on the ground and two waving in the air above his head. Two eye stalks of varying length, one six inches and one two feet, protruded from depressions in his skull. A serpentine tongue darted from side-to-side extending from a long, flat, crocodilian head. Maylan ingested the drool and the spent pieces of meat from his cohort as they fell to the ground.

"Delicious," he said, as he swallowed a mouthful of spittle.

"That's enough to make even me sick," Goryak said. He glared at Maylan.

Maylan looked at him and grunted.

Goryak eyed Maylan. "You are up to something, are you not?"

Maylan snickered.

"Do you know something you should tell me?" Goryak said.

Maylan ignored the question.

"That is it, is it not? You pus laden, belly crawler."

Maylan sneered, "I do not remember you being the boss of me." He slurped the last bit of Goryak's slobber into his mouth and swallowed. His tongue ran around the outer reaches of his mouth as his eyestalks swayed. He stared at Goryak.

"Got any more?" he questioned.

"None for you, slime ball," Goryak replied. "If I have to watch you eat any longer, I will lose everything I have ingested."

Maylan lowered his head. "Are you just going to watch me starve?" he pleaded. "You know I cannot eat that garbage you cook."

"That would be preferable," Goryak mumbled, turning away from the squat creature.

"What did you say, you bug-eyed mastodon?" Maylan demanded.

Goryak wheeled around, his right fist raised high into the air.

Maylan lowered both eyestalks anticipating the blow that struck him dead center of his forehead. His body slammed hard into the ground as its four supports collapsed.

"Do not trifle with me, fish face," Goryak exclaimed. He reached down and lifted the dazed head of Maylan by the underside of his snout. He dropped Maylan's head. It hit the ground with a dull thud. Goryak grunted and turned around to tend his fire and the burnt meat that still drooped over top of it. His bald, irregularly shaped skull encased forward-facing, saucer-sized eyes sunk deep into their sockets. Long, leathery ears protruded from his head at right angles, hanging straight down halfway along their length, flopping as he moved his head. His stout body, wrapped in a black leather jumpsuit stood over seven feet tall.

Maylan raised an eyestalk and lifted his body off the ground. As cumbersome as he appeared, he was surprisingly agile. He leaped from a crouched position, landing on Goryak's back, his teeth sinking deep into the demon's shoulder. Fluorescent pink fluid oozed from the wound. Goryak hissed and grabbed one of Maylan's eyestalks before he could retract it into its socket.

Jhorr had become so enthralled at the scene before him, that he didn't realize he was moving into the light he had so carefully avoided earlier. A bulky foot pressed down on his back, pinning him to the ground.

"What have we here?" the lead-footed stranger inquired. Jhorr felt the pressure of the appendage lift, and a hand large enough to cover his entire back slammed him once again to ground. Its fingers contracted, bunching his clothes into a knot. He could feel warm liquid ooze as claws dug into his flesh.

"AHH!" Jhorr screamed, his back afire from the filthy talons.

The creature shook him violently, opening the lacerations further. "Quiet," his captor growled, "or your head will be next."

Jhorr bit his bottom lip as tears of agony streamed down his face.

It seemed like hours to Jhorr, but after several minutes the creature made his way to the fire with Jhorr still in his grasp. He dropped the bleeding eight-year-old on the ground.

"What in the hell are you sorry sons of dogs doing?" the creature hissed.

Goryak and Maylan ceased their struggle and stared at the newcomer.

"You two have not only shown your true selves to this yearling, but you have allowed him to infiltrate our lair."

Jhorr raised his head and saw the creature as he stepped over his limp body, moving toward the two demons fighting by the fire. The creature's body was shrinking from its immense former self as it walked, into a normal size human being. Goryak and Maylan, looking terrified at the advancing figure, also shrank, taking on human form.

"We did not know," Maylan shrieked, as he knelt down covering his head.

Goryak stood silent, eyes wide. "Forgive us, Dark One," he mumbled.

The newcomer pressed his fist hard into Goryak's face knocking him to the ground.

"Never call me that."

"Forgive me, Sedah," Goryak corrected. "I did not mean to."

Sedah brought his foot down into Goryak's chest, causing the distinct sound of cracking bone. A whoosh of air signaled Goryak's loss of breath. Once his diaphragm ceased its course of spasms, Goryak drew a breath and began to cough.

Sedah hissed. "The Dark One will not take what you have said lightly."

Goryak struggled to his feet.

"Take the yearling to the circle of release," Sedah ordered. "I will send for you."

"Yes, Master," Goryak replied, "right away."

Sedah grabbed Goryak's arm. "Extract what information you can," he said, "but you must not kill the boy. Do you understand?"

"Yes," Goryak said. "It is most clear."

Maylan changed his form once again. He shoveled his nose underneath the boy and tossed him onto his back. His upper pair of arms held Jhorr fast. Goryak, still in human form, jumped onto Maylan's back. The creature scurried out of sight and through the rear entrance of the cave.

Sedah turned to look in the direction Jhorr had come. "The humans, they continue to resist." He chuckled, "No matter."

Chapter Thirty-eight

"WHAT DO YOU SUPPOSE is taking him so long?" Eve asked. "I'm getting worried."

"How long has it been?" Pete asked.

"About two hours," Ben replied. "If he's not back in another hour, we're going in." Ben thought for a moment. "No, we're going now."

He moved to the cave entrance and motioned for Eve and Pete to join him. Pete positioned himself at the opposite side of the opening. Eve stood behind Ben at his left.

Ben placed his index finger on his lips signaling all to be quiet, then conveyed the order they would enter.

Pete slipped through the opening, followed by Ben and Eve.

"Once Pete's eyes adjust, we move out," Ben whispered.

"I'm ready," Pete said.

Pete peered into the darkness, loaded his bow, and moved slowly forward. As he walked, Ben kept a hand on his shoulder and Eve a hand on Ben's.

After several minutes of walking in single file, Ben removed his hand. "I can see now."

"I'm ready, too," Eve said. They slid an arrow shaft notch onto the bow string and tensioned their weapons.

As the three moved down the corridor, Ben could detect the faint glow of a fire. "Get ready," he whispered, and took the lead.

Ben hastened his pace. They came to an abrupt angle in the passageway. As the three made the right-hand turn, they faced an open area. A small bonfire burned. One outline stood by the blaze. The single figure seemed to be warming its hands. They stepped to the edge of the light. As they did, something unnatural gave way under Ben's feet. Looking down, he picked up a child size bow and quiver.

"They've got him," he snarled.

"Got who?" Eve questioned.

"Jhorr," Ben replied. He pulled back his bow, taking careful aim at the lone target. He paused for a moment and lowered his weapon.

"What's wrong?" Pete asked. "Why didn't you shoot?"

"Something's not right," Ben said.

He motioned for his companions to back up. Once they were a safe distance from the light, Ben spoke. "It's a trap."

"How do you know that?" Eve asked. "If we don't do something he will get away."

Ben made calming motions with his hands. "He's not going anywhere."

"And you're sure?" Eve said. "You said yourself that they have Jhorr. What are we going to do?"

"Nothing," Ben replied.

"*Nothing?*" Eve stammered, "we can't stand by and do nothing."

"That's what they want us to do."

Eve stopped. "What do you mean, that's what they want us to do?"

Ben frowned. "Come with me." Ben motioned for Pete to follow. The three walked back to the open area, stopping just short of the light's reach.

"What do you see?" Ben asked.

"The same thing we saw ten minutes ago," Eve said.

"Same here," Pete replied.

"Do you notice anything at all unusual?" Ben asked.

"Wait," Pete said. He stared at the lone figure, turning his head from side to side. He looked at Ben. "He's not moving."

"What?" Eve said. She stared at the figure for several moments.

"He's in the same position he was ten minutes ago," Ben said.

"Are you sure," she said, squinting to bring the outline into focus. "You're right." She faced Ben. "How did you know?"

"Call it a gut feeling," he replied.

Pete smiled. "So what do you have rolling around in that head of yours?"

Ben motioned, drawing the group into a huddle.

Chapter Thirty-nine

MAYLAN HUNCHED HIS BACK, throwing Jhorr to the ground. Jhorr rolled onto his stomach, pushed himself up, and stood wobbling on his feet, displaying an air of defiance.

"You will rue this day," the boy said.

Maylan arched his body sideways, knocking Jhorr to the ground a second time. "Mind your tongue, young one," he growled. "I have eaten bigger snacks than you." Maylan poked a gristly finger into Jhorr's side.

Jhorr smacked it away.

"One bite at the most," Maylan mumbled, "and a scrawny bite at that." He turned, moving several feet from the boy, curled up and then lay down keeping a watchful eye.

Goryak, still in human form, walked up to the boy and helped him to his feet. "Best not antagonize that one," he cautioned. "I cannot promise I could help you if he indulges in the meal before him." Goryak eyed the boy with contempt.

"I do not ask, nor do I expect, any assistance from you," Jhorr said.

Maylan chuckled. Goryak glared at him, causing the quadruped to shrink back.

"I understand your insolence," Goryak said, "but I am here to help you. You must recognize that?"

Jhorr eyed Goryak with distaste.

"It is true," Goryak insisted. "I am not like the other two."

Jhorr smirked. "I would beg your pardon if in any way I have implied that I am a fool."

Goryak ground his teeth and peered through glaring eyes. "Enough of you," he growled.

Jhorr stood expressionless as Goryak grew to his true self. "Now," Goryak said, "What do you think of this?"

"You can disguise an ape in a costume," Jhorr replied, "however; the fact remains he is still an ape." A large hand connected with the side of Jhorr's face. Before he could fall, the same hand landed a blow on the opposite side of the boy's head. Goryak's hand wrapped around the boy's thorax, lifting him to eye level. Jhorr's eyes were swelling. Blood poured from his mouth and nose. The youth coughed and spit out several teeth.

"Best you not provoke an ape such as this," Goryak said. He pulled Jhorr closer. "You are not looking so good, yearling."

Jhorr's head lolled back and forth. "My eyes will soon be too swollen to see," he slurred. "This is preferable to looking upon you."

Goryak's eyes turned to fury. He clinched his fist and raised it to strike.

"Kill him before Sedah orders you to do so" Maylan warned, "and I should think you will become the next casualty in this conflict." Maylan despised Goryak, yet he had grown to know his superior and dreaded the thought of a replacement with a worse disposition.

Maylan ran his feted tongue over his lips. "However, if you insist, I will dispose of the evidence."

Goryak eyed the bleeding rag doll in his hands, and then glanced at Maylan. He huffed and dropped the boy flat on his back. Maylan's eyes brightened, and he crept towards Jhorr.

"Back down, belly crawler," Goryak barked.

Maylan lowered his head and slunk back to his original position. He lay down, dejected at the loss of such an easy meal.

Jhorr moved back and forth between the line of perception and unconsciousness. He closed the narrow slits of his eyes and crossed the line.

Chapter Forty

EVE CRAWLED THE LAST TEN YARDS to where the decoy stood motionless, basking in the dying firelight. She waited an hour for the fire to grow dark. Now accustomed to the darkness, she used the strobe effect emanating from her eyes. Eve took two dead coals and jammed them into what would be the straw figure's eye sockets. She grabbed four more and formed a grin on the decoy's face. *Wait until they get a load of you*, she thought.

The firelight, now gone, save for a few red embers, Eve stood, staring into the newly constructed face. Satisfied with the expression she had pushed into the decoy's head, she pulled a handful of straw from its torso. Retrieving several errant pieces of unburned wood from around the ash pit, Eve scraped together a small pile of embers to restart the fire.

She placed the straw over the glowing coals and the wood on top. As the tender smoldered, Eve ran back along the same path she had bellied her way down earlier.

Avoiding a small rock outcrop and turning to the left, she continued her trek back to Ben and Pete. Eve noticed an outline ahead and increased her pace. As she neared the figure, she tripped and fell into its arms.

"Ben," she exclaimed, as the waiting figure wrapped its arms around her, "good catch."

"Yes, my dear," Sedah sneered, "A good catch indeed."

THE FIRE SWOOSHED back into existence. It grew, blazing as it engulfed the new supply of fuel.

Ben squinted at the sudden burst of yellow. "She never does anything subtly."

Pete smiled. "That should give 'em an idea of who they're dealing with."

With any luck, the right idea, Ben thought.

The blaze illuminated the cave's corridors, removing shadows and exposing the interior.

Pete craned his neck looking toward the fire. "Shouldn't she be back by now?"

"I'm sure she'll be here soon," Ben said, concern creeping into his voice.

"We shouldn't wait too long," Pete said. "We don't know what's out there."

Ben nodded, "Long enough starts right now."

They made their way down the path Eve had taken until they came to the fire.

"This makes no sense at all," Ben said. "There's no sign of her."

"We know she made it here," Pete said. "Something must have happened as she left."

"A very astute observation," Sedah said. "It is most unfortunate you will not live to retrieve your losses."

Ben and Pete turned to see the blur of Sedah's back as he moved at an incredible pace, deeper into the cave.

"Ben," Eve cried, her voice trailing off until she could no longer be heard.

"C'mon," Ben exclaimed. "We've got to follow." Before he could take a step, the corridor and the open area filled with human forms.

"This isn't how I figured it would be," Pete said. "We didn't train for anything like this."

"Get used to it," Ben replied.

The two men retreated as the mob advanced on them. Ben wiped the sweat from his eyebrow with his bicep, all the time keeping tension on his bow.

Ben glanced behind him. "There's a cleft in the cave wall ten paces behind us to the right. When I give the word, we both fire and make for the opening. We should be able to defend ourselves from that position."

"Following you," Pete said. They continued to move backward until they were adjacent to the crevice.

"*Now!*" Ben cried. They fired, both projectiles striking their targets. With a loud screech, the first victim fell to his knees, changing into a six armed tentacle creature and then back to human form. It repeated the cycle several more times before exploding in a red ball of fire. The second creature did the same, except its metamorphosis was that of a feathered lizard.

Ben and Pete slipped into the opening.

"Did you see that?" Pete asked. They leaned against opposite side cave walls facing each other.

"I did," Ben replied. "The difference is that's not what happened when Belac rescued Eve and me from Sedah."

Ben removed another arrow from his quiver and laid it over his bow. "What do you mean?"

"Eve and I were taken captive by Sedah and Eleazor. Belac and his men took out most of Eleazor's cronies with arrows. That's where the results differ from where they are now."

"We took them out with arrows, too. What was the difference?"

"The demons went out in a blast of red fire. The difference being they didn't change back and forth from human to what I assume is their real form before they disintegrated."

Pete thought a moment, "Maybe they're evolving."

"That's a possibility, but evolving into what?"

"Something we won't be able to kill?"

"If that's true, they'll try to stay out of our way until that time comes."

"Unless it comes down to the Tamar," Pete said. "I imagine they'll stop at nothing to protect them."

"Or to kidnap one of us," Ben said.

"Is that why they tried to block us from going after Eve?"

Ben held up a finger to quiet Pete. He pulled his bow tight and nodded toward the entrance. Pete loaded his weapon and nodded back at Ben. The two exited their haven, Pete expecting a legion of demons, and Ben not at all surprised at the sight in front of him. The corridor was empty, the fire, once again, dying.

Ben grimaced and looked at Pete. "I don't think, now I *know*."

SEDAH DROPPED EVE on the ground beside Jhorr. She crawled to the unconscious youngster.

"What have you done to him?"

"Nothing more than will befall you," Sedah cautioned.

Eve rose to her feet and ran toward the creature. Sedah backhanded her, sending her to the ground. Landing flat on her back, Eve rolled over, bringing herself to all fours.

She raised her head. "If that's all you've got, you're gonna have to do better," Eve said, rising and running at him once again. Sedah brought her down again with a second blow.

"We can do this all day," Sedah mused. He squatted down, as Eve lifted up, and reared back on her haunches. "However, I think it best you stay down."

Eve placed her hands on her thighs. "This isn't over." She wiped the blood away from her lip and glared at Sedah.

"Of course it isn't," Sedah said. He raised his huge form to his feet. "Look after this one," he said, "and I do not expect to see the girl in the same condition as the yearling when I return." Sedah turned to leave and then stopped. "If I do," he said, without turning around, "it will not bode well for either of you." He hesitated a moment for effect and then left.

Eve wiped her face once again, and for the first time, noticed that she wasn't alone.

"Goryak, at your service," a tall grotesque figure said, advancing toward her, "and this is Maylan." He directed a hand toward the belly crawler.

Maylan licked his lips, "Pleasure to make your acquaintance."

BEN AND PETE moved cautiously through the open area. They reached the far side and saw one corridor about six feet wide.

"What do you think?" Pete asked, motioning toward the opening. "This way?"

"Looks like the *only* way," Ben said.

Pete nodded, and the two entered the corridor staying close to the sidewalls; Ben to the right and Pete the left.

"What are we looking for?" Pete asked.

"Not sure. I figure we'll know it when we see it."

"Okay, I hope you're—"

"DUCK!" Ben screamed. The two men dropped to the ground as a beach-ball-sized boulder flew over their heads. It landed on the ground behind them and rolled out of the tunnel entrance.

"You mean like that?" Pete stammered.

"Yeah, like that." They rose to one knee, aiming their weapons into the darkness ahead.

"We've got to move," Ben said. "We're sitting ducks if we stay here."

"I'm right behind you."

Ben stood, keeping his head low. "Somehow I'm not so sure that comforts me."

Staring down the hallway, Ben blinked faster than normal, creating more light from his eyes.

"Pete," Ben whispered, "I see three figures. They're at the edge of the light. I'll fire at the first one to the left. That should illuminate the other two."

"I'm with you."

"Take the one to the right of him," Ben said "and I'll take the last one."

"Give the word."

"No word. We don't want to warn them, just watch."

Ben pulled his bow to full tension, and without pausing, let the arrow fly, striking his target at mid-thorax. The demon squealed and changed into an indiscernible shape, multiple times, before exploding in a flash of crimson.

Pete marked the next target and released. The figure transformed into a bear-like aberration, still bathed in the fading light of its predecessor before radiating its own red aura.

Ben's projectile flew after Pete's, striking the last creature. Having already morphed into a snake with multiple arms in answer to the surrounding carnage, the strike culminated in an immediate explosion of scarlet fire.

"Well," Ben said "at least we're heading the right way."

Pete glared at him, "Do ya think?"

Ben patted Pete on the shoulder. "I don't believe it's gonna get any easier from here on out."

Pete shook his head. "I didn't think it would."

Ben chuckled. "Let's get outta here before they throw something down this shaft we can't dodge."

He took several steps forward and froze. Ben motioned for Pete to join him. "See that?" he whispered. Ben pointed to a faint, blue, pulsating light, emanating from the cave wall, adjacent to where the three beings had been.

"What is it?"

"If I'm right, our final destination."

"You mean?"

"Yeah," Ben confirmed, "the Tamar. Those three goons must have stationed themselves here to guard the brood chamber."

"Do we go in?"

"No. We've got to have Eve with us before we attempt an assault." Ben looked around. "They'll be sending someone to check on these three before long and we've got to find Eve and get back here before they do."

Pete nodded and the two men resumed their trek through the corridor. Ben turned to Pete, placing his index finger over his lips, as they neared the brood chamber. A foul stench emanated from the chamber opening, causing Ben to gag and swallow hard to prevent emptying his stomach. He quickened his pace through the offending odor and into clearer air.

Pete joined him with his thumb and forefinger pinching his nose closed. "Something's dead in there," he said.

"Dead would be an improvement," Ben replied, sticking his tongue out. "Let's keep moving."

They traversed the rest of the corridor without incident. It ended outside of the cave after a 90-degree turn, opening into a fenced-in circle, a hundred feet in diameter. The ring had been constructed from stacked stones. The walls ran to a height of twelve feet, with no ceiling, save for trees growing around the perimeter. Leaf-laden branches overhung the enclosure, giving an occasional glimpse of the sky above. Daylight lit the area, causing the two men to squint.

As their eyes became accustomed to the light, Ben froze. He motioned to Pete, and they backtracked until he was sure the darkness concealed their figures from the eyes in the ring.

"What's wrong?" Pete said.

"Shh," Ben cautioned. He pulled Pete down to his knees and pointed through the end of the corridor into the arena. A tall bipedal frog stomped around, ranting at a 12-foot prostrate lizard with six limbs. Several feet away, a disheveled woman consoled a battered boy.

Ben turned to Pete. "You're seeing this, right?"

"Yeah," Pete mumbled, without shifting his eyes. "How are we going to get them out?"

"We've got to get her away from *thing one* and *thing two*. We don't know what'll happen if they blow-up close to Eve."

"*Eve*? Aren't you forgetting someone?"

Ben stared at him and then grasped Pete's question. "I hadn't forgotten about Jhorr. I'm preoccupied with my wife at the moment."

"Sorry, I didn't mean to imply—"

Ben shook his head. "That's okay."

"Have you come up with anything?" Pete asked.

"I think so. Do you remember how Belac kept going on about the Great One?"

"Yeah" Pete said.

"I even talked with Him after Belac saved Eve and me from Eleazor."

"Can you do it again?" Pete asked.

"I'm not sure I remember what to do. When I talked to Him the first time I reconciled with Eve."

"Maybe there's something to it," Pete said.

"How else would you explain the Light?" Ben asked.

"I can't," Pete admitted.

"I just hope that between the two, one of them will help." He stared at the figures in the circle and sighed. "Here goes nothing." Ben steadied himself by placing his hands on his knees. "Mr. Great One," he whispered, "we need to help Eve and Jhorr." Ben paused wondering what else to say. "It's me again. If you could help us out, I sure would appreciate it." He looked at Pete and shrugged.

"Anything yet?" Pete asked.

"I don't think so."

Pete stood up, leaned over, and dusted his pants off. He noticed that Ben wasn't moving. "What's wrong?"

Ben rose to a full upright position, his eyes bright with wonder.

"What is it, Ben, what's wrong?"

"That's it," Ben said, looking at Pete and smiling.

"Please tell me what you're talking about?"

"We've had the answer all along. We just didn't know it."

Pete took Ben by both shoulders. "Why don't you tell me, and we'll both know."

✳ ✳ ✳

"IT HAS TAKEN too long," Belac said. "There is trouble."

"Should we go in?" Nayson asked.

"No. We are not to enter the cave until the three have made all secure unless grave conditions warrant us to do so."

"Why is this so? They may need assistance."

"The three must do this thing themselves. It will prepare them for future events."

"I do not understand," Nayson said.

Belac took a deep breath and sighed. "The ordeal they now face will strengthen and nurture trust in the Great One. This they must acquire before they can proceed upon the path before them."

Nayson nodded.

Belac remained silent for a moment and then began to speak. "Even though entrance is forbidden at this time, we will now leave and gather around the cave opening to make ready."

Nayson smiled, "I will assemble the men."

Belac nodded as Nayson turned to leave. He closed his eyes and uttered,. "Please protect the three."

❊ ❊ ❊

"THE LIGHT," Ben exclaimed, "the Light!"

"What about the light?" Pete said.

"It's the answer. I'll be able to contact her through the Light."

"How?"

"There's no time to explain, just get ready."

"Okay," Pete said, reluctantly as he pondered, *for what?*

Ben moved closer to the corridor exit, staying back far enough to remain out of sight in the darkness. He knelt down, loaded his weapon and brought it out ready to fire. Pete, seeing Ben, did the same.

Ben began to focus his eyes on Eve. He couldn't see the faint yellow flashes dancing on Eve's cheek, but perceived that they were there. Falling into an almost catatonic state of concentration, he attempted to convey his thoughts to her. Beads of sweat broke out on his forehead as his body began to tremble ever so slightly.

Pete helplessly looked at his friend, afraid that he would explode at any moment.

You must take Jhorr and move, unnoticed, further from the damned, Ben thought. It was this message that he suggested to Eve over and over again.

At first, Eve made no notice of her husband's communication. She then began to swat at the air as if a fly were buzzing around her head.

"What is this?" Goryak said, moving closer to Eve. He extended a finger and brushed it sideways through the top of her hair. "Are we losing our mind or just swatting the unseen?"

Eve smacked his hand away. "Trying to relieve myself of your stench."

Goryak reared back with a loud roar of laughter. "Soon, very soon." He turned his attention back to Maylan and continued his tirade.

Ben had dropped his bow and was leaning forward with both hands on the ground, still transmitting his message to Eve. His hair lay plastered to his head as the sweat poured.

"He can't keep this up," Pete mumbled. He thought of going to his friend and putting an end to this, but thought better of it and stayed put.

Eve began to look around, trying to make sense of what she didn't understand and where it was coming from. Moments later, she sat up straight, wrapped an arm around Jhorr, and began to inch toward the corridor entrance, pulling Jhorr with her.

How is she going to move without Mr. Wonderful seeing her, Pete thought.

"Please, Great One," Pete whispered, "if you were ever with us, be with us now."

Eve was making significant progress when it happened. Goryak, in a fit of rage, dropped to one knee, scooped Maylan up in his arms, and threw him to the ground further away from Eve.

Maylan immediately noticed Eve's movement and screamed, pointing at her as Goryak landed on top of him. It would be the last thing he would ever say as Pete's arrow flew true, blowing the belly crawler into oblivion. The blast concussion knocked Goryak forward in Eve's direction.

Ben, still on all fours, totally spent, and unable to assist, stared at the ground. Before Pete could reload, Goryak had gotten to his feet and snatched Eve up in his arms, causing her to drop the boy.

Jhorr lay on the ground, just beginning to regain consciousness in the wake of his protector's exit.

Goryak stood in defiance, yelling for the combatant to show himself. Pete hesitated, unsure whether or not to exit without his companion. "Ben," he hissed, "you've got to get up."

Ben shook his head and looked dazed in Pete's direction.

Pete was waving a hand at him. "Get up!"

"I will rip her head off," Goryak screamed. "Show yourself now!"

Fearing for Eve, Pete slowly exited the cave.

"Ah," Goryak said smugly, "One hardly bigger than the yearling causing so much trouble." He stroked Eve's hair. "Drop your weapon."

Pete extended his arms to the side, as if to ask why, knowing full well if he did, he would be totally helpless against this giant.

Goryak grabbed Eve's head, pulling it hard to the side. "Drop it now or my threat will become a reality."

"Pete, no," Eve exclaimed, "don't do it."

Goryak jerked her head further, causing Eve to yelp.

Pete reluctantly dropped his bow and began to slowly remove his quiver. He dropped it to the ground beside his bow.

"No," Eve whispered, as a tear ran down her cheek, ending on her captor's hand.

Goryak laughed, and with uncanny speed, moved toward Pete taking him to the ground with one swipe of his enormous hand. The monster immediately backed away, unsure of his opponent's capabilities.

Pete groaned, and rolled to his knees, wiping the blood from his lip. Now more sure of himself, the demon moved in once again and knocked Pete's legs from underneath him with one swipe of his arm. After the blow, Goryak retreated, grinning and chuckling as he stumbled around, giddy with pleasure.

Pete lay on the ground, gasping for breath. He rolled onto his stomach, extending his hand toward the tearful form in Goryak's arms.

"Eve," he groaned.

Goryak scraped his ragged feet in the dirt, preparing for a final attack. Jhorr had managed to squirm closer to the creature unnoticed.

An instant before Goryak charged, Jhorr slammed a fist-sized stone onto the giant's foot. The creature screamed and reached for Jhorr, falling backward, and dropping Eve in the process. Eve scooped the boy up and ran toward the corridor entrance.

Goryak jumped to his feet and lunged for Eve. His hand wrapped around her ankle as he fell toward the ground. Before Goryak could tighten his grip, an arrow pierced his throat in midair resulting in a red concussion that knocked Eve to the ground. A fine black dust settled, covering Eve, Jhorr and Pete.

As the air cleared, Eve lifted her beleaguered body off the ground. She noticed a familiar figure out of the corner of her eye. She turned to see Ben down on one knee, still clutching the bow that had dealt the final blow.

Sensing he could do no more, he dropped his head and fell over unconscious.

BEN OPENED HIS EYES and blinked. He sat up and stared at Eve. "How long was I out?"

"About three hours," she said, "as far as I can determine not having a watch."

"Three hours," Ben exclaimed. He whirled around to find Pete, "Didn't you tell her?"

"Tell me what?" Eve asked.

"The Tamar," Ben stammered, "I think they're close to coming out."

"It would have done no good to tell anyone anything until you had recovered enough to go," Pete protested.

"I know," Ben said, rubbing his eyes and shaking his head. "I'm just afraid we'll get there too late." Ben's eyes widened and he grabbed Eve by the shoulders. "Where's Jhorr? Is he okay?"

"I am, in fact all right," Jhorr said. His voice was thick as he mumbled through swollen lips. Jhorr walked in front of Ben, knelt and smiled.

Ben touched the side of his face. His eyes burned with an unbridled hatred."It's a shame they're dead," he hissed. "I would like to have the pleasure of killing them again."

"No, dear Ben," Jhorr said, "They are but gone from this realm. They await the Dark One to lead them. The Tamar will live among us to destroy all that is good."

"Well," Ben said, as he rose to his feet, "time to take out the trash." Ben leaned over and placed his hand on Jhorr's shoulder. "Are you well enough to travel?"

"I would do none other," Jhorr replied.

Ben smiled, "Good boy. You might want these." He untied a small bow and quiver strapped to his back and handed them to Jhorr.

Jhorr's bruised lips managed a meager smile, and he gratefully accepted the implements. "Thank you."

Ben looked at Eve and then at Pete. "Let's go."

They nodded and followed Ben back into the corridor.

As they neared the brood chamber, the now familiar stench permeated the air.

"What is that?" Eve gasped.

"Ah, the fragrance of demon seed," Ben said.

"I never smelled anything like it," Eve said. She gagged twice and threw up a small amount of bile. "It's a good thing my stomach's empty." Eve wiped her mouth and spit.

"Attractive, baby," Ben said.

Eve managed a grim smile. "Thought you'd like it."

Ben stopped and faced his entourage. "We're getting close," he whispered. "Quiet from here on out."

The odor intensified and soon the blue aura glowed in the darkness.

"It doesn't look like they've posted new guards," Pete said.

Ben stopped and spread his arms to keep anyone from continuing on. "No further."

"We can't stop now," Eve protested, "we're almost there."

"No," Pete cautioned. "When Ben stops; we stop."

"What's wrong?" Eve asked.

"Quiet," Ben commanded, in a harsh whisper. "We're not alone." He stood motionless staring into the darkness. Squatting down, he waved an arm instructing everyone to do the same. They complied.

"Where?" Pete whispered.

"With their backs flat up against the cave wall," Ben replied. "I don't think they've seen us." He backed up, coaxing the party to follow. They retreated and stopped just beyond the first turn in the corridor.

Ben dropped to his knees. His three companions did the same, forming a circle.

"It's a good thing they're not equipped with the same directional beacon that's given to us," he said. "I saw five, maybe six,"

"That's great," Eve said, her voice laden with sarcasm, "so what do we do now?"

Pete nudged her.

She looked at him and sighed. "Here we go again."

Ben ground his teeth. "Let's get something straight," he said, looking at Eve. "I'm your husband first, but right now I'm trying to save your butt." Ben's eyes blazed. "Listen and live. Decide otherwise and get us all killed."

Eve lowered her head. "I'm sorry, I didn't mean to—"

"Drop it," Ben said, "there are more important matters right now." He reached down, moving his finger through the sandy cave floor. Ben drew a three-sided square with a round top, indicating the corridor.

"Here's the brood chamber," he said, making a mark on the right hand side of the hallway drawing. "And here is where the five are." He looked at Jhorr. "You're the smallest, and where the black was rubbed from your face, bruises have taken their place, so you're still the darkest." Ben placed a hand on top of Jhorr's head. "Are you up to it?"

"I will do whatever you ask," Jhorr replied.

Ben grinned and shook his head. "Somehow I knew that's what you'd say."

Eve sat silent. She had almost balked at Ben's decision to put Jhorr into harm's way a second time, but thought it best not to question his authority again.

"Listen up," Ben said, "the plan's simple, Jhorr flushes them out and we take them down. Everybody ready?"

Ben looked around with an expression that dared anyone to say no.

The group nodded.

"Good," Ben said. "Jhorr, you first. We'll follow in thirty seconds."

Jhorr disappeared into the darkness. A final yellow flash told Ben the boy had turned the corner and was on his way. He closed his eyes and started the countdown. *One Mississippi, two Mississippi, three Mississippi...*

Chapter Forty-one

"WE HAVE THE GIRL AND THE BOY, Master," Sedah said. "And the sentries?"

"Guards have been posted at the entrance of the nursery, just as you instructed."

"Good," Eleazor said. He closed his eyes and winced. His torso faded to near invisibility, then returned to its solid state. His feet and head followed suit, leaving his bulbous midsection appearing to float in midair.

"The Tamar," Eleazor gasped. "What of the Tamar?"

"Soon," Sedah answered.

"The humans must not make it into the chamber . . ." Eleazor grimaced, lowering his massive form. Once he rose, he wiped the drool from his mouth.

"Is the failsafe in place?" Eleazor asked.

"It is," Sedah replied, satisfied with himself.

Eleazor slid down the wall and onto the ground. "There is little time before I become among the unseen," he said, struggling to get a breath. "I am powerless until this comes to be." He extended a shaky hand toward Sedah. "I must rely on you to carry out my will."

Sedah moved close and took the gargoyle's hand. With lightning speed, Eleazor grabbed the surprised Sedah by the throat, bringing him to within inches of his face.

"Do other than what I have told you," the monster growled, "and when we again meet in my kingdom, I will see you die a thousand times each day for all of eternity."

"Yes, Master," Sedah squeaked, his face taking on a pale color and his saucer-sized eyes bulging from their sockets.

Eleazor released his grip and tossed the near-strangled creature against the wall.

"Away," Eleazor barked, "Leave me in my misery."

"Yes," Sedah gasped. He stood, rubbed his throat and looked at Eleazor one last time before he left.

Chapter Forty-two

J HORR INCHED DOWN the corridor keeping tight to the wall. As he neared the chamber, he paused, pinched his nose, and swallowed the bile that had risen in his throat. He sat there for several minutes until he acclimated to the acrid smell. *Things are not as they should be.*

Jhorr moved to the opposite side of the corridor to avoid the blue glow that emanated from the chamber, he slipped pass the opening undetected. Something in the chamber caught his eye, but it would have to wait. Through his ocular yellow pulses he detected the first target form just inches away. He scanned the area and counted seven figures total.

One more than Ben mentioned. I will need to remove two. Instead of risking unnecessary noise that would alert the enemy, Jhorr left the bow around his neck. He pulled two arrows from his quiver, placed one in his left hand holding it as a dagger and one in his right, poised to throw as a dart.

"Great One, guide my hands," he whispered.

Paying no attention to his proximity for the concussion that would result; he hurled the dart toward it's intended. Jhorr then thrust the makeshift dagger into the foot of the demon closest to him.

THE THREE SET UP their offense ten yards from the brood chamber—Eve's shoulder tight against the right wall of the corridor, Pete to the left wall and Ben directly in the center, weapons loaded and pointing into the darkness.

"Don't forget to crossfire," Ben warned. "Otherwise, your shot may glance off the wall."

"How will we know when to shoot?" Eve nervously asked.

"Sit tight. We'll know," Ben whispered, his body tensing in anticipation.

"But how?" Eve insisted.

A deafening blast filled the chamber with a crimson light, causing the three to duck.

Ben raised his head. "My guess is now." He pulled his bowstring to its breaking point. "FIRE!"

A barrage of six arrows flew, the combatants firing, reloading, and firing again. Five separate strikes and five separate bursts of scarlet filled the chamber, as the sixth arrow passed through the last victim, just after its disintegration. The projectile continued on, bouncing off the cave wall and landing intact in the soft sand.

"Yes!" Eve cried.

The three began to move cautiously forward.

"Jhorr!" Ben called. He ran the last few steps and dropped down beside the prostrate youngster. Eve joined him and began to wipe the hair out of the boy's dirt-covered face.

"He seems to be okay," Eve said, "just unconscious."

"Concussion from the explosion," Ben said.

Another blast ripped through the corridor, pushing Ben and Eve over and covering them with dust. Ben raised his head.

"Missed one," Pete said smiling; his face covered with soot so that only his eyes and teeth were visible.

Ben dropped his head and chuckled.

Jhorr stirred and rose to a sitting position.

"Are you all right, sweetheart?" Eve asked.

Jhorr was looking at her inquisitively shaking his head.

"What's wrong?" she repeated.

Jhorr touched her mouth, pointed to his ear and then shook his head.

Eve cocked her head to the side with a concerned expression. "You can't hear, can you?"

"Shh," Ben cautioned. "They can hear us."

Eve whirled around, "Like no one paid any attention to all the explosions!"

Ben shrugged his shoulders and smiled mischievously.

Eve turned her attention back to Jhorr.

"How's our ward?" Ben asked.

"Well," she said, "other than being deaf as a post, not too bad considering everything he's been through."

"I've seen this before," Ben said. "Occasionally an underwater charge would detonate out of sync. If a diver happened to be too close to the charge, the shock wave from the blast could rupture his eardrums." He placed his hand on Jhorr's shoulder. "Ears heal fast. His hearing should return soon." Ben looked grimly at the boy. "At least I hope so."

* * *

"HOW MANY?" groaned Eleazor.

"Twelve, counting Goryak and Maylan," Sedah said. Nearly sent to the realm of the unseen by a nasty chokehold the last time the Dark One summoned him, Sedah wisely kept his distance.

"The safety of the Tamar is paramount," Eleazor said, wheezing. He leaned over in a fit of choking and coughed up a large white and red ball of slime.

Sedah swallowed hard and backed up a few steps further.

Eleazor caught his breath and sat upright. "If we lose ten times that, it would be worth it." A thick strand of pink drool hung from the corner of his mouth.

"Yes, Master."

Eleazor seemed to settle into a state of semi-consciousness.

Sedah backed away until he could no longer see his host. He then turned and ran.

* * *

"I HUF TO EL OU OMFING," Jhorr struggled to say.

"What?" Ben said. He tried to mouth the word deliberately, hoping Jhorr would understand.

"I aid, I huf to el ou obot da fing ida amber," Jhorr tried again.

"Save your strength," Eve said, also talking in Jhorr's direction.

"No!" Jhorr protested.

"I understood that," Ben said, "and maybe he understood you or he's just saying no because you can't understand him. Or maybe . . ."

"Enough already," Eve said. "No one will understand anything with you rambling like an idiot."

"Sorry," Ben said, "just trying to help."

"I fing is a rap, inda amber."

"Just calm down," Ben urged. "Pete, come here."

Pete bounced over to Ben's side. In an attempt to remove the black residue from his face, cheeks and forehead, he had left a comedy of finger smears crisscrossing his face.

Ben stared at him trying not to laugh. "You look good, ole buddy."

"Yeah, yeah," Pete said, "so what do you want?"

"We're going in," Ben replied. He looked at Eve, "You're with us."

"What about Jhorr?" she asked. "And why the garbled speech? It's not like he's been deaf all his life. He should still be able to speak. "

"He stays here," Ben said. "As far as his speech goes—occasionally with these compression concussions, it will affect certain centers in the brain. With Jhorr it appears his speech center is reacting to the blast."

Jhorr, sensing what was about to happen, spewed line after line of gibberish.

Ben took him by the shoulders. "Jhorr, you must listen." Ben shook his head, realizing that he was expecting a deaf boy to hear him. He looked at Jhorr and mouthed slowly, "Stay here."

Exasperated, Jhorr agreed.

Ben, Eve and Pete entered through the brood chamber doorway and into the blue.

"Ah," Eve protested, "the smell is ten times worse in here."

"Don't worry about the smell," Ben said, "stay focused."

"Ben," Pete said. "There's nothing here but a blue fog. Where are the Tamar?"

Ben moved his head in an arc, scanning the interior of the chamber. He saw what he assumed to be the source of the haze. Ben extended his hand, to warn Pete and Eve to stay back. He walked up to the edge, looked down and saw a hollowed out area in the rock floor. It appeared to be fed by an underground hot spring.

Ben circled the pool, stepping over the outflow trench and paused on the back side, staring into the bowl. The sulfur-laden water boiled in the stone cauldron. Around its edge lay branches of azure colored leaves. In its center, a rotting deer carcass bobbed about as the boiling water tossed it around. Fires dancing at the back of the chamber illuminated the area in an unnatural blue luminescence.

Ben stared into the pool, fascinated by the bobbing carcass. Thoughts flooded his head. *The stench from the sulfur and rotting carcass, I understand. Even the blue color is explainable enough, but why?* As he continued to gaze into the boiling water, a disturbing thought entered his head. *Jhorr had said, 'rap inda amber.'* "What could it mean?" he whispered. Ben pondered for another second and then the answer slammed into his brain.

"Trap," he announced, "trap in the chamber," his voice growing in intensity as he spoke. Ben turned to summon Pete and Eve, instead he saw two formidable creatures emerge from the rock wall and lock his wife and best friend in a deadly embrace.

"The Guardian," Ben barked. He lifted a leg to come to their defense and found that he couldn't move. Six arms then coiled around him to complete his imprisonment.

The two beings that held Pete and Eve sauntered up the small incline to join the creature that held Ben. They stood side-by-side and turned to face the chamber opening. The three watched as a tall human entered through the doorway. He walked up the incline and stood in front of the three.

"Sedah," Eve hissed.

"I am glad to see you remember me, my dear," Sedah said. "Obviously I have impressed you in some way."

"No doubt you have made an impression," Eve spat, "but nothing you'd care to hear."

Sedah placed a finger under her chin. "Perhaps this will change your mind," His form elongated and expanded. Sedah's head bulged to almost three times its original size, developing furry protrusions as it grew. His eyes sunk deep into their sockets while the creature's nose and ears became non-existent save for holes left by each. The mouth extended, forming a wolf-like snout, lined with rows of fangs, in random lengths, protruding at its longest three inches from his face.

Human-sized feet exploded from their soft skinned coverings. His arms and hands swelled as razor sharp claws pierced his fingertips and finished several inches from their origin. Sedah grew to twelve feet before his transformation was complete. A single claw tip pressed precariously underneath Eve's chin. Sedah smiled as a drop of blood oozed from the talon's point and landed on the ground beneath his feet.

"Well," Eve said, "Your impression remains the same, but you sure got ugly."

Sedah grunted and jerked his hand away, opening a small gash that dripped blood. Ben squirmed against his captor's grasp.

"You humans do not understand," Sedah said. "You have no chance to win this battle. The best you can hope for is to die well." He leaned down, moving his head, pausing in front of each of his captives. "I can assure you of at least part of that." He jerked his head back and laughed.

"Dispose of them in the cauldron," he said. As he left the chamber, the last thing the three saw was a human foot leaving through the doorway.

The Guardian holding the three moved robotically toward the stone impression containing the boiling stew of flora and fauna.

Eve looked at Ben. "I didn't think it would end this way. I can't even touch you." Tears of anger streamed down her cheeks.

Ben struggled against the arms that bound him. He felt the tentacles that surrounded his torso tighten their grip.

The Guardian continued their methodical trek toward the pool. Ben observed a small figure slip through the entrance. A second later, a projectile struck the center of his captor's head, disintegrating half of its face. The crumbling rubble fell as sand onto the chamber floor.

Moments later, arrows flew toward Pete and Eve. They landed true, striking the Guardian that held Pete, removing its right arm, and a portion of its shoulder.

Ben looked down, his feet dragging along the ground. He could see the cumbersome feet of his Guardian slide along with a peculiar stride of determination. "The feet," he yelled, "go for the feet!"

Eve and Pete looked to see Ben bring his right foot and then his left down hard on his jailor's feet, turning them to dust. The Guardian wobbled back and forth. Ben dug his heels into the cave floor and pushed, causing the Guardian to fall backward, disintegrating into a pile of gravel-sized rubble.

Ben clamored from the dust as Pete's captor fell on its back, shattering into gravel and freeing his friend from its grasp.

Both men stood helpless as Eve, unable to coax her Guardian to drop rearward, fell forward into the boiling cauldron.

Ben was the first to the pool. Eve lay prostrate stretched across the cauldron, her feet and hands the only thing keeping her out of the water, now boiling with increased vigor from the Guardian's residue. Eve's body sagged closer toward the water, weighed down with the debris on her back.

Ben took her wrists and Pete her ankles, lifting her up, and setting her down beside the pool, choking from the stench.

Ben placed his hands on her cheeks. "Are you all right?" he asked, his hands trembling.

"Yes," she answered, between coughs. Eve's face was bright red from the heat of the water.

Ben dropped to his knees and pulled her close."I thought I had lost you."

Eve wrapped her arms around him. "It ain't gonna be that easy."

Jhorr stumbled up to meet the three, "Ebby ody otay?"

Ben allowed Jhorr's words to circle his gray matter several times before answering.

"Yes," he mouthed slowly, "everybody's okay."

Eve knelt and hugged the boy. Backing away, she stared into his eyes.

"Thank you," she said, carefully enunciating her words.

Jhorr smiled. "Ou elcom."

"He seems to have a much easier time communicating." Ben said.

"I believe he's reading our lips," Eve explained.

JHORR PULLED four leaf-wrapped bundles from a pack tied around his waist and extended three of them to the group.

"You're a life saver," Ben said. He took the packages and unwrapped them, handing one to Pete and one to Eve. He rolled the leaf sandwich wrappings up and handed them to Jhorr. "Hold on to these," he said. "We don't want to leave anything that could give our position away."

Jhorr stuffed them back into his waist pouch.

Ben stopped chewing and stared at Jhorr, unable to speak with his mouth full.

Pete gobbled his down. "Thanks, little buddy," he said, and then burped loudly.

"Certainly," Jhorr replied.

Two heads turned simultaneously. "What?" they said, in unison.

Ben just smiled and nodded.

"Certainly," Jhorr repeated. "It was in answer to Pete's—"

"I know that," Eve interrupted. "Listen to yourself."

Jhorr's face brightened with delight. "I can hear," he exclaimed. He stuffed an index finger in each ear, then opened, and closed his lower jaw, manipulating it from side to side. "Sounds are still somewhat muffled; however, it is much better than total silence."

"Good to have you back," Ben said. He placed a hand on the boy's back. "As nice as this is, the Tamar aren't going to send invitations to their coming out party."

"Any thoughts on how we're going to find them?" Pete asked.

"Well," Ben said, "we know that the little fiasco back there was nothing but a diversion." He looked at Jhorr, "Any ideas?"

"I would think the Dark One would trust no one but himself to guard the Tamar. At the very least he would want to remain close."

"Good observation." Ben rubbed his chin looking at Jhorr and then cautiously posed the boy a second question. "Any thoughts on where that might be?"

"No. However the Tamar requires warmth, like any newborn creature. By my reckoning, we could locate the true brood chamber somewhere along this hot spring."

"Hot spring it is," Ben said. "All right boys and girls, let's saddle up."

Eve looked at Ben with her arms crossed and one corner of her mouth turned up.

"Saddle up?" she said.

"Saddle up," he repeated.

Eve sighed.

Jhorr led the three beside the bubbling tributary, entering the tunnel carved out by the stream itself many thousands of years earlier.

Pete's head nearly scraped the stone above as he walked. "I hope the ceiling doesn't get any lower. If it does I'll be crawling before long."

"Don't worry, big man," Ben said, "we'll drag you along if need be."

"You might be doing that sooner than you think," Pete answered. "If the low ceiling doesn't get me, the heat and humidity boiling off this water will."

Eve wiped the sweat from her forehead. "I'm with you on that one, Petey boy."

After an hour of working their way through the tunnel, they came to a fork in the passageway.

"I'd ask which way," Pete said, "but since the stream continues to the left, and the tunnel to the right, it's pretty obvious. The cooler and much more comfortable tunnel we'll want to avoid in favor of the stream and this heat."

"Didn't want to be too comfortable, now did you?" Ben asked.

"Of course not," Pete replied sarcastically, "though something to drink would be nice." He longingly fixed his eyes on the stream, licking his lips.

"We have been winding through these caves for over an hour now." Eve said. "With the increased heat we're losing more fluid than we've been able to take in."

Ben leaned over and stuck a finger into the fizzy water. He drew it back and pushed the digit into his mouth, paused, spit and then wiped his lips. "Too heavily mineralized to drink." Ben looked up. Water was falling like rain. "That's it," he said, confidently looking at Pete.

"And?" Pete raised an eyebrow.

"The cool air coming from the alternate tunnel is causing all this moisture," Ben explained. "There's enough condensation dripping from the ceiling to give us the water we want. All we need is something to catch it in." He thought for a moment. "Jhorr, give me the leaves."

Jhorr looked at him questioningly, then with a sudden expression of recognition, removed the foliage from his pack. The leaves a short time earlier had served as sandwich wrapping. He handed them to Ben.

Ben uncoiled the roll. He twisted one of the leaves into a funnel. Pinching the small end of the funnel, he placed the larger end against the wall to collect the running water, diverted by the stone irregularities. The container filled quickly. He lifted the constricted end upward and released his fingers. The fluid flowed into his mouth. Ben lowered his head, looking at Pete and Eve with trickles running from each corner of his mouth. He swished, swallowed and then smiled. "Tasty." He handed the coil of leaves to Pete.

"Like this," Ben said and quickly repeated the procedure. He saved this drink for Eve. "Here, sweetie."

She laid her head back and opened her mouth. He raised the funnel over her open lips, releasing the water flow with his fingers.

"Wonderful," she said, moving the side of her finger up her chin, catching an errant drop, and pushing it into her mouth.

The group drank their fill. Pete poured as much over his head as he drank.

"Okay," Pete said, Water coursing down his face. "If I sit here much longer I'm not going to leave."

"Then we've been here long enough," Ben said.

Pete stood and nodded toward the alternate tunnel that he had been sitting in front of, enjoying the cool breeze that flowed down its walls. "Hope to see you soon," he whispered and then turned to face Ben.

Ben touched Jhorr's shoulder. "It's time."

Once again, Jhorr took the lead as the party continued to follow the tributary flowing from the hot spring.

"I didn't think it was possible," Eve said, "but it feels like it's actually getting hotter."

Jhorr stopped, turning his head from side to side. "Do you smell that?"

Ben raised his nose high into the air, taking a deep breath. He stopped abruptly and coughed. "Unfortunately. What is it?"

"The brood chamber," Jhorr said, "the *true* brood chamber."

The party moved closer toward their objective.

"Ah," Pete said, grimacing and pinching his nose. "It's worse than the fake one."

Tears began to run down Ben's cheeks from the acrid odor.

"It stands to reason they would try to disguise the decoy chamber with a similar odor. I've got to tell you the last round of stench comes nowhere close to comparing with this one." He dropped his head and vomited the majority of the water he had previously taken in.

Eve buried her face into her shoulder, in an attempt to quell the stench. "What do we do?" she asked, exposing her face long enough to speak, and then pressing it back into her garment.

"We will stay here a short while," Jhorr said. "We must acclimate ourselves to the odor."

Ben nodded, unable to speak with his hand pressed firmly over his mouth and nose.

The three and Jhorr sat for over an hour. Even after that amount of time they were barely able to continue, though Jhorr tolerated the odor much more so than the rest.

Jhorr led them along the stream until they noticed a blue aura infiltrate their surroundings. He stopped. "We are very close now."

Adrenaline began to course through the three, decreasing the need to cover their noses.

"Jhorr," Eve said, "how is it that you have been able to stand the horrible aroma, when we couldn't?"

"It is what I have lived this portion of my life for," he answered smiling.

"To withstand noxious odors?" Before the words left her mouth, she realized the futility of her question. "No," she said softly, "you're going too—"

"You must not think of such things," Jhorr interrupted. "Concern yourself with the confrontation ahead."

Eve pulled her cupped hand away from her mouth. "I won't let it happen. I will not allow it to happen," she repeated, affirming her previous statement.

At that instant, a deafening thud and ensuing shock wave, compressed by the narrow tunnel nearly knocked the group to the ground. A chorus of muffled voices could be heard echoing throughout the passageway.

"What was that?" Pete asked. He looked around, expecting the tunnel roof to collapse.

Jhorr's eyes widened. "We are too late. It has begun."

"THAT'S WHERE THE SMELL and the blue color are coming from," Ben whispered.

The group stood at the tunnel entrance staring into the brood chamber, absorbing the setting before them. Nine sacs twice the size of an average man hung from the ceiling. Three attendants that appeared to be Guardians held six-foot long two-pronged forks. At regular intervals an attendant would pierce a sac, allowing a thick, putrid, fluorescent blue slime to flow, easing the pressure inside.

"Look," Pete said. "One cocoon is empty."

A deflated pouch, black and shriveled, hung from a single thread still attached to the rock above.

"And there's its former occupant," Eve said.

A tall, slender, black figure devoid of features, other than its two fingered hands, stood unmoving, its arms crossed in front supervising the final gestation of its brothers. Plates that interlocked covered the thing's entire body, giving the creature an air of indestructibility. A single, six inch claw protruded from its otherwise plain left foot.

Ben motioned for the group to fall back. They gathered about 30 feet from the tunnel exit. "Give me suggestions," he said. "We need a plan, and I want everyone's opinion, pro and con."

"I'll start with the obvious," Pete said. "The Tamar are hatching. We need to stop them, but to rush into that chamber would be suicide."

Ben looked at Eve and Jhorr. "Next."

"Maybe we could pick them off one at a time from the tunnel as they break free from their cocoons," Eve suggested.

"Wouldn't work," Ben replied. "We'd get one goon before they figured out where we were, and you can bet that would be the last time this passageway would be used."

"The Guardian, as we have seen," Jhorr began, "are very slow and cumbersome. If we could eliminate the one Tamar, and then reduce the three Guardian, the chamber would be ours to control."

"We could take out the Tamar, as they emerged," Eve said.

"Yes," Ben said. He placed a finger over his lips and thought. "It just might work."

"We must remember that The Dark One is very near," Jhorr warned.

Ben placed a hand on Jhorr's shoulder and sighed. "I don't know what we'd do without you."

"Get used to dirt," Pete interjected.

Ben looked at Pete and grimaced, then turned his attention back to Jhorr. "Your plan may be our only chance."

"I fear you are right," Jhorr said, "but we must make the plan more viable."

"Suggestions I need," Ben said, "If you have any, I'm all ears."

Jhorr looked at Ben. "You have only two small ears."

Ben smiled, "It means I'm ready to listen to you."

"Ah," Jhorr exclaimed. "I understand now. It will take the three of you to eradicate the Tamar. At that time I will begin to reduce the Guardian. Once you have accomplished your task, you will be able to assist me in completing the reduction process."

"I don't like it," Eve said. "I don't like it at all. We can't continue to put this child at risk."

Jhorr touched Eve's face. "It will take each one of us to defeat this enemy."

"I don't like it any more than you do," Ben said, "but he's an integral part of this team."

"Ben's right, Eve," Pete said. "If it weren't for the kid, we'd be well-done, floating next to a rotting deer carcass."

"I know, I know," Eve protested, lowering her head, and rubbing her hair with both hands. She raised her head and looked at Pete. "That doesn't make me any less uneasy."

"Can we go back to where the passageway forked and get something to drink before we get started?" Pete asked. "It can't be over thirty or forty yards down the tunnel and I'm parched."

"Sure," Ben said. "I could use some refreshment myself."

They returned to the condensation flow and gorged themselves.

Pete moved a few feet further up the alternate fork in the passageway than his last visit. He sat down, enjoying the cool air flowing through the tunnel.

"The breeze blowing through here must be surface air," Pete said. "It's too clean to be anything originating from this hell hole."

Ben walked over to Pete and took a deep breath. "I think you're right." Ben laid a hand on Pete's shoulder. "Unfortunately it's time to hit the sauna."

"I knew it wouldn't last," Pete said.

Ben smiled and turned to walk away. Pete stood and grabbed Ben's arm. Ben stopped and turned to face his friend.

"We've been friends for a long time . . ."

"We have," Ben said.

Pete chuckled. "With what's been happening, it might have been a thousand years or more."

Ben smiled, "Could be."

"We've been there and back, but we've had a good run."

"After we're done, make an appointment and we'll talk." Ben said.

"Hmm," Eve grunted. "Before I get dehydrated again, I wonder if you two would like to get started."

"All right people—" Ben started.

"Wait," Jhorr said.

"What is it, Jhorr?" Ben asked. "We need to get back to the chamber."

"There is always time to talk with the Great One," Jhorr said. "Please bear with me, and I will articulate."

"Make it quick," Ben said.

The three closed their eyes as Jhorr spoke.

"Great One, I ask that you would listen to your humble servant. Guide our hands and make our aim true. Allow us to complete the appointed task you have given each of us to fulfill. Be with your servants every step we take. Great One, even though you have given our leader, *the one we know as Ben,* a mission that may seem insurmountable, guide and direct him in all he will say and do. I ask these things in the name and for the sake of the One who lives, Ayen."

"Thank you," Eve said, lifting her head.

"Yeah," Pete said, "that was real nice."

Ben kept his head down.

"Let's go, boss man," Pete said.

"In a minute," Ben said, raising his head. "You two go on. I want to speak with Jhorr."

Eve and Pete nodded, walking a short distance down the tunnel.

"Do you require something from me?" Jhorr asked.

"I do," Ben said. "I wanted to thank you for what you said." He paused a moment. "It touched me."

"I am glad to hear this," Jhorr said, smiling.

"I also wanted to ask you about your last word."

Jhorr looked at him, not understanding.

"Last word?" A concerned expression crossed the boy's face as if he had committed some grievous error.

Ben recognized the look.

"No, you've done nothing wrong. I'd like for you to tell me what the word, *Ayen* means."

"Ah," a relieved Jhorr said. "It is an affirmation to the Great One."

"Affirming what?"

"The Great One's sovereignty. Why do you ask?"

"It's a word I heard you utter, not so long ago, but in a different situation."

"The older Jhorr in the before time you have spoken of?"

"Yes," Ben said, his smile laced with melancholy.

"Tell me of this time." Jhorr now appeared much older and wiser than his years.

"You had announced to your people, of Eve's and my marriage. It was a time of celebration." A sad smile crossed Ben's face, "Unlike now."

"I see," Jhorr said, "however, the word in any situation means the same."

"Thanks." Ben looked toward Pete and Eve, then back at Jhorr. "I think we have a job to do."

Jhorr nodded, "I believe you call it 'taking out the trash'."

"You got it, little buddy."

* * *

JHORR SLIPPED out the tunnel exit and positioned himself behind a cluster of stalagmites.

The Tamar overseer, the first to hatch, jerked its head toward the passageway and took a defensive stance. The three stayed back from the entrance, remaining in the shadows, but close enough to still afford a limited view of the chamber.

"Did you see how fast the Overseer moved?" Eve whispered. She rubbed her palms against her pants, wiping away the sweat, no longer coming just from the heat.

"No, I didn't," Ben said. "It was too quick to follow."

"What are we going to do? We can't fight that thing."

Ben placed a hand on each of her cheeks. "You've got to calm down. We're ready for this."

"I know we think we are, but are we really?"

Eve felt a hand touch her shoulder. She turned to see Pete.

"All I know is that there's something inside of me that wasn't there before." A broad smile spread across his face. "Whatever it is, it tells me that we're ready, and that's good enough for me."

Eve placed her hand on top of Pete's hand. "Okay." She leaned over and kissed Ben. She stood facing the chamber and then turned to face both men. "It's good enough for me, too."

"Now let's get ready before Jhorr thinks we've abandoned him." Ben said. "We'll position ourselves as close to the opening as possible without getting into their line of sight. From there we aim and fire. Jhorr will take the first arrow striking the Tamar as his signal to begin reducing the Guardians."

"That's it?" Pete questioned.

"That's it," Ben replied.

"You'll give the order?" Eve asked.

"Yes, maam," he said. "Once Mister Wonderful is on the ground, we go in, and help Jhorr finish knocking down the dirt piles."

Ben looked into the faces of his companions. "Everyone okay with that?"

Eve and Pete nodded.

"Good," Ben said.

The three gathered around the chamber entrance. Ben knelt down, removed an arrow from his quiver, and laid it across his bow. Pete did the same, followed by Eve. Ben extended his index finger and pointed to himself. He extended two fingers pointing at Eve and three fingers designating Pete as the third to fire. Ben nodded, as did Pete and Eve, signaling all is ready.

Ben started to countdown in a harsh whisper. "Ready, aim . . ."

Chapter Forty-three

"ITRUST THE HUMANS have been eliminated?" Eleazor inquired
"Yes, Master," Sedah replied. "The Overseer has also emerged."
Sedah maintained a respectable distance, remembering his recent
encounters with the Dark One.

"I will depart as soon as the second Tamar bursts from its cocoon."
Eleazor groaned. He leaned over, became virtually transparent, and then
rematerialized once again. He sat back, gasping for air.

Not soon enough for me, Sedah thought.

The Dark One looked at Sedah, raising an eyebrow. "Nor I."

Sedah's eyes grew wide. "Master," he pleaded, "I did not mean . . ."

"Do not grovel," Eleazor interrupted. "As much as it becomes you, I do
not care to listen."

"It will be as you say, Master."

"Now. You will listen carefully to my instructions."

"Yes, Master, I will listen."

"By the time the Tamar are completely loosed I will have begun my
journey away from this wretched place." He winced in pain, doubled over
and grabbed his abdomen. After several moments the Dark One
straightened himself. "And this bothersome form," he finished, with a large
sigh.

A stream of white drool streaked with red ran out the corner of his lips.
He wiped it with a trembling finger and pushed it back into his mouth.

"You must not forget the wooden boxes in the open area," Eleazor
whispered. "They are of the utmost importance."

"I will not forget."

A look of surprise came across the Dark Master's face. He glared at
Sedah, coming to an upright position. "No!" he cried.

"What, Master?" Sedah squawked. "What is wrong?" He dropped to a squat position, placing his disfigured hands, palms out to shield his head from Eleazor's wrath.

Eleazor stood, his legs shaking, scarcely able to support his massive frame. He lumbered toward Sedah, pointing his finger as he walked.

"You told me the humans were no more!" he roared. "The Overseer is . . ." He stopped and cringed. His form faded to a point it hadn't before. He then partially rematerialized. His movement became less steady as he continued his march toward Sedah.

Sedah cowered, still in a defensive position when Eleazor reached him. "I will send you to the Nether Regions, now," Eleazor screamed, as he swung a deadly hand into Sedah's head.

Sedah looked on in wonderment, as the Dark One's hand passed through his skull, without leaving a mark.

Eleazor looked at his hand. "Yes," he whispered. He stood fully upright, pushed his fists upward, and reared his head back roaring, "YEEESSSS!"

He looked down at Sedah. "To the brood chamber! Now!" His form blinked in and out of existence several times and then disappeared with a small puff of matter.

Sedah jumped up as if the Dark One were still there.

"Right away, Master," he voiced, as he ran out of the assembly room.

* * *

"IT HAS BEGUN," Belac said.

Nayson looked into Belac's eyes; "Are they—" Nayson dropped his head and stared at the ground.

"No. The three and Jhorr are still among us for this moment. However, how long they will remain so I cannot say."

Nayson raised his head.

"Can you tell me when we will be able to enter the cave?"

"I cannot." Belac looked at Nayson. "I am also very anxious to help those inside the Den of Evil." Belac broke eye contact with Nayson and stared over his head into oblivion. "Until the time is right, we will remain here."

Nayson nodded sadly, knelt, and once again lowered his head.

* * *

"FIRE!" Ben hissed.

Three arrows left less than a second apart. The first struck its target and shattered. Projectile two touched the same point, bouncing away, but leaving a second chink in the overseer's armor. Number three mimicked the trajectory of the first two sinking deep into the neck of the Overseer.

The creature jerked, sank to the ground, and shook violently. It shriveled into a black wrinkled mass that bubbled and exuded wisps of smoke as it spread in a puddle onto the cave floor.

Eve stood turning a full circle. She noticed she was alone. Ben and Pete were in the chamber, along with Jhorr, taking chunks out of the Guardian. Eve joined the trio, firing, until the masses of vertical stone lay as rubble.

As the last Guardian turned to dust, one of the Tamar sacs moved.

"I am off to keep watch," Jhorr said. "Remember, to shoot as soon as the Tamar passes through the cocoon's skin; you must not give it a chance to develop its outer shell."

"We'll be fine," Ben said. "Keep yourself safe."

Jhorr nodded and left the chamber. The three waited for the Tamar's arrival.

Eve dropped her arms.

"This is worse than the actual fighting."

Ben nodded, but kept his bow ready.

The cocoon pulsated with regularity until a slit developed midway up its side, then all became still.

The three looked at each other and then at the cocoon. Ben rose to a standing position. He took several steps, then turned and looked back at Pete.

Without warning, the cocoon split wide, emanating a similar shock wave as the first had. It spewed a disgusting mixture of thick fluid and rubbery chunks, as it dumped a black, throbbing, slime-covered ball onto the ground. As the ball unraveled, legs extended, hands with two clawed fingers pushed upward, and a featureless head shook into existence. Captivated by the aberrant display, the three delayed shooting almost to the point of no return.

Ben collected his senses, and at the last instance, released. The first two arrows found their mark, plunging deep into the creature's thorax. The third projectile bounced off the now hard exterior shell.

"Oh," Eve exclaimed, covering her ears. "Listen, it's whining like a baby."

"I remember wild cats sounding like that after they'd been shot," Pete said, "except this is a lot more disturbing."

Ben walked over to the creature and nudged it with one foot. The whining trailed off like a deflating balloon exuding its last push of air.

"I can't take seven more like that," Eve said.

"You will not have to," an ominous voice said from behind.

The three whirled around to see Sedah, with Jhorr in his grasp. "I see I have misjudged your prowess in escaping the Guardian in our first meeting." He sauntered closer to the three. "A mistake I will not make a second time."

"Let the boy go," Ben ordered.

"I do not believe you are in a position to bargain," Sedah said, "since I hold the stakes." Sedah grabbed Jhorr's head and twisted until the boy released a high-pitched squeal.

Eve stepped forward, "Let him go, you piece of—"

"Now, now, now, my dear," Sedah interrupted, shaking a finger in her direction. "Saying naughty things will only upset me further." He put his hand to his mouth and rolled his eyes upward as if in deep thought. When he looked back down, he stared at Eve.

"I feel your last comment will cost." Sedah paused. "Yes, I imagine that will do nicely." He took Jhorr's hand, bending the wrist down until it snapped.

Jhorr tried to scream, but could only manage a whimper with Sedah's hand clamped around his mouth.

"Now," Sedah said, his jovial tone gone. "We will sit and wait until each of the Tamar have emerged. After that I will release this precious young one and be on my way."

Ben's blood boiled. After several deep breaths, "Okay, we'll do it your way."

"LOOK," Eve said, "one's moving."

The cocoon bulged, and then split, depositing another creature. This one hardened and stood upright, cautiously moving toward the three.

"What's it doing?" Eve said. She glanced at Sedah, keeping an eye on Jhorr, and then turned, unable to keep her attention away from the newborn creature.

"Not a clue," Ben replied. "Sit tight we'll find out."

The lone Tamar came within six feet of the three. It opened its mouth revealing numerous rows of pointed teeth.

Eve drew back, grabbing Ben with both hands. "I didn't know they had teeth." She pushed her body closer to her husband.

"I didn't know they had a mouth," Pete said. He tightened his grip on his bow. "Bring it, big boy. We'll take you out like we did your brother."

The Tamar crouched down upon hearing Pete's words and began to circle the three hissing as he moved in a sideways motion.

"See how he's moving his arms," Eve said. "He's going to attack."

"He's as scared of us, as you are of him," Ben said.

"How can you be so sure?"

"What you mean is how can *he* be so sure?"

"Whatever, just tell me why you're so positive?"

"We killed the Overseer and one of its siblings," Ben said, keeping a guarded eye on their aggressor. "He knows all right."

"Don't revel in your supposed victory too soon," Sedah said, his arms still clutching Jhorr. A faint moan could be heard from the ailing youngster.

The remaining cocoons moved and split. Within minutes, litter in the form of seven pulsating, wet blobs covered the cave floor.

"We could have taken all these slime balls out," Pete whispered.

"Not without risking Jhorr's life," Ben countered.

"I know," Pete said, lowering his shaking head.

Once the seven Tamar had risen, they joined their companion and encircled the three in similar fashion bearing their teeth and hissing.

"What now?" Pete questioned. "We're out numbered."

Ben kept his eyes on the circling creatures.

"Stay ready."

Pete nodded. Eve clutched her weapon as the eighth Tamar closed the circle.

"Sedah!" Ben screamed.

"What can I do for you," he replied.

"Living up to your promise would be a good start."

"And what promise might that be," Sedah's voice now taking on a hint of sarcasm.

"To let the boy go once your goons were on the loose."

"I agreed to release him, did I not?" Sedah said, looking perplexed. "I will indeed release him, as I have promised." He raised Jhorr high above his head.

"No!" Ben cried.

The Tamar gathered around Sedah and slammed their hands on the cave floor, at the same time uttering a guttural chant.

The three readied their weapons, now moving in slow motion.

"I now join you, Dark One," Sedah exclaimed. He brought the boy down across his knee, crushing his spine.

The three loosed their arrows at the same instant. Sedah exploded in a crimson flash, showering the Tamar with his residue.

"Run, my wards," echoed through the chamber as Sedah's last words.

The three reloaded, singling out one of the newborns.

The Tamar hissed at the three, bearing their teeth, then departed.

"What," Ben said, lowering his bow. "Where'd they go?"

Eve rushed to Jhorr's side clamoring over the chamber floor's rough terrain. Ben and Pete joined her.

"Jhorr!" she exclaimed.

Jhorr opened his eyes and grimaced.

"Don't worry, sweetie, you'll be all right."

"No," Jhorr whispered, "not this time."

"You've got to be," she said.

Ben knelt down. "Jhorr what can we do?"

Jhorr coughed. A trickle of blood ran out the corner of his mouth. He motioned for Ben to come closer.

Ben bent down positioning his ear over Jhorr's mouth.

"You must stop the Tamar. This is what you can do for me."

"It's no use," Ben said. "With their speed, they're out of the cave by now."

"No," Jhorr moaned. "The great light is most certainly in the sky." He coughed again. This time the flow of blood increased. "They cannot leave until the darkness overtakes the light."

"Okay," Ben promised, "but first we have to take care of you."

"No," Jhorr protested, waving his hand. "I am soon to enter the light of the Great One." He glanced down his torso, "Please straighten my legs." His eyes rolled back in his head as Ben aligned his lower extremities.

"Is that better?" Ben asked.

Jhorr's eyes returned to normal.

"I can only perceive it to be," he said. "I can feel nothing in the lower portions."

"Do you want something to drink?" Pete asked.

"That would be nice," Jhorr answered, his voice now stronger.

Pete ran back down the tunnel, picked up, and rolled one of the discarded leaves. He pinched the end and filled it with water and returned.

Jhorr, with Ben and Eve's help, now sat upright with Eve behind him supporting his back.

"Here," Pete said. He placed the small end of the funnel over Jhorr's mouth and opened his fingers.

"Not too much at one time," Eve cautioned.

Pete nodded and closed the funnel once Jhorr's mouth was full.

The boy swallowed.

"Enough." He attempted to raise an unusable hand that flopped, sending him into another round of agonizing pain. Jhorr closed his eyes, absorbed the hurt, and then reopened them. "Thank you," he said, with a fading smile.

"You're welcome," Pete replied. "Can I get you anything else?"

Jhorr shook his head.

"See," Eve said, "you're getting better already. You're even sitting up."

Jhorr placed his good hand on Eve's arm.

"For the moment, to bid you farewell."

"What do you mean? You can stay with us now."

"Dear Eve," Jhorr began, "we have come this far. It is now time for the three to go on alone."

"No!" Eve protested.

Ben tapped her shoulder.

"Let him speak," he said. Eve lowered her head.

"As I said," Jhorr continued, "I have come with you as far as I will go. However, you must continue your hunt for the Tamar and secure the wooden boxes." He closed his eyes, pain searing through his upper torso. Jhorr reopened them, but now they were dull and weak. "It is time. You must not tarry here any longer. There is much to do."

"We won't leave you," Eve declared.

"I am of no importance to your undertaking any longer."

"Don't say that," Eve sobbed, her tears falling on the boy's forehead.

"Do not fret over me," Jhorr said. He expressed surprised curiosity and then smiled. "Your friend, the one you called Stewart. I will soon see him."

"You remember Stewart?" Ben asked, "But how?"

"I do not know. It came to me only now." Jhorr raised his head looking into Ben's eyes. "I will also see you again, much older than I am now, but of this I am sure."

Ben smiled, "I look forward to it."

"As do I." He patted Eve's arm. "Please lay me down," he whispered. "I am tired."

Eve gently laid Jhorr flat on the cave floor. "There you go."

Jhorr smiled. "Thank you," he mouthed.

"Rest well, young one," Ben said.

His words went unnoticed. The boy known as Jhorr was no more.

THE THREE MADE THEIR WAY toward the open area.

"How do you know the crates will still be there?" Pete asked.

"I don't," Ben said, "but we'd better hope they are."

A series of shadows crossed overhead.

Ben froze. "Stop." He scanned the cave walls and up to the ceiling. "Look."

Pete and Eve focused their line of sight on three dark figures hanging from the ceiling. They moved about silently, clinging to the surface of the rock with their hands and feet.

Ben eased an arrow out of his quiver. Pete, anticipating his friend's response, had loaded his weapon, as did Eve.

Without a sound, Ben fired. Two projectiles followed directly behind, Ben's struck the Tamar in the neck, and the trailing two glanced harmlessly off the cave ceiling.

"They're too fast," Pete exclaimed. He reloaded and began to scrutinize his surroundings.

"They're also gone," Ben said, lowering his bow. He placed the second arrow back into his quiver. "If we ever hope to kill another one, we're going to have to take it by total surprise."

"Just like we did the first," Pete stated.

"Exactly," Ben confirmed.

THE THREE STOPPED within ten yards of the corridor's end. Ben dropped to one knee and motioned for Pete and Eve to do the same. The dancing firelight illuminated the open area, bleeding back into the corridor, only feet from where they gathered.

"We could sure use Jhorr right now," Ben said.

"I wish he were here, too," Eve replied.

"No, I meant *use* him. Jhorr was small enough to get closer than we could ever hope to."

"How can you say that," Eve protested. "The child just—" she stopped herself. "I'm sorry."

Ben placed his hand on her shoulder. "It's okay. I miss him as much as you do, but that doesn't change anything."

"I know." Eve sighed. She wiped her eyes and looked at Ben.

"You need to get as flat as you can up against the opposite wall of this passageway," Ben said. "The light's coming in at an angle, and there's less of it on that side. Move as close as you can to the exit and see what's going on in the open area."

Eve nodded."Okay." She rose to her feet.

"No, wait," Ben said. "Too dangerous."

"What do mean, it's too dangerous? You were ready to send me before you thought of me as your wife."

"No," Ben said, standing. "It's not like that at all."

Eve turned to face her husband. "I'm a member of this team and expendable like any one of you." Eve puffed up her chest. "That's how it is, isn't it?"

Ben lowered his head and rubbed his cheek. He raised his head slightly, throwing an eye in her direction. "Yeah," he said, reluctantly.

"Good." She turned to leave and then paused. Whirling around, she kissed him, and then threw a reassuring smile. "I'll be careful."

"You'd better."

Eve moved carefully to the far side of the tunnel. She pressed her back hard into the irregularly shaped wall and began to move toward the light. Within inches of the tunnel entrance, she looked into the open area. There were several fires illuminating the entire space. The crates were still there, but no Tamar or anyone else that she could see. Eve relaxed and walked back to Ben and Pete.

"Well?" Ben said.

"The crates are still there, but nothing else."

"Then why the fires?" Pete asked.

"It's too easy," Ben said. "We don't know how many Tamar may have passed unseen while we were running down the tunnel."

"You think it's a trap?" Eve asked.

"Maybe," Ben replied. "What I do understand is that the Tamar are quick enough to have gotten here before us and warned Eleazor's cronies."

"So what do we do?" Eve questioned.

"Choices are something in rather high demand," Ben said. "Once the sun goes down, the Tamar are gone."

"We're going in?" Pete asked.

"We're going in," Ben replied.

THE ARROW POINT exited the tunnel ahead of its wielder. Ben eased out of the corridor. Pete and Eve followed. Once they were clear, the three moved to a side-by-side position, canvassing a 180 degree arc in front of them. The three moved in unison toward the wooden boxes.

"What gives?" Pete whispered.

"What do you mean?" Ben replied.

"There's nobody here," Pete said.

"Not yet," Ben replied.

"You two finished?" Eve asked.

"Yeah," Ben said, "for now."

"Good," Eve said, "because our friends are back."

"Where?" Ben asked.

"I saw two drop behind the crates and shadows on either end," she reported. "How many shadows, I don't know."

Ben looked at her and smiled, "You saw all that?"

"Yeah while you and Pete were gabbing."

"Good girl," he replied. The three moved closer to their quarry. Once they were within ten yards, Ben looked at Pete and nodded. Pete moved left and Ben to the right. Eve centered herself between the two. From this vantage point she could cover both men.

Ben took two more steps, dropped to one knee, and fired. A fraction of a second later, he fired again. The two projectiles disappeared behind the crate. A glittering burst, and a moment afterward, another lit the area with a brilliant crimson hue.

Eve moved in Ben's direction, side-stepping with increased confidence. To her left, another blast culminated in a sprinkling of red glowing fallout. Two Tamar jumped from behind the crate, landing on top of the wooden surface. Another fell from the ceiling to join its brothers.

Ben, now reloaded, let his arrow go. It struck the closest Tamar in the neck. Eve had positioned herself just to Ben's left. She drew the bowstring back and just before she released, an unseen shadow from behind the crate tackled her. Her arrow bounced end-over-end to the right, dropping harmlessly to the ground.

Ben grabbed the arrow and plunged it into the scaly demon lying on top of Eve. The resulting explosion knocked him backwards and rendered Eve unconscious. Another figure pounced on Ben, and still another on Eve. He felt a furry hand on his face, pushing his head into the ground, and the other pinning down his right shoulder. He pulled his knees into his chest, and pressing the soles of his shoes against the body of his attacker, he kicked out, sending the demon sprawling backwards.

Before his combatant could react, he dissolved into a shower of sparkling dust. In the fading light, Ben could see Pete's smiling face through the haze.

Ben rolled to his left and landed on top of Eve's molester. He wrapped his arms around the thing's neck and threw his weight back. His hands slipped from the slime-covered demon, throwing him backwards. He recovered and embraced the demon once again, this time locking his hands together.

Ben pulled and felt the creature move with him.

"Pete," he screamed, as he twisted sideways releasing the aggressor and sending him spinning to the right. Ben turned away and knelt down, covering his head in anticipation of the explosion. The figure squealed as it turned into ozone, raining down on the cave floor.

Pete jumped from the top of the crate and landed in front of Ben. "You okay?" he asked.

Ben ignored his question. Rising once again, he stepped toward Eve and dropped to his knees hovering over her. Eve's eyes were already open as he placed his hands on the sides of her face.

"Help me up," she mumbled, and then tried to raise her body.

"No," Ben said, putting his hands on her shoulders and pressing her down.

She knocked his hands away.

"No time for chivalry," she said, pulling herself up, and resting on her elbows. She looked at him and raised her eyebrows, "I said help me up!"

"You don't need to get up," Ben said, putting his hands back on her arms.

"Why," she growled, wriggling free of his grasp. "I hope it's not the wife thing again."

Ben stared at her. She glared back at him.

"We will not go through this again." Eve brought herself to an upright position and placing her hands on hips, she looked at Ben with eyes that burned. "We don't know how many more are here, so get over it and get up."

Ben rose when an arrow plucked out of his quiver by a thin translucent hand, thrust the implement through his shoulder. He dropped back down to his knees and wrapped his hand around the shaft.

"Ben!" Eve exclaimed.

Pete whirled and released, sending another demon into the unseen, as crimson residue burst into the air.

Eve threw her bow off her shoulder and nearly fell on Ben trying to lower herself to assist him. She looked at Pete. "He needs help!"

Pete looked down at Eve, still poised with his weapon loaded, and turning in a calculated arc to shield his friends from incoming danger.

"Cover us!"

"I can't leave him!"

"Now," Pete snarled, "or you'll bury us all." He continued his circular trajectory.

Eve reluctantly stood "Okay, I've got the watch." She picked up her weapon and circled.

Pete fell to his knees and assessed his friend's condition.

"The tip," Ben growled. "Break off the tip and get this thing outta me." He rocked forward. "Ah," he groaned, and then rocked back.

Pete grabbed the shaft on either side of Ben's shoulder and without warning, snapped the point; then, with one smooth motion, extracted the arrow. Ben rolled onto his side sweat pouring down his face.

Pete untied a leather cord he had laced to the grip of his bow. Underneath the wrapping was a coarse, spongy material. He tore two pieces out of the end of the substance and rolled them into quarter inch plugs. Pete pulled the neck area of Ben's shirt down to expose his shoulder. He wedged one plug in the entrance wound on his back, and the other into the exit wound, just below his collarbone in the front.

Ben tensed, drawing in a deep breath. His eyes then opened, and his face relaxed. He sat up and stared at Pete.

"What did you do?"

Pete stared back at Ben and began rewrapping the material underneath the leather cord around his bow.

"It's the same stuff that Belac used on my hand after he ran an arrow through it, but I didn't expect it to work so fast."

Ben exposed his shoulder a second time and looked at the moss-like material sealing the wound in his shoulder. He looked back at Pete.

"I'm glad you saved it . . . and thanks."

"No problem, little man."

"Are you okay, sweetie?" Eve asked, still circling the pair on the ground.

"I'm good."

Pete finished wrapping his bow and stood. "I'll take it from here."

"Thanks," Eve said, and knelt down to check her husband. "Are you sure you're all right?"

"Yes, good as new." He leaned over touching her face and smiled. Ben stood and loaded his bow. Eve did the same and rose to stand beside him. Pete looked at both of them and his lips curved into a smile. Before his grin could be completed, a Tamar fell from the ceiling knocking him off the crate and onto the cave floor.

Ben fired, striking the Tamar in the neck. Eve followed with a shot directly behind Ben's. Pete grabbed an arrow from his quiver and plunged it into the neck of the assailant sitting on his chest.

The Tamar jerked and then shriveled into a bubbling mass. Pete pushed it off before the goo could ooze onto him.

Two demons took its place, one grabbing Pete's feet, and the other wrapping a strap of leather around his neck. They moved with uncanny speed toward the tunnel on the opposite side of the open area. Before they could enter, Ben fired, disposing of the demon holding Pete's feet.

Eve released, as Pete and his bearer's disappeared into the tunnel, her arrow disintegrating as it slammed into the stone doorjamb.

"Damn, they're fast," Ben squawked.

"He's gone!" Eve exclaimed.

"Only until I catch up with them," Ben said, as he took off after his friend and entered into the tunnel.

Eve shook her head and followed.

Chapter Forty-four

PETE BEGAN TO LOSE CONSCIOUSNESS as he found himself being dragged deeper into the passageway,the strap around his neck constricting his airflow. Pete felt something lift his feet, and he started moving at a much faster rate.

"He's of no use dead," the newcomer barked.

Pete's shoulders lifted, relieving the pressure on his neck and allowing him to take a deep breath. His body shuddered violently as he filled his lungs. They moved through a series of sharp turns. *I'll never find my way out of here,* he thought.

As his head cleared, his two bearers stopped and dropped him to the ground flat on his back, evacuating his recent intake of air.

Pete gasped for another breath and raised his head. A black, formless face bared its teeth and hissed pushing him back down.

"Stay down human," an eel-like creature said. "Your executioner is mad enough with your kind as it is."

"Unless being torn apart and eaten in pieces is what you would prefer," his companion, a shapeless, pulsating blob with arms and legs said.

The lone Tamar circled Pete, crouching low, and pelting him with low, deliberate barks.

"What does this slime bag want?" Pete asked, glaring at the Tamar.

"This slime bag, as you refer to him, wants to know why you killed three of his brothers," the eel man answered.

"Tell him he'll be number four if I get a chance," Pete said.

The Tamar raised his head and bellowed. "I would be remiss if I did not articulate that you have told him so on your own," the blob said, chuckling.

The Tamar bent down looming over Pete, his head gurgling in an ever-changing mass. "I believe he may let you live another minute if you will disclose your plans. If not, it will not go well with you."

"If I'm going to die anyway what difference does it make?" Pete growled.

"True," the eel man said, "however, the difference lies in how your demise will come to pass."

The Tamar tightened its circle until it reached the prostrate human. It raised its hands bearing a new weapon, dagger like claws. Bellowing once again, it plunged the deadly implements downward.

* * *

"WAIT!" Eve said.

Ben stopped, letting her catch up.

They resumed their search in tandem, following Pete's trail by the drag marks in the sandy cave floor. After jogging for nearly a minute, the trail suddenly ended. They came to a halt and searched for any indication of which way Pete had gone.

Ben walked further along their current direction.

"Nothing," he said, turning around and making his way back to Eve.

"What are these," she said, pointing to irregular indentations in the sand. "They're not natural and they seem to occur at regular intervals."

"Footprints?" Ben queried.

* * *

THE RAZOR-SHARP TALONS pierced the ground beside Pete's head.

"I do not know for any certainty," mused the eel man, "however I imagine you have exercised your one opportunity to comply."

"I fear the next time," the blob said, "the outcome will not be so favorable."

Pete continued to glare at the Tamar. "Just get on with it."

The Tamar seemed to smile at Pete's comment.

"With pleasure," it hissed and raised its hands once again.

Before the creature attacked, an arrow struck it in the neck. It turned with blinding speed and caught the next projectile before being assaulted a second time.

Ben and Eve were now in the chamber and ready to fire again.

"Get them," the Tamar whispered, but this whisper was devilishly deafening.

Two Guardian pushed out of the rock, each subduing one of the humans. This time it held them at arm's length and off the ground to prevent any contact from their legs and feet.

"You don't have to squeeze so tight, sandman," Ben grunted.

The Tamar rushed to the prisoners. The aberration moved back and forth, stroking first Eve's feet and then Ben's.

"Yes," it hissed. "You will now have the pleasure of watching your companion die, and I will come for each of you."

The two demons held Pete down as the Tamar positioned itself behind his head to afford Ben and Eve the best possible view. The black, slender creature stood tall and once again elevated its arms above its head. Uttering a guttural scream, it arched its back, and the chamber filled with a crimson explosion of light and debris.

Ben felt the Guardian that held him disintegrate. He looked to his left and through the dust, saw Eve little by little sliding towards the ground. As Ben's feet touched the cave floor, he ran to her.

They both made their way through the cloud toward their friend and stumbled over something large on the floor. Eve fell over Pete; Ben landed on top of him.

Pete opened his eyes and stared directly into Ben's face. "Good of you to join me." He looked side to side and glared at Ben. "Now do you suppose you could get off before people begin to talk?"

"Sure," Ben said, smiling, "we wouldn't want that." He rolled to the side, stood and helped his friend to his feet.

Eve gave Pete a quick hug. "I thought it was over," she said.

"Not on your life," he said, returning the hug. The dust had settled enough to see around the chamber.

"What happened?" Ben sputtered, spitting particles from his mouth.

"I thought you may require assistance," a familiar voice said.

✱ ✱ ✱

"THE DARKNESS will soon be upon us," the dark creature hissed. "There are but seven who remain. We must see that no more are lost."

"We have learned many of their tactics," a second creature replied, "even their speech. Perhaps we should now confront them."

"No," the first said. "Gather the brothers together. We will meet in the circle of release and make ready our escape. In this way we will do the humans more harm."

"Of course," the second affirmed. "It will be as you have asked."

* * *

"BELAC!" the three cried in unison.

"Yes, my friends, it is I."

The three embraced Belac as six of his fellow combatants gathered around.

"There is little time," he said. "We must make all haste to the open area. The wooden containers we desire are soon to be taken from our grasp."

BEN PEERED into the open area. A horde of demons filled the space. He looked at Belac.

"Once we enter and work through our obstacles," Belac said, "you will make your way through and enter the corridor on the other side."

Ben nodded.

"The Tamar are waiting for darkness," Belac continued. "You will find them at the end of the passageway. It is then you will do what you can to stop them."

"Ready?" Belac questioned.

"Yes," Ben replied.

Ben and Pete entered first and cleared a path through the sea of demons. The creatures pulled back as the humans sent one after another to the realm of the unseen.

Eve followed close behind, with Belac and his men facing the opposite direction protecting their flank. The entire chamber illuminated with a constant barrage of crimson bursts as fine demon dust rained on everyone present.

"I'm almost out of arrows," Ben screamed.

"Wish I could help you," Pete replied, "but I'm almost out myself." Pete felt a weight on his back. Ben felt the same.

"Consider it a loan," Belac said. He fell back to the rear after depositing reloads in each man's quiver.

As the group neared the crates, the sea of demons parted, sending reinforcements to protect the wooden boxes, now on the move.

"Ben," Belac exclaimed. "You three must pursue the Tamar. We will stay and secure the containers."

"Good luck," Ben said.

Belac smiled, "It is much more than that, my friend."

Ben nodded and gathered Pete and Eve to himself. The three left the open area and made their way into the corridor. A torrent of screams and explosions could be heard until they faded, as the three moved deeper into the tunnel.

The three stopped.

"I hope Belac will be all right," Eve said.

"Drop it," Ben demanded. "There's too much to do bringing nothing else into the equation."

Eve opened her mouth to speak and then just nodded.

"A group of the nastiest things we've ever faced are waiting at the end of this tunnel," Ben said. "I need you all to focus."

"Can't kill them standing here," Pete said.

Ben smiled. "You ready?" he said, looking at Eve.

She nodded.

"That's my girl." The three continued down the tunnel until they came to a fenced-in area open to the outside, save for the tree cover.

"This is the same place Goryak and Maylan kept Jhorr and me," Eve said.

"I recognize it," Ben said. "The light is all but gone; where are the Tamar?"

"Two o'clock," Pete said, drawing an arrow from his quiver.

Ben looked to the two o'clock position. Under the heaviest tree cover, crouching near the stonewall were seven black figures. They bounced up and down, as their snake-like song, voiced in unison, filled the area.

"They haven't seen us," Pete whispered.

"We don't have a clear shot," Ben replied. "We must get them moving."

"Not a problem," Pete said, releasing an arrow into their midst. The dark figures divided with lightning speed, most clinging to the stone walls, but one moving to the center of the ring. It raised its head and howled and then crouched in a defensive position.

"There's our target," Ben said. Three arrows hurled toward the lone figure.

"Another one down," Eve exclaimed.

The crouching Tamar waved a hand, knocking the first two arrows to the ground and catching the third between its teeth. It ground the tip and shaft to dust. Turning an intimidating gaze upon its three aggressors, it spat debris from the its mouth that landed as a saliva-soaked wad of sawdust. Wisps of smoke rose from the acrid spittle.

Eve's exhilaration melted into disappointment.

Rising to a fully upright position, the Tamar snarled, levitated and shot upward, burning a path through the foliage. The dark figure exploded into a series of black particles that dispersed in all directions.

"Did you see that?" Eve exclaimed. "The pieces it broke into were darker than the sky itself."

"I saw it," Pete said. "I don't believe it, but I saw it."

The six remaining Tamar followed the first in rapid succession.

"No," Ben screamed, as he pelted the exiting creatures with fire from his bow, the arrows bouncing harmlessly off the intended targets until the last Tamar disappeared.

The three stood staring upward.

"Not good," Ben said, "Not good at all."

Belac entered the arena and joined the warriors. "This battle is done," he said, "however, the war rages on." He led the three out of the tunnel and back to the open area.

* * *

BELAC'S WARRIORS were busy removing the crates.

"We will leave this place and talk while we take nourishment," Belac said.

"The last thing I want right now is food," Ben said. "I have failed."

"No," Belac said, "you must not suffer what you perceive to be a lack of success."

"Yes," Ben replied, "and lost Jhorr in the process."

"Nothing is lost until you give up and allow it to be so," Belac said.

Ben looked at Belac. "I don't understand."

"You will, my friend, you will." Belac led the three out of the cave and back to the settlement.

Chapter Forty-five

EVE TOOK A BITE of food and chewed somberly.

Ben sat silent, his food untouched. "What will happen now?"

"The Tamar have ceased to be," Belac said. "Their essence will spread throughout the Earth contaminating everything they come in contact with."

"In what way?" Pete asked.

"They will spread all manner of plagues," Belac said, "hate, greed, contempt, gluttony and the like. Of the three you destroyed, the first was the Overseer and of no consequence; although it was necessary to afford an opportunity to dispatch the second while still in the brood chamber."

"I'm not sure I understand," Ben said.

"Once a Tamar is destroyed," Belac said, "it no longer lives in this realm or any other, but ceases to be. However, through the ones that remain, the ones who no longer remain may manifest their evil."

"You're losing me again," Ben said.

"Each Tamar has a specific purpose; the second and third you defeated were no different. Their names were Crucif and Golgoth. Even though they are no more, their purpose will come to fruition through the essence of their brothers." Belac lowered his head.

"What?" Ben urged. "What is it?"

Belac raised his head, his eyes moist. "The Living One will come, and through these two, his blood will spill and he will live no more."

"Then we have failed," Ben said, his face falling even further.

"No. You performed as the prophecy foretold. Even though I had hoped for more, I had no right to expect such."

"Prophecy? What prophecy?"

"From the Book of the Chosen."

"Jhorr told us of this book the first time we met. Why didn't he tell us of the prophecy?"

"It has yet to be authored," Belac said.

"I guess that makes as much sense as anything." Ben looked at Belac, his face fallen, screaming with guilt at his inability to save his young friend. "What about Jhorr?"

"Jhorr has fulfilled his purpose."

"How can you just dismiss him like that," Eve protested.

"Dear Eve," Belac said, "Jhorr existed in this when for one reason."

Without a word, Ben's eyes posed his next question.

Belac nodded his understanding. "To live the prophecy, and then to pen the prophecy in the Book of the Chosen."

"You told me it had not been written when we met the older Jhorr," Ben stammered.

"And I told you true. You have yet to meet the old Jhorr that was your guide in the cave, but you will."

"Then who was the Jhorr we met on the Established Place?"

"The same," Belac said, with a smile.

"You're enjoying jerking me around, aren't you?"

"No. I enjoy explaining how the Great One works to achieve his desired outcome. Even though it may seem as folly to you and me, rest assured that it is always for the greater good."

Ben smiled, "Then we weren't a waste of time."

"Hardly," Belac said.

"What will you do now?" Eve asked.

"There is much to do," Belac said. "Now that we have the Andor, the Great One will assure us victory in battle as long as it resides with us."

"You mentioned that it was also vital to our mission," Ben said. "In what way?"

"I cannot say," Belac replied. "You and your companions will know that truth when it comes to fruition."

"We'd better live a good long time," Pete mused. "It'll take half of forever to answer all these questions."

"May we see it?" Eve asked.

"Of course," Belac replied. "Complete your intake of nourishment, and I will show you."

A war cry rose in the distance, startling the party as they ate. Strings of death and confusion surrounded the cry as it filtered through the early evening air.

Belac jerked his head, eyes wide. "We must make all haste."

Before the three could move, Belac was on his feet running toward the chaotic noise.

When Belac and the three reached their intended goal, what they saw drained their faces until white.

By the light of strategically placed torches, numerous holes three feet in diameter littered the area along with the body parts of six of his fallen comrades. Where the Andor had rested, a large hole ten feet or more square was all that remained.

Belac walked into the middle of the carnage. He knelt down closed his eyes and bowed his head. After several moments, he stood and returned to the three.

"The fallen are with the Great One now," he said. "We must make plans to retrieve the Andor at all costs."

Ben moved closer to Belac. "What has happened here?"

Belac stared straight ahead and answered. "These are ones of whom I have not spoken of before. Their very existence is detrimental to every creature's survival."

Eve had fallen to her knees, refusing to accept the reality before her.

Pete joined Ben while he waited for Belac to continue.

Belac turned to face the pair. "The Shadow Ones," was all he said.

Ben and Pete stared at each other, unsure whether to push Belac for more information.

Sensing this, Belac continued. "These creatures are embodied from pure dark evil. They cannot be destroyed; however, are rendered ineffective in the bright daylight."

"How . . . " Ben asked.

"Please," Belac said, "allow me to finish. During times of darkness (dawn until the great light rises and dusk until the great light sets) they are at their most effective. During the day, the light causes them no harm. It merely makes them invisible and unable to affect any man, creature, or thing. The only way to deter them in the darkness is with a massive fire, one as bright as the great light."

He looked at the three. "You may now speak."

Ben, Eve and Pete stood, feeling as though they should raise their hand waiting to be called upon until Ben broke the silence.

"How do we fight against something that's indestructible?"

"We don't," Belac replied.

"Then what?" Pete asked.

"The Shadow Ones have taken the Andor underground where they can better protect it, due to the absence of light. What we must do is expose the Andor to light to force the Shadow Ones to be unable to interfere with our gaining control."

Eve had now joined the party. "What are these beings like?" she asked.

"They are as shadows cast on the ground by any man standing in the great light, but instead, they stand upright. Be not fooled by their frail appearance, as they possess great power, as you can see by the bloodbath that surrounds us."

Again Pete asked, "What do we do?"

"We must take time to plan, beginning now," Belac said. "Before all is lost."

Chapter Forty-six

"WE HAVE DONE as the Dark One enlisted us to do," the dark figure said to another identical to himself.

"You know they will come," the second figure said.

"We will be ready. The first thing we must do is move the Andor as far into the underground catacombs as we can. This will make the object they search for nearly impossible to find."

"Let it be so," the second figure said. "I will gather the brothers and begin immediately."

"Very good, in time I shall join you."

Chapter Forty-seven

ELAC, BEN, EVE, PETE AND THREE of Belac's men took turns lowering into the cave through the hole used to steal the Andor. Seven others remained above to trace the same path that the ones below would traverse.

Belac handed each of his men two wooden branches and kept two for himself to use as torches. Once they were lit, he spoke. "You must remember the Andor is not to be touched. It must be carried by the poles inserted through the rings on each side. This is also the same for the Shadow Ones. If they touch the Andor they will cease to be."

As the group moved deeper into the cave, they struck the ceiling with a long wooden rod. The men above would place an ear to the ground to follow them as they progressed.

"We will halt for a moment," Belac said. "The torches are growing dim and we must replenish the fuel supply." He opened a bag and pulled several strips of cloths smeared with a black substance that smelled of petroleum. He wrapped the cloth around his torch. At once, the fire light increased. He did the same for the three of his comrades and then the group continued on.

"Will the torches help us against the Shadow Ones in the caves as we search for the Andor?" Ben asked.

"In a minor way," Belac replied, "if your skill is such that you are able to touch them with the flame."

"Is this the reason we have the torches instead of using the night vision instilled within us?" Ben asked.

Belac nodded. "We will rely on both."

The group continued deeper into the underground lair. As they traveled through the tunnel, it divided, heading in different directions leaving a menagerie of catacombs. They came to a halt with no clear direction to search.

Belac pulled more of the strips from his bag and wrapped the torches increasing the light throughout the immediate area.

"Gather the group closer together," Belac ordered. "We must intensify the light into a single component, to battle our enemy."

Several shadow creatures danced in and out of the group's vision as they moved closer and then further away from the firelight. As they did so, the torch bearers would swing their burning weapons in unison, causing portions of the creatures to disappear and forcing them to back away.

The group moved with intent following the retreating creatures, all the while developing an insight of where their quarry lay.

"I sense we are growing closer," Belac said, extending his hand to stop Ben, Eve and Pete's progress.

Belac's three men took the lead, their torchlight fading. Volton, who traveled ahead of the rest, left the ground without warning. Amar reacted, thrusting his torch into the shadow creature holding his friend. The flame startled the creature, causing the spot it touched on its dark form to disappear; however, the gesture came too late as Volton slammed into the ceiling hard enough to shatter his spine and flatten the back of his head. He fell to the ground with a sickening thud that left him twitching as his involuntary nervous system protested one final time.

"Everyone back!" Belac bellowed.

Each one complied, regrouping ten yards further back.

"We must not leave Volton's body," his comrade, Blaine, insisted.

"First, we must concern ourselves with the living," Belac said. He moved to within several feet of Volton's body. Ben joined him, retrieving the torches of the dead. Belac removed the last of the strips from his bag and refueled the torches one last time.

"I can see it," Ben said. He pointed to a lone object, the light reflecting off its golden exterior.

Belac took the wooden rod and tapped against the ceiling. After several moments and a series of muffled taps, the precise location could be determined from above. Belac did this three more times. With the sound of Belac's taps, his men located the corresponding spots above. These four points formed the corners of a square about 30 feet by 30 feet.

The men scraped the layer of top soil, leaving a square of exposed rock that was the ceiling above the three, Belac, and his two men.

The men above them gathered great quantities of fire wood. Filling in the square with the tinder and piling it to a height of six feet, they ignited the mound of fuel. Once the fire was blazing they fanned with huge leaves, which acted like a bellows. It increased the heat to an extreme level.

After several hours, Ben could detect the heat radiating down from the ceiling and a red glow deep within the stone.

"The heat intensifies the immediate area," he said to Belac, "we should evacuate to a safer place."

Belac tapped the ceiling with his wooden rod, signaling the next stage. The ones above then cleared most of the ash from the stone. A horde of men with buckets of water soaked the stone; it turned to steam as it contacted the super-heated rock.

Below, Belac readied his men by moving them back further from the heated portion of the ceiling.

The men above continued to dump water on the exposed stone. This caused the rock to contract, at first triggering slight fissures and cracks until the entire roof buckled, collapsing onto the catacomb floor.

The now absent ceiling allowed the noon day sun to flood the area containing the Andor.

* * *

"I'M VERY SORRY once again for your loss," Ben said.

Belac nodded. "Volton was the closest of friends. He will be missed; however, he is in the care of the Great One."

"I know that brings you much comfort," Eve said, she paused, a melancholy expression accompanied by a sad smile spread across her face.

The entire area was abuzz with activity. The Andor was removed and taken to a more secure position.

Something akin to stonemasons were busy taking the shattered pieces of ceiling and forming a barrier around the open hole to prevent any unaware passerby's from falling in.

"Belac?" Eve asked. "I didn't get a good look at the Andor. May I see what we had fought so hard to retain?"

"Of course, dear one," Belac replied, "it would honor me to show you."

AFTER A SHORT WALK, they entered a small clearing. Up against a sheer cliff face sat the grand article. Its placement was in such a way as to receive the maximum amount of sunlight during the day.

"Impressive," Pete said.

Ben stared in total admiration.

"How will you protect it during the evening hours?" Ben asked.

"There must be an extreme fire kept raging during the time of darkness," Belac replied.

"What about the cliff itself?" Pete asked.

"As the cliff retains heat from the night time fire, this will dissuade any attempt to bore through the rock." Belac said. "So in this way, by keeping the Andor tight to the stone face of the cliff, it will afford protection from that direction."

"It's beautiful," Eve admired, "Is that gold?"

"Yes," Belac replied. "You may move closer but are forbidden to touch."

"What happens if I do?" Eve asked. She was almost giddy, something akin to intoxication.

"You would cease to be," Belac stated.

Eve's eyes widened. "Talk about a sobering thought," she said, her smile having gone. "I now remember your words in the cave disclosing that information."

The Andor was a rectangular box, six feet long and three feet wide, standing waist high. It was beautifully adorned with gold carvings and sported a winged figure on either end. Two poles laced through brass rings allowed the Andor to be carried without being touched by human hands.

"Can you tell us anything about its purpose as it pertains to us?" Ben asked.

"Only that the laws contained within are being transposed onto parchment for you to take when you leave," Belac replied.

"Which brings me to my next question," Ben said. "Where do we go from here?"

"I am but one stop on your journey," Belac said. "It is not for me to say where, when or how. You must follow your Inner Guide. You may stay here as long as you wish." Belac paused, staring at Ben for a moment. "However, I do not believe that will be the case."

"We will stay long enough to recover from our ordeal," Ben said. "Then I feel we must leave."

"You will have ample provisions and be supplied with pack animals."

"Thank you, Belac, and I mean for everything."

"It is I who should thank you," Belac said. The two men locked hands on forearms.

"In two risings of the great light we shall meet again and prepare for your departure," Belac said.

"Until then," Ben said.

Chapter Forty-eight

EN ROSE EARLY to an overcast, blustery day.

"Come back to bed," Eve said, yawning. "Why are you up so early?"

"Too much on my mind, babe." Ben sat down and kissed her on the forehead. "Go back to sleep. You'll have plenty to do later."

"Where are you going so early?" Eve asked.

"Don't know." Ben sat staring at the floor. "We've been through so much, it's hard to believe most of it, much less imagine having to endure anymore."

"It's okay," Eve said. "We've faced some pretty impossible odds. We have what it takes to keep pushing through."

"It's more than having what it takes, we've proved that." Ben said. "I've come to terms with being the leader." He wrapped his hands gently around her face. "That means I'm responsible for two lives other than my own, and one of those lives just happens to be my wife."

"I think I speak for Pete when I say this. You've had some tough decisions to make that weren't always popular but turned out to be the right ones. And you've kept us safe." Eve looked deep into his eyes, "We'll follow wherever you go."

Ben smiled and nodded. "Thanks." He stood up. "Now do like I told you and go back to sleep."

"No argument there," Eve replied.

As he left, she squeezed her pillow and watched him go. Before long, she was once again sleeping; however, this time her dreams were laden with uncomfortable thoughts made real in her fantasy world.

WHEN EVE OPENED her eyes several hours later, she dressed and searched for her party. She found Ben, Pete and Belac in a stable of sorts packing supplies and loading two horses with the parcels.

"Well, good morning, sleepy head," Ben said, smiling.

"So nice of you to join us," Pete chimed in.

"I've had enough of you two already," Eve said and then turned to Belac. She smiled, "Good morning, Belac. How are you?"

"I do well this morning," Belac replied.

Ben had left the others and stood staring at the sky. Darker clouds had moved in at an alarming rate."It looks like we might be in for some nasty weather."

Belac frowned but said nothing. *If you only knew what the future holds,* he thought. *Unfortunately I do not and will be of no help beyond this when . . . Sadly the three must face this on their own.*

Pete and Eve joined Ben. The mass of clouds began to swirl forming ominous shapes that seemed to take on a life separate from the mother storm. It was as if sentient beings were growing, feeding off a central host. Once they reached a certain size they would break away and begin a menacing dance making their way ground-ward.

The three hesitated almost to the point of disaster.

"Look out!" Ben roared, grabbing Eve. He jerked her out of the way. just before one of the diving aberrations could dig a clawed hand into her back.

"Even though the entities are formed from water vapor," Belac said, "make no mistake—they are as deadly as you believe them to be."

"What do we do," Ben yelled, attempting to be heard over the roar of the wind.

"Follow me," Belac said, "and stay close." He grabbed the reins of two of the horses and motioned for the three to join him in between the two animals. Belac led them from underneath the stable cover and headed for a stone building two hundred feet away.

Eve looked at Ben with pure fear in her eyes.

Ben stared back as if to say *don't worry I'm here for you.*

In an instant, one horse left the ground taking Belac with him, his hand wrapped in the reins. Belac released the leather rope and dropped to the ground before reaching a dangerous altitude.

As the equine rose further into the air, a host of creatures massed around it pulling it to shreds. Eve gagged while red droplets fell as rain.

Belac motioned for everyone to squat low beside their remaining sacrificial beast. Ben detected the unmistakable sound of a thin sheet of metal wobbling through the clouds at the whim of the wind itself. The piece flew over his head. He could sense an attempt to communicate, and then it vanished.

"Well," Ben said to himself, "looks like Chester's back, for good or for bad I'm sure I'll find out soon enough."

Just as they reached the stone building, the second horse suffered a similar fate as the first, with one exception. The full head fell from the sky landing in the doorway, splattering blood and brain matter.

Now that they were safely within the building, the storm died; sunshine taking its place. Belac looked at the decapitated remains of the horse he once called Lacer. This was an animal he was extremely fond of, and felt the deed was carried out to further intimidate the three.

Eve moved to a corner and dry heaved, having not eaten breakfast.

Ben stood bent over, hands on his knees, and shaking his head in disbelief.

Pete moved to Belac's side. "What was that?"

"A storm is brewing," Belac replied, still staring at his fallen comrade's head.

"A storm," Ben questioned. "What did we just go through?"

"A sign of things to come," Belac said. He turned to face the three. "We must in all haste make ready your departure. Even now the dark forces that would waylay your journey have gathered."

Ben opened his mouth to speak.

Belac raised his hand. "There will be no more conversation. I have told you all I can tell you for I know no more. Now, please, time is of the essence. You must be on your way."

THE THREE AND BELAC completed packing the needed provisions.

"Belac," Eve inquired, "there's something I've been meaning to ask you."

"Yes, dear one," Belac replied.

"Why have we not seen but a few of your people? I know there must be more."

"Indeed you are correct. The ones necessary to serve are the ones you have seen. We do this to prevent what you would call cross-contamination of our two cultures. Please do not take offense at my words, for it is a necessary thing we do. We have reached that point in our existence; you will reach the same upon the completion of your journey."

Belac looked around checking the two pack animals and the three horses that would bear the travelers. "All seems in order."

Ben walked up to Belac, "I guess this is it."

Belac nodded. The two men hugged. "To be sure."

Eve and Pete joined the two men both receiving hugs and bidding each other farewell.

A distant rumble thundered, catching the attention of all. Ben looked at Belac questioning him with his eyes.

"Yes," Belac answered, "the storm."

The three mounted their horses. "Thanks for everything, ole friend," Ben said.

"Remember me," Belac replied, "for you and yours I shall never forget."

A tear ran down Eve's cheek as they turned and left. A cool blast of air covered her, keeping the recollection of the previous storm firmly embedded within her memory.

Several men and women, previously hidden, now brought themselves into view, joining Belac.

"Will they be successful in their journey?" one inquired.

"I cannot say," Belac replied. "It is up to them and their trust in the Great One." The rumble moved closer, gaining in volume, and then subsided. As it faded to nothing, a large lightning-bolt followed by a deafening thunder-clap signified its retreat.

Belac nodded somberly, "I am afraid the storm has begun."

About the Author

 **Lynn Steigleder** was born in Richmond, Virginia. He spent most of his young adult life as a supervisor in the field of construction and fabrication. When Lynn's department was outsourced within two months of his diagnosis of multiple sclerosis, he realized the need to transition into a new career path.

During a fishing trip, his son suggested that he consider writing as a career, having enjoyed short stories written by his father in years past. Lynn agreed to the challenge and his first novel, *Rising Tide*, was accepted for publication. Lynn has continued to work on the *Rising Tide* series. *Eden's Wake* is the second book in the series, and he has more in the draft stage close to completion.

Other Books by Lynn Steigleder

The Rising Tide Series

Rising Tide (Book One in the *Rising Tide* Series)

Another blast ripped through the Orion, cutting all power and knocking him to the floor. Ben lifted himself off the deck and found it was impossible to stand. He crawled to the COM panel. "Marty! All systems down! All systems down! "With a category six hurricane above and his habitat below destroyed by the blast, Ben finds himself alone in a decompression chamber. Suddenly, he receives a mysterious message. Dash, dash, dot, dot, dot, a seven. S.E.E.K.C.7. Is he dreaming, or is someone trying to reach him? In Rising Tide, Steigleder depicts a world in which land is at a premium due to the advancing sea, and where man's attempt to adapt has led to a decay of morality and survival of the fittest. In the midst of the ocean, a crew of criminally-minded profiteers rescues a stranded diver, Ben Adams. Is the rescue just a fortunate coincidence for Ben, or has he been led to this rendezvous by fate for a common goal? Rising Tide is a novel of rebirth for a world corrupted by evil.

Eden's Wake (Book Two in the *Rising Tide* Series)

Ben's best friend is killed in an underwater implosion on a dying world. Living to die again, the two men reunite and battle for an ancient artifact, a relic which will ensure this planet's survival. Ben crosses a threshold. The world he leaves—doomed; the world he enters—reborn. His wife, Eve, and their bumbling charge, Eleazor, follow Ben through the doorway and blindly into the void.